FOLLOW THE NEW GRASS

**Center Point
Large Print**

**This Large Print Book carries the
Seal of Approval of N.A.V.H.**

FOLLOW THE NEW GRASS

Cliff Farrell

CENTER POINT PUBLISHING
THORNDIKE, MAINE

This Center Point Large Print edition
is published in the year 2005 by arrangement with
Golden West Literary Agency.

The text of this Large Print edition is unabridged. In other
aspects, this book may vary from the original edition. Printed in
Thailand. Set in 16-point Times New Roman type.

ISBN 1-58547-582-3

Library of Congress Cataloging-in-Publication Data

Farrell, Cliff.
    Follow the new grass / Cliff Farrell.--Center Point large print ed.
        p. cm.
    ISBN 1-58547-582-3 (lib. bdg. : alk. paper)
    1. Large type books. I. Title.

PS3556.A766F65 2005
813'.54--dc22

2004026757

TO MARIE AND BILL
THEIR EFFORTS A LONG TIME AGO
MADE THIS BOOK POSSIBLE

FOLLOW THE NEW GRASS

1

Spring and its moods were as unpredictable as the whims of a headstrong woman here in the high slants of the Wardrums. Eastward, far away and far below, where the country leveled and sobered and lost its wild young beauty in the monotony of the plains, the horizon offered an emerald tinge.

Below that sky the country was greening, but in the Wardrums only the quaking aspen were showing signs of life; first greening was still a week or ten days away.

Indeed the greening might be longer delayed, for a chill and hostile wind was flowing down from the snow-drowned peaks; the sun had lost its warmth. A faint haze was deepening above the high rim, presaging a change of weather, and perhaps snow before another day.

The man who called himself Jay Webb raked the brim of his hat lower, and hiked a guarding shoulder against this wind as he turned his grulla horse to retrace his way down the mountain to his ranch. He had climbed almost to the snow line, a rifle in his boot, on the long chance that he might sight a loafer wolf that had hamstrung one of his yearlings the previous night.

Even after five years' experience with this climate he had been deluded by the bright morning sun into starting this hunt shirtsleeved, and without a brush coat on the saddle. He would never, he reflected with wry good humor, learn the ways of this northern range. That brought the jarring and unwanted thought that, if this were so, then he was ways fated to be an alien.

Abruptly the content of the morning's ride was dimmed. He had seen no sign of the loafer, and had almost forgotten the purpose of his journey. For, during these hours of lax and aimless scrabbling through timber and over ridges, the belief had lain pleasantly on him that he had at last become a part of this challenging country. He had fallen to dreaming of a future that he had never expected to see.

For a long time he had lived only on the surface of this region, unable to shake off the thought that his presence here was but an interlude in his life. Now he was seeing every peak and every run of the land as a part of his yesterdays and his tomorrows. They had become friends, instead of mere places of refuge for him. The country had grown into him, and he had grown into it. He never wanted to leave it. He never again wanted to think of himself as an alien here.

Still, the day was flawed for him. A flatness that was the reflection of harsh and juiceless memories came into his eyes, and they were slate gray instead of hazel.

"Let's go home, Chink," he said to the mouse-colored horse.

The gravity lingered with him as he followed the lee of hogback ridge downward, where he had shelter from the sharpening drive of the wind. A return of a long-known wariness and unease tightened him in the saddle.

A tall, flat-shouldered man, he had the lank legs, pinched hips and whipstock waist of a lifetime horseman. Straight-browed, dark-haired, with a thrust to his jaw and chin, the lean planes of his face were deeply burnished by sun and wind. These same elements had bleached the ends of his hair to a tawny color where they showed beneath the band of his crim-brimmed, weathered range hat. He wore a flannel shirt, faded by many washings to a neutral hue, dark woolen trousers, comfortably creased to the form of the saddle and cuffed high to clear his boots, one of which carried a blunted rowel.

He resented this change of mood, for he saw clearly now that it would always be this way with him. There would always be this spoiling memory to crop up in his mind and bring him straighter in the saddle and tighten his throat. The regrets of those past years would never leave him.

Carrying this resignation he let the horse pick its own way. Presently the animal leveled off on the faded ruts of the old Fort Relief trail, little used since the previous fall. Turning north along this, a curve brought them out on a bold shoulder of the mountain that gave a hawk's view of all the Wardrum country.

Ten miles to the east Spearhead's buildings were scattered among the timber above the river ford, which was now spanned by a wooden wagon bridge. Half a dozen trails veined the landscape with Spearhead as their heart. A packstring, gnat-size at this distance, was fording the river to save toll. In the opposite direction a freighter crawled toward the benches—probably old Claus Hupman hauling supplies to Yellow House.

Yellow House was in sight in the middle distance to the south, standing amid its mature windbreaks of poplars and cottonwoods and a wide scatter of work buildings and corrals. Yellow House's Pitchfork was the pioneer brand in the Wardrums, and the years were mellowing the peeled pine walls of the headquarters building to a silvery hue.

Jay had been told that Cheyenne and Gros Ventre and Brule lance heads and arrow barbs were still preserved in the walls of Yellow House as relics of its violent past.

Eastward, beyond town, where the Ox Bow River began its long sweep northward into the plains, the thinning sun caught the fresher glint of a new spread. This was the third year on this range for Hodge McColl's Chainlink, but he was spreading out, planting his line camps to challenge Pitchfork and the small outfits that pooled the graze in the middle benches.

Then movement nearer at hand brought Jay's attention swinging back, and he watched three riders round a switchback below him. They were ascending this same trail, and punishing their horses, but they had more than a mile of stiff climbing ahead of them to reach Jay's position. The bulky man in the lead was Hodge McColl.

The scrape of hooves diverted Jay. Frank Spain rode

into view on the trail only a hundred yards away.

Frank's face wore the ashen tinge of panic. His first reaction at this unexpected encounter with Jay sent him driving for the holster gun he wore. But the motion was the reflex of edged nerves, for recognition came, and he let the half-drawn weapon slide back into its sheath. A wild flame broke the flat stare of his dark eyes. It was the rushing hope of a man who had given himself up as lost and now saw rescue near.

Frank's horse had been pushed beyond any humane limit. When he let the animal stop it dropped its head between spread legs and began to tremble.

Frank's voice was shrill. "No man ever hit better luck when he needed it. I've got to borrow your horse, Jess. I'm . . ."

"Watch the name!" Jay said. "You slipped, Frank. I'm Jay Webb, remember?"

"For God's sake, don't preach to me now. I'm in big trouble. There are two . . ."

"Three," Jay said. "And they're coming fast."

"I need your horse," Frank said frenziedly. "I'd do the same for you if it was the other way around. You can't turn me down. You know that."

"Don't threaten me, Frank," Jay said.

"It's McColl! Him an' me had trouble, and . . ."

"You asked to trade horses," Jay cut him off. "That's all I want to know—and all I need to know."

He dismounted as he spoke, stripped the saddle and headstall from the grulla and set them on a trailside boulder.

"You've got less than ten minutes, Frank," he said.

13

Frank Spain frantically shifted rig to Jay's horse. His panic began to ease. With a fairly fresh mount under him he would be over the pass before dark and Brule Basin, beyond, was big and wild. Frank felt that he was safe—for the time at least—and he had never been one to look into the future. He owned a little cattle outfit on Latigo Creek. Dark-haired, with a wisp of mustache, handsome and with a gift for small talk, Frank had always found women easy to master. That had always been his pride and his trouble, and that probably was the source of his trouble now.

"Better take to the brush," Frank warned. "It will save explanations."

"I'll see," Jay said.

Frank swung aboard the grulla, then remembered something. "Good Lord! Dallas is arriving on tomorrow's stage. I almost forgot. Will you meet her, Je—Jay? The Castle Bend stage."

"Dallas?"

"Dallas Carver. The girl I met last fall in Kansas City. Remember me telling you about her? She's coming to Spearhead to marry me."

"Marry?"

Frank said petulantly, "What's wrong with that?"

"Wait! What will I tell her, Frank?"

"Anything. You'll think of something."

"Damn it, Frank!" Jay said. "Why did you get into grief at a time like this?"

Frank headed away. "Tell her she'll hear from me when the sign is right," he called back. "Tell her to wait for me."

Then he was gone from sight. This Dallas Carver, Jay reflected, probably would wait for him. All women did, for Frank. Jay stood a moment, debating his own course. He might avoid awkward explanations by taking to the brush, as Frank had advised. But there was also the possibility such a maneuver would put him in the position of deliberately drawing pursuit on himself in order to give Frank more leeway.

There were reasons why he wanted to avoid serious trouble, not only with Hodge McColl, but with anyone. For six years, he had been steering clear of friction with other men. He had been so successful that he had become convinced that he had really succeeded in burying his past.

He decided to stand his ground, picking that course as the lesser of two evils. He had not brought a side gun, and now he carried his rifle into the brush, hiding it where it would be out of reach and out of sight.

Returning, he began working on the suffering bay, massaging its twitching flanks and legs with the saddle blanket. The animal began to respond a trifle.

He was at this task when the three pursuers rode up. Their horses were also in bad shape. They pulled up, and the only sound was the blowing of the exhausted animals as they sized up the situation.

Hodge McColl's glance swung to Jay's saddle on the boulder, and he instantly knew the story. His sharp eyes, small and black in a fleshy, brown face, lifted angrily and scanned the mountainside above.

He must have glimpsed Frank on some promontory above, for he swung up the rifle that he carried slung in his arm. Evidently the chance for a shot had already passed, for he reluctantly lowered the gun without firing.

McColl then slacked back in the saddle, and said, "It looks like we had the ride for nothing, boys."

A deep and unsatisfied fury was roweling him as he dismounted. He took his time loosening the cinches to aid his horse. His riders followed suit.

He studied Jay with a rough deliberation. He was a wide-chested, rock-solid man. He wore a fawn-colored hat, foxed saddle breeches stuffed into half-boots, and a beaded elkskin vest over a plaid shirt. A bone-handled gun was slung in a carved-leather holster.

McColl had founded his brand in Texas, popping his first mavericks from the brush below the Nueces River, bulldogging them with his own great strength and burning the Chainlink brand on their hides with a heated cinch ring. Willful and arrogant, he also had the shrewdness and the patience never to play a losing hand. Frank Spain had evaded him this time, but McColl was the kind who would wait for the next deal.

Accompanying him were Sam Leathers, a slab-muscled, blocky man who had a reputation as a bare-knuckle prize fighter in roundup camps and trail towns, and a saturnine cowboy named Buck Clay.

McColl finished his survey of Jay. "The name's Webb, if I recollect right," he said heavily. "You run a brand on Slide Crick? The Rocking J?"

Jay nodded. He was beginning to regret that he had

not taken to the brush after all.

"You made a poor horse trade," McColl said. "That bay will never earn his keep again."

"It wasn't a trade," Jay shrugged. "Only a loan."

"It was still a bad bargain," McColl said. "Wasn't it, Sam?"

"Mighty poor," Sam Leathers spoke up as he understood what this was leading to.

"Frank Spain must be a pretty close tillicum of yours that you'd be willing to walk home with a ruined horse just to help him out of a ruckus," McColl said.

"We've never had trouble."

"You've never had trouble with me either—until now."

Jay picked up his saddle, slung it on his shoulder. "A hull is the damnedest thing to pack over a distance," he remarked mildly. "Harder to hang onto than a watermelon."

Sam Leathers shoved forward. "He's too proud for his shadow, Hodge," he said, anxious to anticipate his boss's wishes. "Let me cut him down a notch."

"Hold off a minute, Sam," McColl said.

McColl studied Jay again, puzzled by his mildness. Jay was as tall as McColl, but many pounds lighter. His eyes were almost a lazy blue now, but there was no real humility in them. Nor was there any weakness in the set of his mouth. McColl had bumped into men with eyes and mouth like that who possessed an amazing capacity for temper and violence.

"Did Frank Spain mention why he was sullin' a

horse to stay ahead of me?" McColl asked.

"No."

"And you didn't ask?"

"It was Frank's worry. Not mine."

"You could be wrong there too, Webb."

"I've made my share of wrong guesses in the past," Jay admitted.

"Maybe you helped Frank because you don't like your new neighbors in this range?"

Jay meditated that a moment. "Likely it was the horse I was concerned about the most. I never care to see anything abused—horses, men or women."

"So you know it was a woman that started this?"

"Frank's troubles usually wear petticoats," Jay shrugged.

McColl appraised him again, trying to sift an evasion out of Jay's manner. Then, as though dissatisfied with what he had found, he nodded to Leathers. "All right, Sam. Try him out for size. He is a mite proud."

Leathers moved in eagerly. "Next time, Webb, stay clear of affairs that ain't your worry," he said.

"Watch yourself, Sam," McColl warned sharply.

Leathers measured Jay carefully as he advanced. He expected opposition. Jay stood balancing the saddle on his shoulder. He understood that he had his choice. McColl was testing him to learn where he really stood, and if he might be dangerous. Jay had stayed carefully clear of both Pitchfork and Chain when it became clear that a struggle for supremacy was coming, and now McColl was trying to force his hand.

He made no attempt at defense, nor did he retreat.

Leathers, amazed at the ease with which he was to have his way, launched a punch.

Jay could have rolled the blow, or could have side-stepped it entirely. He did neither. Leathers' fist crashed on the base of his jaw. The force of it drove him back in a staggering fall. The saddle skidded on its horn into a clump of brush off the trail.

Jay was dazed, but had the presence of mind to fold his legs against his body in case Leathers came at him with his boots.

Leathers had such an intention, but McColl spoke, "Don't play your luck too far, Sam."

"I oughta fix him for keeps," Leathers said. "He's doggin' it."

"Maybe I'm doing you a favor, Sam," McColl said. "Maybe I'm saving you trouble another day."

Leathers laughed scornfully. Angry now at his boss he walked impatiently to his horse.

McColl looked down at Jay who was sitting up, blood coursing from the corner of his mouth. "You got off cheap, Webb," he said.

McColl walked to his horse, pulled in the cinches. "I guess we can make it back to town if we take it slow," he said to his companions.

He mounted, eyed Jay again with remote perplexity, then led Leathers and Buck Clay away down the trail. McColl was still not satisfied with the answers Jay had given him.

Jay sat braced on his arms. Presently the dizziness faded, and his jaw began to throb. But he had been lucky. His jawbone was intact and so were his teeth.

He finally got to his feet. He was uncertain on his legs, and grasped the limb of a scrub oak until he steadied.

His hat had fallen. He bent to pick it up, but that brought back the dizziness and he nearly fell.

A clear, cool voice spoke behind him. "At least you didn't have to turn the other cheek."

2

Jay turned. A young woman, mounted on a chunky, short-coupled sorrel mare, sat on the trail only a dozen yards away She was gazing at him with neither pity nor approval. Her eyes were a deep amber shade and disconcertingly direct.

Jay knew Lily Benton by little more than sight. He had spoken to her for the first time the previous fall when she had visited the wagon while he was riding with the Pitchfork crew at beef roundup. Since then he had encountered her infrequently on the trail or in town, lifting his hat and giving her only the customary polite greeting as they passed.

She was the only child of Barney Benton, who had brought the first herd of longhorns up from Texas into the Wardrums. Barney Benton had fought the Cheyennes and the Sioux for this range, and he had built Yellow House, with loopholes in its fresh-cut log walls. Some twelve thousand head of cattle now grazed the country in the Benton Pitchfork iron.

Lily Benton had been attending finishing schools in the East and in Europe during the greater part of the five years Jay had been in the country. She had been in France the previous spring when her father had died at Yellow House.

Barney Benton had been stricken in his bed six months before his death, but he had given strict orders that the news be kept from his daughter. He had carried a bullet near his heart for twenty years—a big, round slug that had been fired from a brass-bound trade gun by some Indian warrior during a raid on Yellow House. That slug, which no doctor had dared to remove because of its position, had finally killed him.

Lily Benton had hurried home from abroad to mourn her father and to take charge of Pitchfork, which she had inherited, for her mother had been killed by an arrow in the same fight in which her father had received the wound that brought his death years later.

She apparently had just come up the Fort Relief trail, and that meant she must have encountered McColl and his men.

She guessed Jay's thoughts. She said, "No. Hodge McColl didn't see me. I wasn't on the trail. I was higher up on the mountain. I saw them chasing Frank Spain before you spotted them, so I stayed out of sight in the timber."

She added, dryly, "I saw everything that happened. It was very interesting."

Jay made another attempt at picking up his hat. This time he was successful. The deliberate manner in which Lily Benton sat there, a faint, ironic smile on her mouth, nettled him. And it touched off a vague uneasiness within him.

She waited for him to speak. When he did not, her smile widened a trifle. "It must be even more painful to deliberately stand and let a man biff you on the jaw than to be beaten up in the heat of an honest fight," she observed. "Sort of like waiting for the guillotine to fall. Did all your past life flash before your eyes while you waited for Sam Leathers to knock your head off? They say that's what happens at such a time."

Jay got his hat on his head, making an effort of it. Under cover of that motion he gave her a quick and closer inspection. She was baiting him—and with a studied purpose. He was almost sure of that.

"I can't figure why they picked on me," he said querulously. Then he added boastfully, It's a happy thing for Sam Leathers he had two men to back him up. Otherwise I wouldn't have let him run over me roughshod."

"At least, for once in your life, you know how it feels to be meek," Lily Benton said.

Jay came inwardly to a knife-edge alert. But he continued to maintain his bumbling pose. "All I know is I loaned a horse to Frank Spain because his own mount was sulled—dead tuckered out," he said complainingly, "and for that Chain is ready to gang me. I didn't figure to get mixed up in any trouble. I don't even know what started it."

"Knowing Frank Spain, you probably can guess," Lily Benton said. "It was a woman, of course. It usually is when men go gunning for each other."

Jay was certain of one thing. He wanted to end this talk, get rid of Lily Benton and her searching, amber eyes. He did not like the way she was sizing him up. It was as though she was asking herself something, coming to a final and irrevocable decision about him.

He gazed up at her with a broad and knowing look. "So that's how it is," he said.

Lily Benton sensed his purpose. In spite of that she found herself sharply annoyed. "Your inference is insulting," she said crisply. "They weren't fighting over me."

Jay surveyed her from head to foot with the same deliberation she was using on him, measuring her for a weakness that would give him an advantage over her. "They could do worse," he commented.

Lily Benton's nose went up slightly. She had the type of a small nose that gave emphasis to that gesture. "Thank you," she said acidly. "Or was it intended as a compliment?"

She was a strikingly handsome young woman. She had a generous mouth and her cheeks were soft beneath good cheekbones, and her skin was tanned a clear golden hue. She was not tall, but possessed a sturdiness of figure. She was assured in the saddle, her body lithely responsive to every movement of the none-too-gentle mare.

She was bareheaded against all convention. Also, in defiance of custom, she wore her thick, chestnut hair clipped at shoulder length.

She had on a tight-bodiced waist of dove gray, fitted with cloth-covered red buttons. Over that she wore an open, short jacket of black fox fur. These garments were completely feminine on a figure of which Lily Benton had no cause to be ashamed. It was evident she wore no stays, and needed none, and that also was an offense to other and less fortunate women in this range. But she was a woman whom men turned to watch with appreciation.

There was one more item that offended propriety in the Wardrums. Her dark riding skirt was full cut and had several flounces below the knee. This garment gave her the semblance of being decorously attired when she was dismounted, but it was evident now that she was riding astride.

That meant the skirt was one of those divided affairs that was the cause of so much talk. Only common women dared ride anything but sidesaddle.

"What do you call that thing you're wearing?" Jay asked. "A skirt, or a pair of pants?"

He expected her to recoil with shock at such rudeness. At least he was certain this would put her to flight.

Lily Benton was unruffled. She had endured Jay's inspection calmly, her tight smile unchanged. In her turn she had taken advantage of this chance to analyze him at close quarters. What she saw caused her heart to slow a little. A doubt edged into her mind—a doubt that she knew—would swell into icy panic if she lost her grip on herself.

She saw his brown leanness and his height. He could be no more than four or five years older than herself, but in his eyes was a timeless shadow and about his

24

mouth the lines of a vast and bitter knowledge of life. Here was a man who had his secrets.

She had seen him hide his rifle, and there were none of the customary signs of wear along the seam of his trousers common to men in this range where carrying a weighted holster was the rule rather than the exception. Thinking back, she could never recall having seen him carrying a side arm.

She resolutely forced the doubt and the panic away and continued to fence with him, using a rapier against his broadsword. She showed him only her strength, and none of her inner conflict.

"Whether they're called pants or a skirt hardly seems important," she shrugged. "By one name or another they're comfortable."

"Maybe you don't know what people say about women who ride around in clothes like that?" Jay said.

"If you want to tell me, I'll listen," she said. "I'm curious to learn if you've been discussing me."

Jay dropped the subject. He had gained no advantage over her. He was remembering the words of a cowboy in Spearhead the day Lily Benton had alighted from the stage after her return from Europe to take over direction of Pitchfork.

"You'd think she was the Queen of Sheba," the cowboy had said. "Three trunkloads of clothes, an' if that wasn't fancy-woman paint on her face then I'm color-blind. Barney Benton spent the price o' two thousand head o' prime steers educatin' her, an' all he's got for his money is a fast woman. They say her main idea in goin' to Europe was to marry one o' them half-baked counts or earls, but even them mavericks couldn't stand her. Gawd! Who'd want her, even with her shape? She's got a tongue that cuts worsen the popper on a bullwhip, an' a skillet-throwin' temper. I've heard say she can roll a cigarette like a man an' that she hits the bottle. She's spoiled, and now she's soured because she's afeared of bein' an old maid."

The speaker had been one of Hodge McColl's Chain riders. But his remarks had only brought him trouble. A rawboned cowhand named Yancey Tolliver, who worked for Pitchfork, had taken exception to his statements. In the fist fight that followed the Chain rider had been taken to a bloody trimming.

However, Jay had since heard that Hodge McColl himself wasn't as hard to please. McColl had been a frequent caller at Yellow House since Barney Benton's death. He and Lily Benton were often seen riding the trails together.

Lily Benton's mare was so impatient she now dismounted, holding the reins, in order to give her full attention to Jay.

"I didn't happen here by accident," she said. "I want to talk to you."

Jay began rolling a cigarette. "Yeah?"

"I rode to your place this morning. I saw the wolf kill, and saw that you had headed for the high country. So I headed in the same direction."

"Yeah?"

"I want you to work for me—for Pitchfork."

Inwardly Jay tightened. Outwardly he only appeared

26

surprised—and he was surprised. "You short of riders?" he asked.

"I'm short of the kind of riders I need," she said.

"I might help out at Pitchfork a little in a pinch," Jay conceded. "Though it would only be part-time. I've got my own place to look after."

"This would be full-time."

This wasn't a request. This was an order. And she was sure of herself.

"The pay will be three hundred dollars a month," she went on, and now in her voice was the rushing tension of a girl who was taking her risk and burning her bridges behind her.

"Three hundred? Ma'am, you must have the wrong man in mind. I . . ."

"And I can use four or five more men just like you. I'll pay them a hundred a month. The money will go through your hands. You can pay them what you please."

Jay's gaze thinned, but he continued desperately to play his humble part. "You don't pay your own foreman more than eighty," he protested. "You can hire any top hand in the country for thirty."

"You're the man I want."

"That kind of money usually has to be earned the hard way," Jay said slowly. "Through gunsmoke."

For the first time he had gained an advantage over her, and unexpectedly. For her resolution faltered. A dread formed in her eyes. Then she made her final decision. She said, "You are no stranger to gunsmoke."

"You seem to have read my brand wrong," Jay said. "You just saw Sam Leathers cuff me around. Why would you pick on a man like me to draw pay as a gunhand? I don't even pack a six-shooter."

"You can drop the hillbilly pose," she said. "It doesn't go well with your appearance anyway. Even Hodge McColl wasn't completely fooled. He couldn't understand why you didn't fight back."

After a moment, she added, "But I know."

Jay stood a long minute, staring out over the vast roll of distance. "Just what do you know?" he finally asked.

She spoke soberly. "I was sitting on the gallery of the Alamo Hotel in Concho, Texas, on a hot July night nearly six years ago when a man named Jess Steele rode by. I had traveled there with Dad. He was buying cattle. Jess Steele said to me, 'Lady, you better go inside. There might be shooting in this street soon.'"

For a time the only sound was the vacant droning of the chill wind through the brush.

"A few minutes later," Lily Benton went on, "the shooting came. Only two shots were fired. Mason Lomack, owner of the Double Arrow ranch out of Concho, and his son, Vince, were murdered. They were shot in the back through a window as they sat in a saloon."

Again the long silence. "You will call me Miss Benton," she said. "I will, of course, always refer to you as Jay Webb, the name you now choose to use . . . provided our association is satisfactory to me."

And she added, ". . . Otherwise I will call you by

your real name . . . Jess Steele."

"You could be mistaken," Jay said heavily, after a time. "Maybe I only look like this Jess Steele."

"It was your voice that gave you away. I did not even see your face that night in Concho. It was too dark as you rode by. Do you remember one evening last fall when you were riding with one of my Pitchfork wagons at beef roundup? It was just after dark, as it had been that night in Concho. I had come out to the wagon from Yellow House, for I wanted to talk to my foreman about a business matter.

"You were on the cocktail trick with the herd, and I unintentionally almost rode into the cattle on bedground while I was hunting the wagon. You intercepted me in time. You said, 'Lady, you better learn to sing out when you're around bunched cattle at night. You might spook them if you blundered into some skittery steer in the darkness.'"

She paused, then went on, "A man's appearance might change some in six years, but not his voice. I had always remembered the voice I heard that night in Concho. I've awakened many times at night, hearing it. After all, the killing of two men isn't a matter one forgets easily. It was coincidence that you would speak to me a second time in darkness, and using words somewhat similar to the ones I heard in Concho —an unfortunate coincidence for you."

"Beef roundup was eight months ago," Jay said. "If I am what you say I am—a murderer—you waited a long time to pounce."

"I had to make absolutely sure, of course," she said

29

steadily. "That took time."

"And how did you make sure?"

"I checked on the description under which the law is hunting Jess Steele for murder."

Jay's head came up, and his eyes asked her a sharp and bitter question.

"Don't be alarmed," she said. "I was discreet. I did not go directly to the law for the information. I knew that might arouse curiosity and lead to complications. I went to Concho myself and found what I wanted without consulting anyone."

"To Concho?"

"Last winter," she nodded. "I was supposed to be in Chicago on a pleasure and business trip. Instead I made the stage trip to Texas. I used an assumed name, posing as the daughter of an army officer en route to El Paso. I stopped in Concho twenty-four hours. At the same Alamo Hotel. But I was not recognized. Six years changes a woman's appearance too, you know. I had a hunch I would find what I wanted at the post-office. That's one of the places reward posters are usually displayed. And I was right. I found it there on the bulletin board —a poster bearing your description, and others giving the descriptions of other men who used to ride with you. The posters were old and yellow, but the fact they were still on the board shows that you haven't been forgotten by the law."

"And so you are sure?" Jay said grimly.

"It was easy to see that the voice fitted the man. I can understand how you escaped identification so long. Evidently you were not a vain man in your youth. There seems to have been no photograph of you in existence. At least there was no picture of you on the law dodger. Only a general description that would fit a lot of men '. . . About six feet tall, weight about one hundred and eighty, dark hair, straight nose and jaw, lean build and probably bullet scars on body, but locations unknown. Fairly well educated, and with gray-blue eyes. Attractive to women.' Apparently you must have left some broken hearts among the ladies in Texas, according to that last item."

Then she added slowly, "And the poster had this warning at the end, 'This man is very fast with a gun and will shoot to kill. Take no chances.' "

She quit talking for a time. At last she said, "That's how I made sure. And I am sure—beyond any shadow of a doubt."

"You spent months checking on me, made a trip in midwinter of hundreds of miles by stage," Jay said. "This Jess Steele seems to be very important to you."

"He is a weapon placed in my hands by chance," she said. "A valuable weapon, if his record as a fighting man is to be believed. It was worth the trouble if he measures up to his reputation."

"You made sure who I was many weeks ago," Jay said. "Why did you wait until now?"

"I had hoped I would not be forced to take this step."

"And if you had decided you did not need me you would have exposed me?" Jay questioned.

She said only one word, "Perhaps."

"I could refuse," Jay said in a monotone. "I could pull out of this range."

"Yes. That means abandoning your ranch and the brand you've built up. You own more than three hundred head of stock, I believe. It means you'd be back where you were six years ago when you rode out of the Concho country with a price on your head. The reward Wyatt Lomack posted for the man who killed his father and brother still stands. Five thousand dollars in gold for you, dead. Ten thousand dollars in gold or cattle if you are delivered to him alive so that he can hang you."

3

Their eyes met, and their wills clashed. Lily Benton was unyielding.

"Now that I've learned to know you better," Jay said, "I'd imagine that you would prefer the gold. And ten thousand dollars sounds like it would be your price a couple of times over."

Again she refused to show anger, knowing he was still testing her for weakness. "You are worth more than ten thousand dollars to me," she said. "You and your talent with a gun."

"Who is it you want killed?" Jay demanded harshly.

Her mouth tightened. She edged back a pace, and he saw that she was suddenly afraid of him.

"Don't ever dare talk to me in that manner," she exclaimed.

"You're hiring Jess Steele," he reminded her derisively. "You're hiring his gun."

"This is what I want," she said hurriedly. "You will be my range boss. You're to see that Pitchfork has its fair share of graze . . . the graze we've always used. But I am sure it can be done without killing men. I want no gunplay. You must understand that clearly."

"You want your cake, but you don't want eggs broken," Jay said ironically. "You can't stop a bullet by merely saying you don't want anyone's life on your conscience. Does the other side know there is to be no gunplay?"

"If gunplay is forced on us," Lily Benton said huskily, "I will stand by you."

"With a knife at my back."

"If necessary . . . yes. One way or another I do not intend to be crowded out of this range."

"Hodge McColl is the only one who is crowding you."

She said nothing. Jay said jeeringly, "That means you're going to try to stop McColl. But they say you and Hodge . . ."

"Damnation on what they say!" she blazed. "Pitchfork pioneered this range. My father fought the tribes to hold this country. He would turn over in his grave if I let myself be shoved out of it now."

Jay's cold smile did not change. "I've heard that you could marry into Chain. And you already own Pitchfork."

She had the pride to refuse to answer that.

"I take it that Hodge isn't the marrying kind," Jay said. "He wants you, and he wants Pitchfork too, but he only intends to keep Pitchfork permanently."

The temper she had been holding in check broke out of control now. She moved nearer and swung a palm at his face with total fury. Jay caught her wrist in time and checked the blow. He was suddenly keenly aware of her supple strength.

They stood an instant, eye to eye, matching their determination, and finding no retreat in either.

Then Jay released her and stepped back. "A man's jaw will stand only so much," he said. "Once a day is plenty."

"Keep your insinuations to yourself," she said, breathing hard. "Let's understand each other. I'm hiring you to put the fear of wrath in Hodge McColl and Chain . . . not to judge me on my personal matters. I'm ashamed of myself for even wanting to lay a hand on a man like you."

"You don't have to touch pitch to be defiled," Jay said. "You're hiring a killer. That makes you an accessory in the eyes of the law. Always keep that in mind."

She forced her temper under restraint again. "You will make your headquarters at Yellow House. Your cattle can be worked along with Pitchfork and the pool. I do not expect you to abandon your ranch. I'll give orders to the crew, accordingly."

"If I'm to be your range boss I'll give the orders."

"Please do not use the indefinite. You are my range boss. That is decided."

"You seem to have decided also that I'm to hire a gun crew," Jay said. "I know no such people and wouldn't hire them if I did. A man who would take a hundred dollars to fight on my side could be bought by the opposition for a dollar more."

"And for a dollar more than three hundred a month, perhaps," she said.

"That's your problem," Jay remarked.

"But in your case the price you would pay if you double-deal on me might be a little high," she reminded him. "Sid Ferris is still with Wyatt Lomack in Texas. If Lomack doesn't hang you, Sid Ferris will kill you."

She turned, caught a stirrup and mounted. "I'll be expecting you in the morning at Yellow House, ready to take over our duties. We should be preparing to drift the stock out of the lower country. This weather won't hold long. Spring will come with a rush."

She forced the mare nearer. "The mare can carry double," she said. "I'll take you to your place."

"I prefer to walk," Jay said stonily.

"As you wish," she shrugged. "I will send Will Overmire to your place as soon as possible."

"Overmire? I never needed a doctor to tend a bruised jaw before. I'll survive this one."

"I'll send Will anyway. You can trust him."

She wheeled to ride away, leaving Jay puzzled. She had no sooner turned her back on him, than she twisted sharply around in the saddle again, and glanced at the boulders where Jay had hidden his rifle.

A sudden apprehension had chilled her. "I forgot to mention," she said quickly, "that if anything happens to me I have left a letter with a friend, which is to be opened in case of my sudden death. You are mentioned in that letter. Any bad luck that comes to me will be your bad luck also. It is important to you that I stay alive."

She turned deliberately again and rode away. She maintained that confident pose as she followed the gooseneck curves of the rough trail downward. But once she knew she was safely out of Jay's sight she sagged in the saddle and was suddenly all jangling nerves and fighting off hysteria.

She used her spurs and the offended mare broke into a wild gallop. Lily Benton rode as though pursued by demons, and kept looking over her shoulder.

Behind her Jay listened to the sudden clatter of hooves, heard them fade into silence. He stood there a long time, bitter defeat in his eyes. Just when he had become convinced that he was safe all the solid ground had been cut from under him, and the old, desperate sensation of sinking, always sinking, was back with him again.

Little by little, over the stretch of six years, the ever-quivering watchfulness of a hunted thing had subsided in him. For many months now he had been sleeping soundly at nights, no longer springing up, gun in hand, at the scrabble of a pack rat, or the creaking of a wind-tossed tree.

The sight of a strange horseman in the distance had ceased to bring the old, icy readiness into his eyes; he had learned to ride straight ahead to meet passers-by without feeling that in the next instant he might be called upon to shoot first to stay alive. He had lately been traveling into town whenever he pleased, instead of choosing the protecting, distorting half-light of dusk, or darkness, for his visits.

Now, upon him again was the gaunting weight of danger, the bitterness and the futility. He was again Jess Steele, gunman, wanted for murder. Six years had changed him. It had added ten pounds to his once sparse frame, tightened the line of his mouth, laid a taciturn armor on him. The fiery zeal of young idealism, he was sure, was dead forever, leaving only the cold residue that goes with defeat. He had led a lost cause, but now he was mature, and he wanted no more lost causes.

But he was still a man with a price on his head. And now he had a price on his gun.

There was only one way out. He must leave this range now—at once—to escape from Lily Benton and her plans. That meant giving up his ranch and the fruits of five years of careful work. And he was just getting his real start.

He turned, looked at the majestic mountains, an empty and protesting loneliness in his eyes. He remembered the pleasure of the morning's ride, and his kinship with this country that had shielded him so long. Now his roots had been torn up by a woman's will, and there would be no peace and no security for him here again. And, he reflected, there would be none anywhere now that a woman knew his secret.

He finally became aware that the wind was knifing into him; his hands were numb. He appraised Frank's jaded bay and decided the animal was able to travel and might, with care, recover completely.

He got his rifle and shouldered the saddle again.

Leading the drooping bay, he began walking.

Presently he left the trail, and cut across the face of the mountain northward. Pausing at times to rest the horse, he picked a route across a rockslide where a marmot whistled a challenge at them. Climbing a ridge, they then angled down a long mountainside through buckbrush and fir, and presently reached the pocket of a shallow canyon. Here a cold snow-water stream rumbled noisily from pool to pool over the ribs of exposed bedrock.

This was Slide Creek, Jay's home stream. The gray-white skeletons of the quakies stood in huddled silence, their first buds subdued now by the return of cold weather. Higher up the waning day was massing its shadows in the depths of the spruce and lodge-poles, for the sun was now below the haze-shrouded rim.

He let the bay drink briefly, then headed down-stream. Soon the canyon faded into a wide, natural meadow. Box elder and willows grew here, along with the aspen, and the stream gentled and slid in easy loops beneath undercut grass banks where fat trout lurked.

At the east end of this clearing stood the shake-roofed cabin that Jay had bought from a homesteader who had originally proved up on this flat.

Jay pulled up, staring. Faint heat haze showed above the kitchen pipe. Someone had a fire going in his kitchen—a careful fire of clean quakie wood, hot and at full draft so that it would give only a minimum of smoke.

Jay now stood confronted with the possibility that he did not dare even return to his house to get what belongings he could carry on a pack saddle. For he meant to pull out after dark and travel fast.

He debated it for a motionless minute. Reason told him that it must be only some passing rider who had stopped to cook a meal and find a bunk for the night. He made his decision and moved ahead again.

He led the bay to his slab-built shelter shed south of the house and swung open the hinged door. Five horses, gaunt, sinewy and with eyes bloodshot from hard riding, were tied inside the shed, crowding the place. They were eating wild hay from his stacks.

Saddle and girth rub had worn their shaggy, unpicked winter coats into patchwork. One horse, a dun, had a long, scabbed-over welt on its right haunch. That might be a bullet burn. Mud was matted in strings on the long hair under their bellies and caked on their fetlocks. They wore brands he had never before read. Hard-used saddle gear was on the trees and wall pegs.

Jay made room for the weary bay, put feed in its reach, then walked to the house.

He called out at the proper distance, though he knew his approach was known, for he had glimpsed movement at a window.

A man's voice answered from inside the house. "All right, Jess."

He opened the door, stepped in, closing it quickly. Four men, unshaven, rough-garbed, and as trailworn as their horses, returned his stare soberly.

39

He knew these men, had grown up with them in Texas. He had fought side by side with them, seen their kinfolk die, watched their women weep over open graves.

"I guessed it when I saw the horses," he said.

4

Ben Tracy stood tiredly leaning against the frame of the door that led into the main room. He was a long-flanked, square-jawed, weather-roughened man. Jay saw that six years had laid a tinge of frost on Ben's stubble of sandy beard.

Ben's red-headed younger brother, Steve, was at the cookstove, frying beefsteaks from Jay's cooler. "Howdy, highpockets," Steve said, his freckled face grinning. "You've put on some tallow."

Jay and Steve were the same age and had been close comrades since childhood. Tom Faye, the stocky, dark-eyed, quiet one, was at a table, a coffee mug in his hands. Mario Rodriguez, lithe, smiling, calm, was rolling a huskpaper cigarette. Mario smoothed the quirlie carefully, reached from his heel squat, touched a shaving to the glowing bars of the stove grate, and drew smoke into his lungs.

"*Buenos días,* Jess!" Mario said. "You have been fighting, no? You have the very beautiful jaw."

Jay shook hands with them, one by one. There was an unspoken world of meaning in the fierce strength of their grasp.

Beyond Ben Tracy Jay saw someone lying in his bed in the main room. He pushed past Ben and said, "Ward!"

This was his brother. Ward Steele was two years younger than Jay but he looked gaunt and aged. He lay pale, limp, the waste of fever dulling his blue eyes.

Ward pulled a grin to his lips. That required mighty effort. "Sorry I got to shake lying down, Jess," he murmured.

Jay's voice was unsure. "What's the matter, kid? Growing pains?"

"A touch of lead poison," Ward said.

Jay pulled back the blanket. A bandage was wound around Ward's body. A soiled bandage.

"It tickled a rib," Ward said.

Jay wheeled on Ben Tracy. "How long?" he demanded.

"Six days."

"Six? Good God!"

"Julesburg," Ben said. "Somebody must have recognized us there. We came in after dark for a solid meal, an' had to leave in a hurry. They smoked us up before we got clear, but only Ward was hit. Two days later, at a little cow town, we talked a doctor into looking him over. The fellow got the bullet out, and Ward felt better. But the doc also put the marshals on us again. We had two days of steady riding before we cooled our trail. That was rough on the boy."

Jay had a new thought. "Did anyone see you come here today?"

They all turned swiftly, a demanding question in

their eyes. "Not that we know of," Ben said slowly. "Though we got here at mid-morning. Had to take a chance on broad daylight. Ward needed to get into a bunk."

"How did you know where to locate me?" Jay asked.

Suddenly the room was very quiet. "That letter," Ben said slowly. "That letter you sent to my mother at Concho more'n a month ago. It said you were in trouble and gave directions. You took a chance, Jay. They might still be watching Mom's mail, even after six years. Wyatt Lomack is a bulldog. And so is Sid Ferris."

"Did you see this letter?" Jay demanded sharply.

Tension built up in the room. "No," Ben said softly. "Mom sent us the message verbally by a friend of mine. She had memorized it and burned it, for it was dangerous to have around."

"Was it in a man's handwriting?"

All of them were on their feet now. Even Ward was trying to sit up in his bunk. Mario lifted his gun belt from the back of a chair, strapped it on.

Ben drew from an inner pocket a small object. "This was enclosed with the letter, Jess. That's why Mom never doubted it had come from you. She likely had never seen your handwriting anyway. But this picture was enough for her—and for the rest of us too. We knew you always used to carry it with you. Mom sent it to me to be returned to you."

The object he handed Jay was a small tintype picture of a sweet-faced woman and a lank-mustached man and two small boys, all garbed in their Sunday best, and standing in the rigid pose typical of the early-day photography.

This was Jay's father and mother, and Jay, himself, at the age of six, and Ward.

Jay stared unbelievingly at that old tintype that had been about the only memento of the past that he had cherished. Then he strode across the room and rummaged in the homemade desk that contained his tally books and ranch records.

Finally he straightened. "That picture was in my wallet when I rode out of Concho that night. I had kept it hidden in this desk for years. But now it is gone."

He added softly, "I didn't write that letter."

"A deadfall," Ben said, his voice metallic. "An' we stepped into it like fat possums.

"Maybe the party is starting already," Steve spoke, peering from a window. "Somebody coming up the trail. A long reach buckboard with a buggy top. Roan team. Looks like only one man, though."

Jay moved to the window. The rig was entering the flat, coming from down-bench. The lone occupant was Dr. Will Overmire.

All of this suddenly fitted into a pattern in Jay's mind. "Maybe it's no deadfall," he said. "But it might be the death of all of us before it's over."

He was remembering his talk with Lily Benton. He knew now why she had been so certain he would find the crew of fighting men she wanted. She was responsible for that letter to Ben Tracy's mother and the removal of the tintype from his desk.

And she had known, during their talk, that these men had arrived at his ranch with a wounded rider among them. This was why she had insisted on a doctor.

Lily Benton knew what all of them had been, and what they were now. She had mentioned that Jay was not the only one described in the faded law dodgers she had read in the post office at Concho.

It all came back vividly, grimly to Jay. Here, in this room, were assembled the survivors of the losing side of the Fence Cutters' war that had been fought so bitterly in the Concho country in the past.

They had all been small brand owners in the Concho when Mason Lomack and his two sons moved in with ten thousand head of Sonora Reds out of Mexico that they had vented into their Double Arrow brand.

The Lomacks had brought with them a dozen fighting men under the direction of the deadly Sid Ferris, and soon they were fencing off shoestring ranchers like Jay from water and all decent graze.

Jay Webb—in those days, Jess Steele—had led the Fence Cutters, snipping wire to open up water and range for their failing stock.

But the majority of them were men with families, and the Lomack riders fought at night, shooting up homes, burning them and terrorizing women and children.

It had been an open secret that Mason Lomack had made an offer of $1,000 to any man who killed Jess Steele.

Even some of the Fence Cutters had tried to collect

44

that bounty. Men whom Jay had trusted had attempted to betray him. But they had not been fast enough. Jay had learned what it meant to see them go down through the haze of his own gunsmoke, the Judas-terror in their eyes.

Soon, other more kindly men were avoiding Jay, turning off the trails at his approach. He was no longer welcome at many of the homes he had helped defend. He was Jess Steele, gunman, killer.

By that time only a handful of the original Fence Cutters organization was left. These men were the hard, unbreakable core of the lost cause. Their ranch houses were in ashes, their brands wiped out. Ben Tracy had lost his wife. Tom Faye had buried a sister after a raid by the Lomack night riders. Mario Rodriguez had seen his parents die.

Mason Lomack's Double Arrow ranged at will, and finally fences were no longer needed, for the state had made it a prison offense to cut stock wire. Lomack had the law on his side, but he did not have the courage to file open charges against Jay and his comrades. Still, they bore the whispered taint of outlaws.

The climax came when Mason Lomack and his eldest son, Vince, were killed as they sat at a table in a saloon in Concho. Two shots, fired through a rear window into their backs, had struck them down.

Jay had been in Concho that night. Mason Lomack had sent word he wanted to talk to him. Lomack, now that the fight was won, was anxious to make peace with the men he had ruined but could not conquer. He wanted no avengers in the range to raid his herds and keep the feud alive.

For the sake of Ben Tracy's mother, and a few others who had hung on through disaster, Jay had decided to listen to Lomack's offer.

He remembered the vague figure of the young girl who had been sitting on the gallery of the Alamo Hotel as he rode past that night, and his warning to her. She had worn a white dress and she had a ribbon in her hair. He recalled that clearly.

Riding on he had swung off the street to the tie rail in the vacant lot alongside the Palace Bar. He was wary that this might be a trap, and he had his gun in his hand as he slid from his horse. Then two shots were fired at the rear of the building out of his sight.

From the shouting he had realized that Mason and Vince Lomack had been killed. He knew what that meant. He had hit the saddle, and headed out of town. But he was glimpsed and recognized by men who came running from the Palace, and they opened up on him.

Jay still carried the scar of a bullet that had raked his ribs, but he had shaken off immediate pursuit in the darkness.

He had sent word to the others, warning them to go into hiding, for he knew now they would all be out-lawed. He had drawn pursuit on himself for days, deliberately leading the trail northward as far as Colorado before making a real effort to blind his tracks.

That had given the others time to quit the Concho alive. Wyatt Lomack, the surviving son, had filed charges against all of them, and put rewards on their heads. He offered $5,000 for the capture of Ben and the others, $5,000 on Jay dead, and $10,000 if he were delivered alive so that Wyatt could personally hang him.

Jay had spent a year on the move, ranging as far as Canada, before he settled in this remote Wardrum country. Stories had drifted up from Texas telling that the old Fence Cutters survivors had gone entirely wolf. Ben Tracy was their leader, and Ward was one of them. They were charged with running wet cattle across the river into Mexico, running them back again at the other points to be sold to ranchers in other ranges who were not particular about their source of supply.

Jay believed these stories, for Wyatt Lomack's Double Arrow was the sufferer in these border-hopping raids. But soon the long riders, as they came to be called, were accused of train robberies and bank and stagecoach holdups in Kansas and New Mexico and Oklahoma. They were paying the price of notoriety. Every crime was being laid at their door.

Now they were here in the Wardrums, lean, wary men set on hair triggers, as they listened to the rattle of the doctor's rig as it approached the house. Ben Tracy looked twenty years older. Even Mario, though he still sported his sideburns and small mustache, had lost his debonair air of perpetual youth.

This, Jay reflected, is the look of the wolf. And this, no doubt, was how he looked to them. For that meeting with Lily Benton had stripped away the ease into which years of safety had lulled him. In him again, and edging to the surface was the tension and the suspicion, and the watchfulness . . . the cold and deadly readiness to lash back at the first sign of danger.

Jay turned from the window. "That man is a doctor. Stay out of sight while I talk to him. He may not be dangerous."

He walked out the door. Will Overmire drew up at the pole rail before the house. Without so much as a nod to Jay he alighted and tethered his team. Then he got his medical case from the buckboard.

Now he looked at Jay. His gaze held a chill neutrality. About the same age and height as Jay, Will Overmire had sensitive, well-bred features and intense dark eyes beneath a strong forehead.

Jay said carefully, "What brings you here, Doc?"

Overmire winced. He detested being referred to as Doc, but he was growing resigned to it in this wild region.

"I met Miss Benton on the trail," he said. "She told me a doctor was needed here."

"What else did Miss Benton say?"

Will Overmire did not answer. But his glance shifted to the house. Jay watched that, and made his decision. "All right," he said. "You seem to know it's more than a moused jaw. Come in."

He led the way, and as he entered he said to the men inside, "This is Will Overmire, a doctor from Spearhead. I'll explain this later."

Distaste was in Will Overmire's face. But he showed no surprise at finding the house so crowded and that confirmed Jay's guess that Lily Benton had fore-warned him.

Jay nodded toward the bunk. Overmire walked to Ward's side, drew back the blanket. Then he pulled off his coat, and rolled back the starched cuffs of his sleeves. He opened the bag. Presently he asked for warm water, and afterwards he worked in silence.

Jay stood across the room, a shoulder tilted against a wall, moving occasionally to help Overmire when the doctor beckoned.

Ben Tracy crowded the doorway to the kitchen, watching in silence. Ben's face was grim, dubious. He did not like this. Steve and Tom and Mario sat without talk in the kitchen, letting Ben and Jay decide this matter.

After a time Overmire straightened. Ward was moaning now, mumbling incoherently.

"He seems in more pain," Jay said.

"He's feeling it more," Will Overmire said. "He's fighting it now. That gives him a chance. A slim one, but a chance."

"He's that bad?"

"He was dying when I came in."

"Dying?"

"He would not have lived through the day," Over-mire said. "This man is suffering from shock, exhaustion, exposure and loss of blood. He has a badly shattered rib and pneumonia. All that he has in his favor is that he is young and tough."

He added, "I've done all I can for today." He cleaned and sterilized his instruments at the stove, closed his medicine case and rolled down his sleeves. He pulled on his coat and reached for his fleece-lined weather jacket.

"You're staying here, Doc," Ben Tracy said quietly.

Overmire gave Ben a long and scornful look, then picked up his bag, turned toward the door.

Ben blocked his path. "Sorry, Doc," he said. "We can't let you go. You know that."

"He won't talk," Jay said.

"Why not?" Ben challenged.

Jay looked at Overmire. "How did she get your scalp, Overmire?" he asked. "What kind of a club does Lily Benton hold over you?"

"I happen to be Miss Benton's friend," Overmire said icily. "I have a deep respect for her."

"You haven't known her long, then?"

"Long enough. I first met Miss Benton back east, when I was an intern."

This man, Jay surmised, was in love with Lily Benton. If so, that answered the question, often discussed in Spearhead, as to why a young, obviously talented doctor like Will Overmire had chosen to hang his shingle in this remote range.

Jay motioned Ben to stand aside. "Let's hope your respect is justified, Overmire," he said.

Overmire smiled disdainfully, walked past Ben and out of the house to his rig. He freed the team and climbed to the seat.

Jay had followed him. "What are the boy's chances?" he asked.

"One in ten, I'd say. But I could be wrong. They say

only the good die young."

"When will you see him again?"

"Tomorrow, if possible. He should sleep through most of the night. Whenever he arouses, a little beef broth should be ready. Aside from that give him nothing but water, and only a sip at a time."

"I'm in your debt, Overmire," Jay said. "I would prefer to stay obligated to you."

Overmire swung his team. "I should lose my certificate for this," he said. "I've already lost my self-respect."

He drove away without a backward glance.

5

Jay walked back to the house.

"Who is this señorita, this Lily Benton?" Mario Rodriguez asked. "If she is young and pretty, then I am interested."

"She's my future boss," Jay said. "At least until Ward is able to travel."

They eyed him. "Lily Benton was responsible for that letter to your mother, Ben," Jay said. "She knows I am Jess Steele. And she knows who all of you are."

"Does that doctor know too?"

"I doubt it. He probably is sure only that we are outlaws or gunmen. That belief was branded all over him."

"Even so, he knows too much, and so does this Lily Benton," Ben said. "Anyone else?"

"Yes. Frank Spain."

"Frank Spain?"

"I suppose it was inevitable someone would come into this range who would know me," Jay said. "Frank showed up as a roundup hand three years ago. He stayed on in this country. He's got a little cattle claim on Latigo Creek, which is over the next ridge south of me."

They looked wary. "Frank is happy-go-lucky," Jay said, "and still has petticoat fever. But he was a Fence Cutter too, though he quit the fight early and left Texas. His father and a couple of cousins rode with us for a time. None of the Spains ever turned against us. I don't think Frank ever will either. In fact he's proud he was a Fence Cutter."

"How did this Lily Benton deal herself in?" Ben asked.

They listened while Jay told them of his meeting that day with Frank Spain and Hodge McColl. Then he recounted in exact detail his talk with Lily Benton and her amazing demand.

"I thought she had underestimated me," Jay concluded. "But I was the one who did the underestimating. I came here, intending to load a pack horse and hit the long trail again. I took it for granted that she didn't believe I would give up my outfit to escape from her. But all the time she knew you were here, and that one of you was badly wounded. She knew that would hold me here."

Ben reflectively rubbed his bristle of beard. "Between the six of us," he said, "we're worth considerable money on the hoof. At least $15,000. She must have something much better in mind to pass up that much sure money."

"This Wardrum country has as rich a graze as I've seen," Jay said. "Lily Benton runs about 12,000 head, and pools the country south of me with five small outfits that tally about 2,000 more cattle among them. But this range south of the Ox Bow River is open to homestead, and settlers are moving in, now that the railroad has reached Castle Bend. The country north of the river was Cheyenne reserve until a couple of years ago, but the Cheyennes have taken reservation farther north. The reserve will be opened some day, and probably will be for grazing only. That is virgin grass, and rich. It will triple Lily Benton's range if she can get priority on the top graze. Fifteen thousand is a small ante. She is shooting for a million. And so is Hodge McColl. The fight for this south range is only the side show. The north graze is the big prize."

"Did you say she was attractive? Mario persisted. "This Señorita Lily Benton?"

"You can take your chances, Mario," Jay said. "She's already brought Hodge McColl and the doctor to heel. The field is still open. I wouldn't say she was ugly. She's got a shape and knows it. But, remember, Mario, when you dine with the devil you've got to use a long spoon."

Tom Faye spoke, "Do you figure to earn this gun money she's offering?"

"No, but I may have to string along with the play until Ward pulls through." And Jay added quietly, "If

53

he does pull through. Overmire said the odds were against him."

"Seems like we'll need a long spoon in each hand," Tom observed. "We're playin' one devil ag'in another. I've heard of Hodge McColl. He got his start in Texas, if I recollect right."

"Not 'we,'" Jay said. "You men will ride. I'll stay with Ward, and we'll join you later."

"When we ride we'll ride together," Ben Tracy said flatly.

That was the way it stood, for there was no changing their decision.

It was not until he was rolling his bedtime smoke that Jay remembered Frank Spain's request that he meet a girl who was to arrive at Spearhead the next day to marry him. Jay vaguely recalled the name of Frank's fiancée. Dallas Carver.

Frank had spoken enthusiastically to Jay some months earlier of a girl he had met during a trip to Kansas City. Frank was always involved in some affair of the heart and Jay had taken it for granted that this was another of Frank's passing fancies. Evidently Dallas Carver must be something special to intrigue Frank to the point of marriage.

Jay felt a remote pity for this Dallas Carver who was evidently en route to Spearhead to face disillusionment and humiliation.

He owed it to Frank to meet the stage, but Lily Benton had ordered him to report to her at Yellow House in the morning. It would be dangerous to offend her, for she held the power of life and death over him, and over the other men who lay in their blankets, sleeping with the deadness of exhaustion.

However he decided he could make the trip to town and do what he could to explain to Frank's fiancée, then ride to Yellow House in the afternoon.

Occasionally Ward moaned in his stupor. Invariably, before he could stir, Jay would hear one of the others arouse from their heavy sleep, hurry to the bed and sit in the faint glow of the turned-down lamp, murmuring encouragement, or swearing in sympathy with Ward's misery.

Daybreak came, raw and cheerless. Cold rain and sleet flurries slashed against the walls at intervals, and the driving wind rattled the doors. The high spires of the Wardrums were lost in the overcast. Up there it was snowing steadily, no doubt, while the plains were probably swept by rain. These middle benches had both kinds of weather on this day, and likely would see worse before nightfall.

Ward aroused at times, then would sink back into his pain-racked stupor. His weakness was frightening. Ben Tracy fed him, his big, hard-knuckled hands shaking with the tension of his care.

The broth evidently was good medicine, for Ward fully aroused for a time. He looked at Ben, and said in a thin voice, "I never had any luck. By rights I ought to have a nurse that wore skirts and didn't need a shave. One with taffy-colored hair, and the right glow in her eyes. You're enough to set a man back, Ben."

Then he fell asleep again.

Afterwards Jay pulled on a brush jacket and gloves and picked up his slicker. He had shaved, though it was a patchwork operation, for his jaw was still swollen.

He stood a moment, considering. Then he unlocked a case on the wall in which he kept his rifle and bird gun and other effects.

A six-shooter, which he carried occasionally while working cattle, hung in a rough bullhide holster. It was a wooden-handled .44 of standard make, its grip scarred by use as a hammer for pounding coffee beans and jerky in many overnight camps. This gun was the commonplace, all-purpose tool of the working cowman.

Jay hesitated, then drew out a second gun, wrapped in an oiled cloth. This weapon was a different proposition. Black-handled, with a seven-inch barrel dyed a dull blue-black, it lay in his hand wickedly sleek, perfectly balanced. With it was a waxed cutaway holster, known in range parlance as a half-breed. The holster was fitted with a belt and tie-down whangs.

This was the gun Jay had carried during his fighting days. He had not used it in more than five years. He gazed at it for a time. Then he slowly, carefully cleaned it, tried the action. He loaded it and buckled it on. Its weight lay tight against his thigh.

Ben and the others watched in silence. There was no need for talk.

Jay had rarely worn a side gun since he had fled Texas, and never in town or at roundup wagons where he was in contact with other men. He had avoided

56

even the normal, minor disputes of active, hard-working riders.

He never again wanted to use in earnest the special speed that he had once developed to the ultimate degree by constant practice. Gun skill had kept him alive in his fighting days, but it had exacted its penalty. No respectable girl in the Concho would be seen in his company in those days.

Now this was happening to him again.

He said, "We'll know more after I talk to Lily Benton."

He picked his top horse, a sorrel, from his string that was huddled in the lee of the shelter shed. Saddling, he rode down the trail toward Spearhead. He had a gunny sack lashed on the cantle. He was not equipped to feed so many men, and needed supplies. This was his final excuse for deciding to be in Spearhead when the Castle Bend stage arrived.

Gusts of rain struck at him occasionally. The weather was coming from the north now, and the temperature was falling. He began sighting a few cattle in the brush as he descended the trail. These were mainly his own Rocking J's, which, lacking lower range, wintered in this area. With them were some of Frank Spain's Rafter S stock, and a few of Lily Benton's Pitchforks. The Pitchforks were early drifters, well off their regular range, for the bulk of the Pitchfork cattle were still in the lower country south and east.

He rode lax, his head turtled in the fleece-lined collar of his jacket, his slicker unfrogged.

He reached the fork where the Yellow House trail

funneled in from the south. Frank Spain's place on Latigo Creek was only two miles from this point, off the Yellow House trail.

Jay's horse was moving at a steady shuffle when its head lifted, and its ears came to an instant alert.

It might have been a deer moving in the brush. Twenty-four hours earlier Jay would hardly have aroused from his own thoughts at such a common occurrence.

But now his nerves jangled. That throwback to his old life saved him. He caught the glint of gun steel in the half-light of the lowering day.

He was moving, falling from the saddle on the off-side of his horse as the bullet came, with a gush of saffron flame, from a brush-grown boulder off the trail.

A savage force punched his left shoulder, whirling him as he pitched to the ground. He landed on a knee and a hand, but he clung to the reins with his left hand, and it was the sorrel, rearing, that lifted him back to his feet.

Already he had flipped up the skirt of his brush coat, and his gun was in his hand, rising.

His horse, panicked by the shot, was fighting to escape. Its resistance swung it so that its bulk shielded him from the person back of the boulder.

Jay held the horse thus, following the backing animal toward the rock. Then he glimpsed a man's head.

Jay fired, shooting beneath the rearing horse's belly. And that was the only shot he needed, for he felt an instinctive sureness as he tripped the hammer that he had centered his target.

A second bullet came from the boulder, but it must have been the result of reflex action, for it was fired upward. The head disappeared.

Jay continued to use the horse as a shield as he moved warily around the rock, pushing through the small brush. At last he stood looking down at a man in a black slicker who lay twisted there on the rain-wet mat of pine needles, hands and feet still quivering.

Then the quivering stopped in the terrible finality of death. Back in the timber a horse was racing off, empty stirrups kicking it into greater panic. Mechanically Jay noted its brand. The animal wore Lily Benton's Pitchfork iron.

The horse vanished from sight and sound. The wind had stilled momentarily. Brooding silence came in the timber, marked only by the drip from the recent gusts of rain.

It had all happened with such swiftness that Jay's reactions had been only the fast reflexes of a hunted thing protecting its own life.

Now he looked at the long-muzzled gun in his hand. "I've still got it—the speed," he thought with a man's instinctive pride in his own power.

Then the horror came. The gun sagged to his side, and he stood gaunt and lonely, torn by heartsick protest. He had laid aside that balanced gun more than five years ago, vowing never to wear it again. But circumstances had crowded him into carrying it once more, and already the old pattern was beginning—kill or be killed.

He finally bent over the dead man. His bullet had struck above the right eye. He had to study the face before recollection came. He recalled the man vaguely as a cowhand named Dave Hollister who rode for Lily Benton's Pitchfork. He could not remember exchanging more than a nod and a casual word with Hollister on the few occasions they had met.

Jay stood, trying to sift something rational out of this attempt to cut him down. His first thought was that Lily Benton had decided to get rid of him for the sake of her own safety. But it did not seem reasonable that she would lose her nerve and want him killed now after spending months of effort to force him to serve her purpose.

Jay holstered his gun and examined his shoulder. He found a rip in his slicker and brush jacket. There was a faint red welt where the slug had burned his skin.

He mounted, leaving Hollister's body lying in the brush. Whoever had sent Hollister probably would know where to look for him. For Jay was sure someone had sent the man to bushwhack him. The attempt on his life could hardly have had any connection with his being wanted for murder, for he would have been worth twice as much delivered alive to Wyatt Lomack, as dead.

He rode blindly for a time. Then he looked again at his right hand in wonder and protest. The physical reaction came then. He began to shake inside, uncontrollably. He turned off the trail, slid from the saddle and was sick.

He calmed at last, and rode on toward Spearhead.

It was well past noon when he turned into the head of Custer Street, the sorrel picking its way with distaste through the wheel-whipped batter of mud. The duck-board and plank sidewalks were nearly deserted. The biting wind had driven Spearhead mainly indoors.

Jay saw that two new business enterprises had opened since his last visit, and carpenters were spiking the framework of another structure that had the promise of being a sizeable freight warehouse. The planer in Herdman's lumber mill laid a flat and busy drone over the town, and he met the clean tang of sawdust. Spearhead was growing, now that the railroad was within reach.

From the timber east of town the wind brought the ragged call of the old army bugle that Hank Cass used as a stage horn. Hank was pulling in on time with the run from Case Bend.

Jay stabled his horse in shelter at Charlie Beals's livery. Charlie eyed his bruised jaw, and said, "It's gittin' so a man don't dare stand up for his friends in these parts."

Apparently word of what had happened on the Fort Relief trail had reached Spearhead.

Leaving the livery Jay walked as far as Al Pettit's harness shop, opposite the stage station. He paused in the overhang of the shop door, his eyes fixed on a new saddle Al had on display inside the shop. But he was not seeing the saddle. He was seeing Dave Hollister through the gunsmoke. He was still quivering at the knees.

Hank Cass's bugle had brought Ma Monday to the

door of her Pioneer House, which adjoined the stage station. Ma, an ample, garrulous woman, with a complexion perpetually reddened by hot cookstoves, was removing her apron and brushing at her graying hair as she prepared to welcome guests and drain from them all gossip.

Fred Dobbs stirred in the stage office, and a hostler came from the barn. A few other stragglers showed up. Stage arrival, with its possible look at new faces, was always a luxurious break in Spearhead's drifting day.

Otis Haskell's slender, dark-haired wife stepped from the bank a few doors from where Jay stood. Otis had followed her to the door and now stood, showing Spearhead a proud and sure smile as he watched his wife walk away.

But it occurred to Jay that the smile had no depth. Otis, a balding, kindly man in his late forties, had confounded Spearhead by bringing home from Cheyenne a bride twenty years younger than himself, and now, after more than two years of marriage he still seemed surprised, and uncertain of his luck.

Amelia had been a waitress when Otis had met and married her. A thin-cheeked, olive-complexioned girl, slim but shapely of figure, her dark, intense eyes were always hopefully aware of any masculine attention. She still carried herself defiantly, for the women of Spearhead had never forgiven her for marrying Otis. She had a market basket on her arm as an excuse for being on the street, but Jay surmised that it was loneliness that had brought her here.

Otis pampered her. At first she had dressed gaudily,

but she had learned repression in that art also, and now garbed herself in studied good taste. She had gone to Lily Benton when she had realized that something was wrong. Lily had helped her select her wardrobe, taught her the value of repression. That was another item that feminine Spearhead held against both her and Lily Benton.

To Jay, there always had been a strain and a tension in Amelia, as though she were trapped and unable to find the right key to her freedom. Now he sensed that the burning urgency within her was greater than ever as she walked toward him, the wind whipping her skirt against her legs.

He saw now that she intended to speak to him, though they always had been strangers. A question was forming in Amelia's eyes, a question that was desperate and pleading.

But at that moment the slap of hooves sounded close by. Hedge McColl and Sam Leathers rode abreast of them, heading for Pat Slattery's bar beyond the stage station.

Amelia's glance swung from Jay to McColl. Her eyes and McColl's met and held for a moment, then broke apart. McColl rode on past without a flicker of expression or a backward glance.

A hopeless defeat came into Amelia's face. She dropped her head, clutched her market basket tighter and hurried by Jay without a word.

But Sam Leathers' crooked mouth had shaped briefly in a moist and knowing grin. He wiped this away hastily, and attempted to appear vastly and righteously unaware of Amelia as he followed McColl toward Slattery's.

Jay suddenly knew for sure the identity of the woman who was involved in the trouble between Frank Spain and Hodge McColl.

He guessed that rumor of what had happened to him on the Fort Relief trail had been heard by Amelia. Driven by that wildness that had placed her in this situation, she had almost made the mistake of accosting him openly to ask him about that meeting with McColl and about Frank Spain. But she had thought better of it in time. Either that or the sight of McColl had deterred her.

Jay watched her walk rapidly away, heading in the direction of the big, Eastern-styled house that Otis had built for her on the south fringe of town.

Then Hank Cass brought the muddy stage into town, bringing it to a stop with a final flourish at the station platform.

Four muscle-stiff passengers alighted. The fifth and last was a young woman, who stepped easily to the dry planks beneath the wooden station awning, refusing the offer of help from hopeful men. She stood there, shaking out her dark traveling skirt. She touched her small bonnet into place and looked around expectantly.

6

Jay picked his way across the muddy street and approached her. He lifted his hat. "Miss Carver?"

She turned questioningly. "Yes?"

Jay had not expected anything like this. He had anticipated comeliness, for Frank's taste had always run to brash, full beauty in his women. Dallas Carver was more than comely. She was extraordinarily beautiful, but hers was the finely cut perfection of a cameo.

She was inspecting him with eyes that were a cool sea green under delicate brows. Her face was narrow with a singular attractiveness, her cheeks thin under strong cheekbones, and her skin was a very pale ivory. Her hair was a finely spun pale gold, and she had slender, expressive hands.

She seemed taller than average, but Jay decided this was mainly because she carried herself so straight. She was exceedingly well formed and graceful, but, above all, he was aware of an inner composure that strengthened her.

"I'm Jay Webb, a friend of Frank's," he said, keeping his voice down, for bystanders were watching and listening avidly. "He asked me to meet you."

Her glance rested briefly and dubiously on his bruised jaw. However, what decision she made about him she kept reserved, for her eyes remained noncommittal.

"Why didn't Frank come in person?" she asked.

"He was called away on important business."

Dallas Carver's face became instantly expressionless, masking her thoughts. "How important?"

"Enough to take him away at a time like this," Jay assured her.

He saw smirking grins on the faces of the listeners. Everyone in Spearhead, of course, must know that Frank Spain and Hodge McColl were in a shooting feud and that McColl had driven Frank into hiding in the mountains. The chances were they knew that a woman was the cause of the trouble and also that Frank had expected to be married and that this was his fiancée.

Jay warned Dallas Carver with his eyes not to speak. She stiffened a little, and at once was on her guard.

"Right now," Jay said, "what you need is a meal and a chance to freshen up. Ma Monday sets the best table in the West, and she has hotel accommodations."

She eyed him again, measuring him against her own doubts. Her glance swung to the onlookers, and what she saw there brought a tinge of resentful color into her throat.

She nodded. "Perhaps that would be best."

The stage boot had been unloaded. She pointed out a leather traveling case and a handbag. "I'll send for my trunk later," she said.

She laid a hand on his arm as Jay, carrying the luggage, walked her to the Pioneer House. "Tell no one anything," he murmured. "Ma Monday is the biggest gossip in a week's ride."

"Forewarned is forearmed," she said softly. "What

is this trouble that Frank has got himself involved in?"

"Trouble?"

"Is it a woman?" she asked bluntly.

"I imagine, after seeing you, that you are the only woman Frank would ever get into trouble over," Jay said.

She smiled a little tightly. "I know Frank," she said.

They entered the Pioneer's small lobby. Jay had to surrender her to Ma Monday who was in a flutter of anxiety to get this comely visitor in her grasp and prospect her for information.

"You poor, poor dear!" Ma gushed. "I'll take mighty good care of you, depend on that."

Dallas gave Jay a resigned glance as she suffered Ma to lead her up the worn wooden stairs to the second floor.

Ma ushered her to a front room whose window overlooked Custer Street. It contained a bed, washstand, dresser, cane-seated chairs and rag rugs. Mamie Schneider, the hired girl, brought up Dallas' luggage.

Ma bustled around, arranging the blinds, pouring water in the china basin. "Men," she sighed, "are women's burden. I declare, they ain't to be trusted. Not a single one of 'em. I know. Wasn't I married myself, twice? Buried two husbands, an' I don't want another."

A cold anger began to pulse in Dallas, but outwardly she showed Ma only a helpless perplexity. She removed her coat and bonnet, opened the luggage, and, after appraising the weather through the window, laid out a heavy dark skirt and a warm waist and jacket. She pulled off her traveling dress.

"My, but you're the purtiest thing," Ma said dolefully. "Frank Spain ought to be ashamed of himself."

"Ashamed? Why?"

"Didn't Jay Webb tell you?" Ma demanded eagerly.

The anger grew in Dallas, but with the skill of a practiced actress, she maintained her pose of bewilderment. "Tell me what?" she asked. "I don't understand."

"You wouldn't, you poor little lamb. You came here to marry Frank Spain, didn't you? Ain't you the girl he met in Kansas City? Frank told everybody about you."

"Why, yes. Frank and I are engaged."

Ma placed her hands on her ample hips. "Well, then, it's only right that you should know the truth. If Jay Webb won't tell you, then I will. Frank has got himself into a peck of trouble with Hodge McColl, an' has had to skedaddle off into hidin' in the hills."

Dallas gazed with genuine shock. "Who is Hodge McColl?"

"You'll learn soon enough," Ma said. "McColl owns the Chainlink outfit. A big cattle ranch."

"But . . . but what was the trouble about?"

"What's trouble generally about when two men go gunnin' for each other?" Ma said grimly.

"You mean a . . . a woman?"

Ma patted Dallas soothingly on the shoulder. "Now don't take it too hard. It's happened before to plenty of decent women, an' it'll happen ag'in as long as men are what they are."

The fury was a raging fire in Dallas now. But she

compelled herself to endure Ma's sympathy, for she had to learn more. "Who is the woman?" she asked.

"Now, now," Ma said a trifle uncertainly. "What difference would it make, knowin' that? She wouldn't be your kind anyway, I reckon."

Dallas forced herself to maintain her helpless pose. She began nervously brushing her hair. Her hands were shaking. Then she realized Ma Monday was watching her with cat-and-mouse delight, marking every surge of emotion she displayed so that she could describe it later to others. Ma would like nothing better than to drive her into hysteria and a storm of tears.

Dallas' hand steadied, and suddenly she again had full control of her will and her emotions. It had always been this way with her in matters of self-discipline.

"You mean she's some common woman?" she asked.

"Ain't that the kind that always start trouble among men?" Ma sniffed.

"How do you know all this?"

"People talk," Ma shrugged.

"Then this is . . . is generally known?"

"A little ripple travels fur in a small frogpond," Ma said. "Everybody knows most everything that goes on in these parts."

"When did all this start?"

"Couldn't say when it started," Ma admitted. "Likely it's been simmerin' for a long time. It come to a boil yesterday when McColl went gunnin' fer Frank.

Seems like Frank got wind of it in time, an' lit out fer the mountains. McColl an' two cowboys chased him. Frank's horse fagged out, but he happened to run into Jay Webb. They traded horses an' that saved Frank's neck. He got away. I reckon Jay Webb is mighty sorry he got mixed up in it. They beat him up."

"Beat him up?"

"You saw that jaw Jay is carryin', didn't you?"

"Do you mean this person, Hodge McColl, did that to Mr. Webb because he helped Frank?"

" 'Twasn't exactly Hodge, though he ordered it done. He's got men who're paid to do that kind of work. Sam Leathers did the chastisin'. Sam was in town last night an' drinkin'. He told the whole story. Sam said Jay Webb didn't even dare fight back. I reckon Jay was smart at that."

"Smart?"

"It only would have made it worse on himself," Ma explained. " 'Tain't healthy to oppose Hodge McColl."

"Why? Is McColl some sort of a ruffian?"

"Not the way Hodge looks at it," Ma shrugged. "But he aims to own all this range, and he's goin' to succeed, if you ask me. He's just about got Pitchfork on the run."

"Pitchfork?"

Ma sighed. "I keep forgittin' you're a stranger. Pitchfork is a big cattle outfit owned now by a snobbish girl named Lily Benton. Pitchfork was founded by her father, an' was top dog in the Wardrums 'til Hodge moved in an' started takin' over the graze. Hodge will run Pitchfork clean out of the country in another year, the way things are goin'."

"You mean this man McColl is stealing the other person's range?"

"Stealin'?" Ma laughed tolerantly. "Well, I reckon Lily Benton looks at it that way."

"What about the law?"

"Law?" Ma scoffed. "Why, you poor dear, this ain't the East. There's a deputy marshal at Castle Bend, but that's nigh on to a hundred miles away, an' he only gits paid in fees. There's easier ways to earn fees than to mix into trouble way up here. Anyway it ain't hardly stealin' in the eyes of the law. This is all open range south of the Ox Bow River, available to homestead. It's a case of dog eat dog right now. Any cowman who's strong enough to take an' hold the graze is in a position to use it as long as he ain't homesteaded out of it."

"That sounds incredible."

"My land, you do use four-bit words, don't you?" Ma said. "But then you was a schoolmarm, if I recall rightly. I reckon it does sound a little skeery to you, but that's the way it is. This here is frontier country an' still sufferin' from growin' colic. 'Twon't be long until the law moves in. When that happens the outfit that controls the lion's share will be sittin' purty, an' will likely keep what it has. McColl knows that, an' so does Lily Benton. That's why Lily is facin' ruination. McColl is too much for even her to handle."

"This man, McColl, must be an overbearing person," Dallas said. "What does he look like?"

"Speakin' of the devil," Ma exclaimed. "Here's your

71

chance to see fer yourself. There's Hodge McColl down there in the street this very minute."

Ma had been standing by the window, and now she was pointing. Dallas moved to her side.

Hodge McColl had left Slattery's bar, and was strolling the opposite sidewalk, a cigar in his teeth.

Dallas' eyes were intent as she studied him. She marked his solid bulk and his assurance, and noted that he spent money on his garb. Here, she reflected, was a man sure of his own prowess.

Then McColl's glance came up to the window, singling her out. He gazed at her with a full and appraising deliberation, a bold question in his bright, black eyes.

Dallas had the sensation of being stripped naked and evaluated by this arrogant man. She understood that McColl had purposely appeared in the street, guessing that he would be pointed out to her. Annoyed, she realized she had stepped into that trap. She had pleased McColl's vanity by showing this interest in him.

Then she met the challenge fiercely, almost gladly. Here, at last, was something tangible with which to come to grips. She refused to show him any weakness by retreating from the window. She remained there, her slim face cold, her green eyes returning his calculating stare.

McColl's white teeth showed in a pleased laugh. He lifted a hand, bearing the cigar, touched the brim of his hat in acknowledgment and continued on down the street. Dallas held the sure promise that he would see to it that their paths crossed again.

She remained at the window a few moments longer, watching McColl, studying him with the same, precise care she would give to an expensive purchase that might be brought within her means.

But when she turned away, all this was gone and she showed Ma only a womanly confusion. "A rude person," she said. "His appearance matches your description of his methods."

"There're plenty of girls," Ma said slyly, "that'd be mighty happy to have Hodge McColl look at them like he jest looked at you. Hodge is goin' places, an' is well fixed already. An' he ain't married—yet."

Dallas turned a cool glance on Ma, and Ma had the grace to flush. "It was just a passin' thought," Ma said hurriedly. "But a girl could do worse. Lily Benton has got her cap set fer Hodge, an' I'd like to see her git left."

"Lily Benton? But I understood you to say that McColl was stealing range from a woman named Lily Benton."

"I reckon Lily figures the only way she kin save herself is to marry Hodge," Ma snorted.

"You don't seem to approve of Lily Benton," Dallas observed.

"What respectable woman would stand up for a gal that traipses around in public ridin' a horse like a man, an' with her hair bobbed short like a red-light woman's."

Ma lowered her voice to a scandalized whisper. "An' they say Lily Benton smokes an' drinks."

"I can't imagine even Hodge McColl marryin' a

woman like that," Dallas said.

"Oh, she's not bad-lookin' in her own way," Ma acknowledged. "An' she knows how to swing herself so as to rile up a man's worst nature. She kin act the part of a lady too, if she's of a mind. Her paw sent her to high-toned schools, hopin' to make somethin' out of her."

Ma added, "But you're purtier, an' you're refined. That's plain to see. An' Hodge McColl ain't blind."

Dallas sat on the side of the bed and began changing stockings. When Ma saw that her remark was going to be pointedly ignored she said, "But I reckon you'll be goin' back home right away, Miss Carver?"

Dallas arose, holding her skirts above her knees, viewing her stockings in the mirror. Her legs were very good, and she knew it. "What does Jay Webb do for a living?" she asked.

"Jay Webb? Oh, him. Why, I figured you knew him, bein' as he met you at the stage."

"Frank had mentioned him to me a time or two in his letters. I understood that they were good friends. From his appearance, Mr. Webb seems to be a cowboy."

Ma, miffed at her inability to goad Dallas into talking about herself, said shortly, "Jay Webb owns a little outfit up on Slide Crick, about fifteen miles west of town. He started with a patched saddle a few years back, but I hear he's got a fair little bunch of beef in his brand now."

"A rancher?"

"He's got a long ways to go before he'll amount to anything as a cowman," Ma said disparagingly. "An',

74

anyway, he'll be gobbled up by McColl before he gits much further."

"Apparently Mr. McColl is the sun around which this range revolves. He's out to steal the Benton woman's ranch and Jay Webb's also."

"Jay don't count right now," Ma said. "He's small potatoes. But he won't last long after McColl takes care of Lily Benton an' the pool. With Pitchfork gone, Hodge will step on little independent outfits like Jay Webb's an' squash him as he would a tumblebug under his boot."

"What about Frank's ranch?"

"I reckon he's in the same boat with Jay Webb," Ma said sympathetically. "I don't want to discourage you, my dear, fer you've got enough misery on your hands, but that's the way it is. Frank ain't in the Pitchfork pool. Neither is Jay Webb. Their graze is cut off from the main range by rough country, so they handle their cattle independently. But that won't save 'em in the long run. McColl will crowd 'em out when he gits around to it."

"It seems to me all this would make Frank and Jay Webb allies of this Benton woman against McColl," Dallas said.

"Wal," Ma said, getting her chance to drive a hon-eyed barb into Dallas, "Frank ain't likely to be much help, with him already hidin' out from McColl. An' Jay Webb ain't never took sides with either Lily Benton or McColl. Ain't likely to, either. If you ask me, Jay Webb is a little short on backbone. Quite a bit short, if you want to know."

Dallas looked at Ma. "You mean he is afraid of McColl?"

"He let Sam Leathers punch him around without liftin' a hand to defend himself, didn't he? He's never offered to help Lily Benton. Never even packs a gun. Leastwise I never seen one on him. Likely he's afeared of havin' to use it. That's one way of avoidin' trouble, I suppose. Keeps to himself like he was skeered of his own shadow. Lily Benton can't count on any help from Jay Webb, an' I guess she knows it."

Dallas knew Ma was wrong in one particular. Jay Webb was carrying a gun today, at least. She had seen the shape of a holster weapon beneath his slicker when he had met her at the stage station.

She said, "That reminds me that Mr. Webb probably is waiting for me in the dining room. Please be kind enough to tell him I'll be down in a few minutes.

Ma, chagrined, realized she was being dismissed. She blinked, looked hurt, then left the room with a swish of calico. Ma had come here to pump this green-eyed girl, and now was realizing that, instead, she had been pumped herself. She had learned nothing about Dallas or her plans for the future, but Dallas had learned considerable from her. This was a new experience for Ma Monday.

Ma would have had considerable consolation if she could have seen Dallas after the door closed between them.

Dallas stood an instant, and then she let the fury and the injured pride have its way with her. She breathed in a choked voice, "Damn you! Damn all of you!"

She seized up a spare pillow case that Ma had left on the dresser and tore it to ribbons. Her nails ripped the cloth with the savagery of a tiger.

She stamped the shreds beneath her slippers and then the tears came, hot, scalding tears of injured vanity, tears that were the residue of a consuming thirst for vengeance on this town that had humiliated her.

Then, with characteristic abruptness, she gained control of herself. She walked at last to the window and stood there, the tears drying on her cheeks, the high drumming of her pulse easing in her throat.

She gazed at Spearhead with eyes that were composed again and purposeful. She estimated the town.

The band saw in the lumber mill was whining steadily. A twelve-mule jerk-line freight wagon and trailer with loads bulging under lashed tarps was straining into town off the Castle Bend trail. Somewhere carpenters' hammers were thudding, and she saw the rafters of a new, sizeable structure rising above the roofs of the older buildings.

Lights glowed on this gloomy day in Otis Haskell's bank, and its name—Spearhead Security Bank—was done in conservative gilt letters on the plate-glass window. There were customers in the bank, and in Mort Skelly's mercantile, and all the freight-yards were busy.

Beyond, beneath the roof of clouds, the timbered benches stretched into the distance, meeting the bulk of the Wardrums, whose upper reaches were buried in the storm. Here was a raw, new country that was beginning to pulse and stir and build, a country where a man's or a woman's opportunities were measured only by the strength of ambition, and by the drive of his or her will. From what Ma Monday had said, here was a country for the taking.

Presently Dallas turned away from the window, a deep and icy meditation in her eyes. She went to the mirror and carefully removed all traces of the tears.

When she turned to the door to go down to find Jay Webb she was serene and self-possessed again—and very beautiful.

7

Jay, after leaving Dallas in Ma Monday's hands, filled his grub sack at Mort Skelly's store, added a jug of whisky and a bottle of brandy to the order, and carried the sack to the livery. He debated a moment, then removed his gun belt and stuffed the weapon into the sack also.

He returned to the Pioneer House. The dining room opened off the lobby. Patrons were being served at the long table, family style, by Mamie Schneider. Smaller tables, with oilcloth covers, lined the walls, and a base-burner warmed the room. A gust of cold rain slapped the windows.

Jay took a chair at a small table and told Mamie he would wait before ordering. He sat wondering what he would say to Dallas Carver. She would surely leave

Spearhead. There was no other course for a woman of pride.

Now the memory of that blazing moment of gunplay, and of Dave Hollister's body lying in the rain-sodden brush, returned with choking impact.

He went over, word by word, his talk with Lily Benton, seeking some clue that would link her with Hollister's attempt to bushwhack him.

Only one thing seemed sure. Lily Benton was dangerous. She was fighting for high stakes, and she evidently would use any weapon at her command. She was letting McColl court her, and at the same time was using her knowledge of Jay's true identity to defeat him.

Lily Benton was highly intelligent, and evidently unscrupulous. The subterfuge by which she had lured the long riders hundreds of miles north had required imagination and long planning. It also marked her as a gambler, for she believed she was staking her life on this venture.

To her Jay and the long riders were outlaws, murderers. She was gambling on the chance that the letter she had written would deter them from silencing her permanently.

Then Dallas Carver entered the dining room. She had changed to a pleated skirt and hip-length jacket with puffed sleeves, and a choke-collared pale green waist. She wore no hat and her hair, parted in the center, was drawn into two neat, plaited coils at the back. In this dim light her hair was almost platinum.

She singled him out and came walking to the table.

She carried herself rigidly straight, and he saw the pallor of outraged pride in her face.

She knew! Jay understood that Ma Monday had talked, torturing her with sugary sympathy.

Jay seated her. Dallas Carver's expression was neutral—warned, but waiting.

"Damn women," Jay murmured wryly. "They've all got a cruel streak in 'em."

"Yes," Dallas said. "We're our own worst enemies."

"You're being watched," Jay said. "Everyone in town knows. Don't give them the satisfaction of showing how you feel."

"Who was the other woman?" Dallas asked steadily.

"Didn't Ma tell you that too?"

"No. I'm sure she doesn't know. That is a trial to her. She's beside herself to find out."

"That's something at least," Jay said reflectively. "Maybe it isn't such open knowledge after all."

"Who is she?"

"Answering that would put me in the same class with Ma Monday."

"Then you do know who she is?"

Jay said, "Whoever she is, I feel that it is past and done with."

Dallas did not persist. Mamie Schneider came to the table, and said, "Chicken, beef stew, venison, elk or beefsteaks. The stew's good, and with dumplin's."

"The beefsteak," Dallas said. "Rare."

After Mamie went away she studied Jay again. "Ma Monday didn't seem to know much about you, either," she said. "I did some fishing on my own account, but didn't land anything of any size. At least Ma didn't say too much against you. That may be a point in your favor, or it may only mean you're a friend of Ma's. In that case it's a point against you."

"I came into this range five years ago," Jay said. "Bought a pre-empted claim, and have built up a small cattle brand. Frank came in two years later and did the same. Being neighbors, we often threw in together. Frank had mentioned you, but frankly, I didn't know it was marrying serious with you two. He asked me yesterday to meet you."

"Now I know almost as much about you as Ma Monday does," she remarked lightly. "Why did you let McColl humble you without defending yourself?"

"That is known as following the line of least resistance," Jay said.

"Your words and your appearance do not match," she said. "You don't look like a man accustomed to knuckling down."

"Would you like coffee now?" Jay asked.

She smiled. "All right. I'll quit fishing—for the moment at least."

Then she asked, "How far is it to Frank's place?"

"A dozen miles."

"Then I could reach it before dark?" She watched the expression on Jay's face. "You don't approve?"

"Why do you want to go out there?" Jay asked.

"I don't intend to stay here and let these people pick my flesh," she said. "Frank is away. There could be no scandal in my staying there—at least not in the minds of decent persons."

81

"One hurt won't cure another."

She was a very direct person. "You mean Frank isn't exactly the kind of a man I thought him to be?"

"Go back home," Jay said flatly. "You'll only break your heart here."

She smiled again, but without amusement. "People like to pick flesh in Missouri too. I taught school there for two years. I came from the East originally. I had opportunities for marriage. Solid young men, but dull. Then Frank came along. I met him at Kansas City when he was there selling a carload of beef. I was on a shopping trip. He followed me back to Minters, where I taught school. A handsome cattleman, and with his talk of big, new country and high mountains and sure wealth. His singling me out did not add to my popularity with the other girls at Minters. Nor the young men either. Now, you're advising me to go back there, jilted."

"Pride is a rough taskmaster," Jay said.

"You may as well tell me the name of the other woman," she said. "I'll learn it eventually of course."

"You're determined to stay, then?"

"I will stay until I talk to Frank, at least. Now, will you help me hire transportation, and I'd appreciate it if you would show me the way to Frank's place."

Jay glanced out at the bleak sky. "We'll have to make tracks," he said. "There's snow and cold in that sky."

Mamie brought the meal then, and they began eating in silence. Spur chains jingled. Sam Leathers entered the dining room, accompanied by two more of McColl's riders.

Leathers had been drinking. He marked out Jay and Dallas Carver, and said something to his comrades, grinning.

They took a nearby table. Leathers spoke, louder. "A feller no sooner goes rabbitin' into the hills than another jigger begins makin' time with his gal."

Dallas gave no sign that she had heard. Jay carefully finished his steak and the dried apple pie that Mamie brought.

Leathers made other remarks. Dallas finally murmured, "I gather that this is the man who gave you that bruised jaw yesterday as punishment for helping Frank."

"Will you have more coffee?" Jay asked easily.

"No," she said, preparing to arise. "I'm always being put off with coffee when you don't care to answer my questions."

Jay walked with her to the stairs. "Dress for heavy weather," he warned her. "Warm stuff against the skin, and something that will stop the wind. Sometimes we get a real blizzard in this country, even this late in season."

He added, as an afterthought, "In case I can't make the trip today, wait until you hear from me."

Worry pinched her forehead. "Don't let that ruffian goad you into fighting him. That's what he wants."

"Pride has sharp spurs," Jay said, "for both of us."

She hesitated, then reluctantly mounted the stairs.

Jay walked back to where Sam Leathers sat. He said, "Let's go outside, Sam. No use wrecking Ma's furniture."

83

Leathers was astonished. "I'll be damned!" he marveled. Then he shoved away from the table, came to his feet with an eager grunt. His cloudy eyes began to flame.

Jay led the way through the kitchen and to a space away from the trash barrels back of the building. He hung his coat on the fence of an adjoining wagon yard. Leathers had already shed his saddle coat. The two Chain riders and three or four more diners had followed them, and stood waiting in the lee of the building out of the cold wind.

Jay said, "All right, Sam."

"This'll be fun," Leathers said, and walked in, his fists clubbed, his thick arms guarding his body.

Jay let Leathers rush him, and start the first swing. He shoulder blocked the blow, destroyed the power of the left that Leathers tried to cross to the body. He drove a right and left to Leathers' stomach at close quarters.

Leathers backhanded him, then raked an elbow against his jaw. Leathers lashed out with his foot, but missed his target.

Jay said, "That's how you want it, Sam."

He moved in fast, taking punishment, but he broke through and found the opening he wanted. He hooked a left to the throat and that rocked Leathers back, and sank a right below the heart. He heard the damaging rush of breath from Leathers' lungs.

Leathers clamped arms around him, trying to gain time for a breather. Jay broke free with a violence that sent Leathers staggering against the trash barrels. Jay followed him. Panic showed in Leathers. Jay was faster, stronger, and the man knew it.

Jay caught Leathers by the hair with his left, side-stepped as the man tried to knee him. Holding him thus, he drove a right to the jaw.

The power faded completely out of Leathers. He began to buckle at the knees. Jay said, "Man, you ought to stay in training. You're soft as butter."

He knocked Leathers out then with another punch to the heart.

Leathers pitched forward on his face, and doubled up, gasping. Jay leaned against the corral a moment until the high throb of his pulse eased in his throat. He wiped his lips. He was aware that blood was streaming down his face.

Hodge McColl, striding fast, came around the corner of the building. McColl pulled up, staring at Leathers' writhing body. Damn it, Sam," he said, aggrieved, "I warned you he looked like hard forma-tion."

"He just wanted his fun, Hodge," Jay said.

He got his hat and coat and walked into Ma Monday's kitchen. He looked at the pale faces of Ma and Mamie Schneider, then went to the dish trough and pumped water into a basin and washed away the blood.

Mamie brought court plaster. "You've got a bad cut on your cheek and another on your chin," she said. "I'll do what I can."

Afterwards Jay went back to the lobby. Dallas was waiting, wearing a heavy weather coat, and with her luggage ready. He saw that she had on a riding habit beneath the coat.

"A man's ride causes considerable wear and tear on his face at times, she said.

"But heals the soul," Jay said. "I'll fetch horses from the livery. It would be better if we rode saddleback instead of by buggy, if you can manage. We might have to take to the timber for shelter."

"I'll make out," she nodded, "though horsemanship isn't one of my better accomplishments."

Jay walked to the livery, rigged his sorrel and rented a black gelding that Charlie said was broken to sidesaddle. He rented the saddle also.

He rode through a driving wind to the Pioneer House and Dallas came out, adjusting a hood over her hair. He lashed the traveling case to his own saddle, also with the gunny sack of supplies, hoping the sorrel would stand for it, and tied her smaller handbag on the gelding.

Jay knew that all of Spearhead was watching as they rode out of town, and that tongues would be wagging at full gallop. Dallas knew it too, for he again saw the tinge of anger in her cheeks.

Then they were bucking the wind. A mile out of town the first gust of gritty snow hit them, and Jay wrapped his slicker around her.

"We're in for it," he said. "Do you want to turn back?"

"No," she said. "I never like to turn back."

They had the snow in their faces for nearly two hours. The horses began to rebel, and, whenever it was feasible, Jay left the trail, following the shelter of timber.

Dusk came before they reached the Yellow House fork, and the storm was opening up in earnest. Snow drove at them with birdshot force; it was growing bitterly cold.

Dallas had uttered no complaint, but Jay now saw that she was tiring and that she was frightened. He pulled up in the lee of wind-bent fir. He had to shout to make himself heard. "It's only about two miles. We turn south here on this trail, and will have more timber to break the wind."

She nodded, forced a smile. Jay used the romal ends to force the horses again into the lash of the wind. He looked back at the fork of the trail, curtained now by whirling snow in the darkening finish of the day. He could picture the storm moaning over Dave Hollister's body, which he had left lying in the brush only a stone's throw from this point. The snow would be drifting over it now, covering it little by little. The futile sickness rose in him again.

Tumultuous darkness came, but the snow offered contrast with the black mass of the wind-whipped timber so that the trail remained plain. Presently Jay made out the side road that branched through thick timber toward Frank's place.

They followed this for a mile, then emerged into the open sweep of a flat on Latigo Creek where Frank had lived in a two-room log house.

Jay pulled up, peering. Frank's cabin should be in sight against the snow. He seized the bridle of the gelding and spurred ahead, forcing the animal with him.

Then, amid the wind and snow, he became aware of the sooty scent of charred wood. At the same instant his sorrel stumbled and shied back from obstacles underfoot.

Jay now made out the black smear of wind-drifted ashes that stained the new snow. Even Frank's saddle shed was gone, and there was no sign of his pole corral.

He turned to Dallas and shouted, "Frank's place has burned down."

Then he wheeled the horses and rode back into the shelter of the timber where he could make himself heard more easily. "That was the house we stumbled onto," he said. "There's nothing left but charred logs and ashes. Even the corral is gone." He added slowly, "A corral wouldn't burn. It was pulled down."

"I imagine this is the work of the man called Hodge McColl," Dallas said. "Mrs. Monday let me understand that Frank would never dare return to this range as long as McColl held a grudge against him."

"Well, we can't stay here," Jay said. "It would be tough making it back to town on tired horses. My own place is only three miles across country, but more than double that by trail, and we couldn't make it by the short cut tonight. However there's a hay shack about two miles south off the Yellow House trail at lace called Eagle Creek. That's our best bet. McColl built that shack, but it will be deserted at this time of year. It'll offer shelter at least. This storm may blow over by morning."

They fought their way back to the Yellow House road, turned south, and endured the storm's rough hand for a weary, numbing plod. Then they entered a clearing, and Jay swung the horses off the road.

He was thankful when the outline of the shack that McColl had built for his haying crews loomed out of the darkness. This was a real blizzard now. High country weather had moved down into the middle range for this night at least.

A dugout stood in a cutbank near the creek more than a hundred yards from the shack, built by some trapper in the early days. Jay rode to the dugout, slid from the saddle and lifted Dallas down. She was so chilled he had to support her with an arm around her while he prodded the horses into the dugout where they would have shelter from the wind.

She stumbled numbly as she tried to move with him away from that place. He said, "This has been too rough on you," then lifted her and carried her to the pole-built sack.

He set her on her feet and freed the wooden pin that held the door hasp, and guided her into the icy, black interior.

He closed the door against the storm, and managed to unbuckle his saddle coat and fumble for matches. He got a match going and finally located a lamp that still had age-yellowed oil in its dusty glass base.

The feeble light strengthened as the wick began to draw oil. The shapes of a rusty, grease-streaked cook-stove, a long, plank table and two benches, and four double-bunks, slung with rawhide, lifted out of the shadows.

Dallas said consolingly, "Tonight it looks like a palace."

A fair supply of wood remained in the packing box alongside the stove. Jay got a fire going, and presently the pitch began to offer a steady and pushing flame.

Jay removed the stove lids, and they huddled over the stove, with hands spread above the fire, letting the first grateful assurance of warmth and security flow through them.

"I've got a sack of grub in the dugout," Jay said. "But no blankets. We'll have to tough it out. At least we won't go hungry."

He looked directly at her. "I'll bunk in the dugout, of course."

"That would be a useless hardship," she said with equal directness. "You would freeze there. It will make no difference anyway. Spearhead suspected the worst when we rode out of town together, and will continue to prefer to think that way, no matter what you or I do. I intend to sleep on that table, if you will be kind enough to drag it nearer the stove. You can have the benches."

"Don't judge this country by Ma Monday," Jay said.

"I imagine Spearhead is no better, and no worse, than other communities," she observed. "They all have their Ma Mondays, and their Jay Webbs, too."

"Meaning that you are sure you are safe from me?"

A sudden, gay impertinence danced in her eyes. "If I answered that in the proper way it might be a chal-

90

lenge to your masculine pride," she said. "And it would also be a reflection on my own charm. No woman likes to feel safe from a man."

8

On the morning of that day, Lily Benton sat at the great, square, spur-scarred desk in the room at Yellow House that served as the ranch business office. A framed portrait of her parents hung above the desk. There were antler racks for guns and hats, and game pelt rugs, and a magnificent set of longhorns over the door.

Lily had the payroll to make out, the monthly bills to care for, and Sabrina Moon's grocery list to sign. Letters from cattle buyers and sellers, and circulars from the stock association and market reports lay unopened on the desk, along with ledgers and tally and brand books.

She had been there more than an hour, trying to work, but now she gave it up and merely sat very still, gazing out at the trail, which curved from the timber a quarter of a mile north of the house, and mounted to the ranch in a gentle loop.

All this time she had been waiting for Jay Webb to come riding up that trail in obedience to her demand, but it was mid-morning now, and the road still remained empty.

She thought, "I can't just sit here waiting. I'll start jibbering. I've got to know."

But she did remain there watching. The east window overlooked the major portion of the ranch spread. The crew bunkhouse was in sight a hundred yards away, near the poplars that lined the irrigation ditch. The bunkhouse was mainly deserted now, for the majority of the winter crew was still on duty at the line and drift camps in the lower country, and the four riders who worked out of the home ranch were absent. Lem Riddle, the cook, was in town, enjoying a two-day drunk before the spring work started.

Beyond the bunkhouse she could see Pooley Moon working in the open tunnel of the wagon shed, stretching new canvas on the bed wagon and chuck wagon in preparation for the season that would soon be upon them.

There were other buildings, built of logs, or chinked cedar poles, or slabs, mellowing and weathering comfortably with the years. A flume brought water across the horse pasture, spilling a clear liquid sheet into a big, cedar-built tank from which smaller flumes and pipes diverted it to the various ranch purposes.

In the pasture a quarter of a mile away Yancey Tolliver was schooling young horses. He had half a dozen in his morning class, and was letting one pupil learn the smell of a saddle blanket and the pinch of a surcingle around its belly. Yancey, a sliver of a man, with hairpin legs, took pride in gentling horses without breaking their spirit.

Al Shepherd came from the small log house that had been built as quarters for that ranch foreman, and walked away somewhere beyond the bunkhouse out of sight.

Al had been with Yellow House ten years, and Lily's father had made him foreman two years previously. Solid of shoulder and jaw, graying at the temples, Al looked to be all granite and leather. He had on his usual worn buckskin vest over his clean gray flannel shirt. His dark woolen trousers were stuffed into his boots.

He was a man who lived inside himself. Though he had never said so in words, Lily was well aware that he looked upon her attempt to take her father's place as preposterous.

Then Sabrina Moon came into the room, interrupting Lily's meditation. Sabrina carried a tray bearing a steaming mug of coffee, a thin elksteak that was crisply chicken-fried, and hot soda biscuits, each with a melting button of butter spilling over its brown top. There was wild honey and wild plum preserves.

Angular, firm-chinned, Sabrina wore a pin-neat calico dress and a gingham apron with its hem starched to the crackling point. Her graying hair, as always, was drawn into a forehead-tightening bun, and she wore steel-rimmed spectacles.

She slapped the tray belligerently before Lily. "You're downin' this grub, young lady, even if I have to stand here an' stuff it into you like I used to do when you was a tad. I declare, you ain't et enough in the past few days to keep a chipmunk alive. You hardly touched your breakfast this mornin'."

"It's my figure," Lily said. "There comes a time

when every girl realizes she is growing too broad in certain places. Then . . ."

"Eat!" Sabrina commanded uncompromisingly. "It ain't your figger you're frettin' about. It's got somethin' to do with hirin' this Jay Webb as range boss. I've seen you do some outlandish things in your life, but that takes the cake . . ."

Then a sudden, stunning thought caused Sabrina's stern blue eyes to widen in horror. "See here, young lady! You ain't gone an' fell in love with this fellow, now have you?"

Lily stared, then sagged back in the chair, and began to laugh helplessly, almost hysterically. "Oh, Sabrina!"

Sabrina scowled at her, worried. She and her husband, Pooley Moon, had been with Pitchfork before Lily was born, Pooley as rider, and Sabrina as housekeeper. Sabrina had been a second mother to Lily since the death of Ann Benton.

"I don't recollect you ever mentionin' this Jay Webb until you come home yesterday an' announced out of a blue sky that you was hirin' him to run things here," Sabrina said. "Where'd you meet him? An' when?"

Lily forced herself to tackle the food. "I met him yesterday."

"You meet a man for the first time, an' hire him to run your outfit for you. That don't make sense, an' you know it. It wasn't up on the Fort Relief trail that you happened to bump into Jay Webb, now was it?"

Lily looked quickly at Sabrina.

"You was gone most o' the day, an' there was white

94

clay mud on the mare when you come home," Sabrina said grimly. "Ain't much white clay in the country except up high on that trail. In addition, Yancey Tolliver was in town last night an' told about hearin' Sam Leathers brag in a saloon that he had beat up your Jay Webb on that trail yesterday, an' he didn't even dare to fight back."

"They say Sam Leathers always talks big when he's drinking," Lily said.

"I got a hunch you know he was tellin' the truth," Sabrina challenged. "Maybe you even seen what happened up there."

"Perhaps I did," Lily admitted.

"You see a man turn craven in front of Hodge McColl, an' so you hire him as your range boss. That don't add up to anything sane."

Lily arose, impulsively kissed Sabrina on the cheek. "There's nothing sane in any of this," she said.

Sabrina cleared her throat, and suddenly had to dry her spectacles. "You do soften a person, don't you?" she said. "An' you're in bad trouble, ain't you child? Jay Webb is an outlaw, ain't he?"

Lily drew back, turned to the desk again.

"You don't have to answer that," Sabrina said. "But I see what I see, an' I know what I know. You may have met Jay Webb for the first time only yesterday, but you've had this thing in mind long before that. As fur back as last February, at least. I've seen it preyin' on you. At first I thought it was only Hodge McColl that you was thinkin' about. Now I know it was this other thing."

"Am I as open as all that?" Lily asked protestingly.

"To me you are. You might fool other people, but you can't fool me. Where did you go last February when you was supposed to be in Chicago?"

Lily looked at her silently.

"You didn't go to Chicago," Sabrina went on. "You'd have called on the McReadys. They're old friends. But I got a letter from Jenny McReady a few weeks ago, an' she never mentioned you bein' there. So I know you never went near Chicago."

"I can't tell you where I went, Sabrina. It's . . . it's best you don't know."

"That means that what you know is dangerous," Sabrina sighed. "You're afraid of Jay Webb, an' afraid of what you know about him."

"Please don't cross-examine me," Lily said desperately.

"You ain't the only one that's bein' close-mouthed about things that are goin' on around here," Sabrina grumbled. "Even my own husband is mixed up in whatever you're up to. So is Yancey Tolliver. Oh, I've noticed that they've been away a lot lately on some mysterious business. But I ain't never been able to git a single word out of them as to where they go. When a woman's own husband won't confide in her, then it's mighty serious."

"I'm not talking," Lily said.

Sabrina was silent for a moment. "I reckon you'll tell me in your own good time," she finally sighed. "You're like your paw. You take after your mother in your good looks, but you got Barney Benton's bull-headed mind. You don't share your troubles. You let 'em build up inside you until they explode."

"I'll explode if I try to force any more food down me," Lily said.

"Well, you et enough to keep you goin' a little while. If you git any thinner even Hodge McColl will lose interest in you. Men don't hanker to hold a bag o' bones in their arms. There's no warmth to it."

"That sounds indecent," Lily said in mock horror.

"Don't try to play innocent an' shocked with me, young lady," Sabrina sniffed. "I reckon Hodge McColl won't be the first man you've kissed."

"A scandalous thing to say."

"I've heard about all them men with shoe polish on their hair that tagged around after you when you was in Europe. From what Jenny McReady told me, you could have had your pick of half a dozen titles over there. The McReadys was there when you was galli-vantin' in Paris an' them other places, remember. All that hand-kissin'. I don't doubt but that some of 'em went a little further too."

"It happens that Hodge McColl isn't on my kissing list, hand or otherwise," Lily said. "At least not yet."

"An' I hope I never live to see the day when he gits there," Sabrina snapped, and slammed the dishes on the tray.

She headed for the door. "There, I've said it, an' I mean what I said. Hodge McColl is courtin' you with one hand, tryin' to softsoap you while he's robbin' you with the other. There ain't anything lower'n deceit like that. A hand-kisser with polished hair would be

97

better than him for a husband."

Sabrina closed the door emphatically behind her as she left the room. Her crisp footsteps faded in the direction of the kitchen, and then the house became silent.

Lily sat for a long time in that silence, without moving. She looked up at the picture of her parents, and fell to studying the strength in her father's face.

A phrase from somewhere ran through her mind. The loneliness of command. She was lonely enough. All the weight of decision was on her shoulders, and there could be no shifting.

She was playing with fire and knew it. She was attempting to force desperate men to work for her by holding over them the threat of the gallows or prison, and her only protection from them was the letter she had told Jay Webb she had written, which would expose his past and put the law on his trail if anything happened to her.

But, if they were desperate men, then desperation was driving her also. The death of her father had tossed her into a situation with which she had found herself unable to cope by normal means. Barney Benton had never shared his responsibilities with her, and she had taken it for granted that Pitchfork's foundations were solid and everlasting.

Then she discovered that those foundations had been only as strong as her father's strength. Hodge McColl had started his encroachments the instant Barney Benton was stricken. Lily had learned that during the six months of her father's illness McColl had made heavy inroads. Al Shepherd, for all his granite exterior, apparently was afraid of McColl and his tough crew. That left only Pooley Moon and Yancey Tolliver. They were loyal to the core, and she could count on them, but they were not fibered as leaders. And, without leadership, the remainder of the crew was merely a band of men who drew their pay and waited to make sure which way the wind blew.

The anger that worked in her now was the long, gnawing anger of helplessness over nearly a year's time. She had at first depended on Al Shepherd, expecting him to stop McColl in the only way he could be stopped—by equal toughness and violence. But Shepherd had made only a few weak protests to McColl that accomplished nothing.

McColl had continued to drift his cattle deeper into the graze that had always been Pitchfork's. He now claimed all the lower range from Pipestone Creek to the Ox Bow, and it was evident that he would be moving this year into the summer graze in the upper benches. When that happened Pitchfork would be finished. Lily would be forced to sell off cattle for which there was no graze—or marry McColl.

Resentfully she recalled Jay Webb's opinion of her chances of saving herself by marriage. He had said that McColl wanted both Lily and Pitchfork, but intended only to keep Pitchfork permanently. She knew Jay was wrong. She had a woman's sureness in her own power in that category, at least. She could marry McColl, if she so decided. After all, he was only a man, with a man's desires and a man's weaknesses.

But another path had opened the night she had identified Jay's voice as the voice of Jess Steele. The thought that here was the kind of a man who could stop McColl had leaped into her mind instantly.

The idea had repelled her for a time. But the seed had been planted, and it germinated. Fed by her desperation it had driven her to make that trip to Concho to prove beyond all doubt there was no mistake in her identification.

But it had also become clear to her that one man was not enough. While in Concho she had learned that the mother of the Tracy brothers still lived nearby, and that had inspired the method by which she had lured the long riders to the Wardrums.

At that point she had been forced to take Pooley Moon into her confidence. She had browbeaten Pooley into writing the letter to Hattie Tracy. She had searched the desk in Jay's ranch house one day when he was absent, and had taken examples of his handwriting. She had also found the tintype in the desk, and had guessed it was a family portrait.

Pooley had sweated for hours on the letter, trying without too much success to imitate Jay's handwriting, and Lily had gambled on the probability that Hattie Tracy would be unfamiliar with Jay's penmanship, but would instantly recognize the picture as genuine.

Lily had thought of the possibility that Hattie Tracy's mail might be watched by the law, and she had concealed the letter and picture in a patent-medicine almanac and remailed it to Mrs. Tracy.

She had detailed Pooley and Yancey Tolliver to keep an eye on Jay's ranch and to report to her if any strange riders appeared there. She had doubted that the long riders would respond to that forged appeal, but the bond that had linked them to Jess Steele had proved still strong.

She had not given Yancey any reason for his assignment. That was for his own safety. But it happened that Lily herself had been watching Jay's ranch the previous morning when the five men had come like ghosts out of the timber and taken refuge in Jay's house.

The presence of a desperately wounded man among them was an unexpected factor. Then she realized it might be an advantage in her favor. They would be less likely to abandon a comrade and flee out of her reach. It was a practical viewpoint. She conceded that. But she could not afford to do otherwise.

She had sent Will Overmire to do what he could for the wounded man. That thought eased her conscience a trifle. She had been fortunate in encountering Will on the trail shortly after her talk with Jay Webb.

Lily's eyes softened as she let her mind rest on Will Overmire. He was the one soothing influence in her turmoiled world now. Will had studied her gravely when she had asked that he say nothing about what he would find at Jay's ranch.

"Lily," Will had said in his cultured voice, "there is a lawlessness in you that could get out of hand. I've seen the change in you lately. The worry, and the increasing determination. You are the kind that might go to the last extreme to fight for what you believe is your right. You could become hard and ruthless. That would be a pity, for you were created to please men, not use them for your purposes. You could walk in the clouds with beauty."

"I could hardly walk in the clouds with a broken pride dragging me down," Lily had said.

"I will always see only the beauty in you," he had said wistfully. "You know that."

"You are too willing to overlook my faults, Will. That is a mistake. You must see me as I really am, not just half of me. If I am hard and ruthless you must take that into account in estimating me."

He had listened gravely to the gentleness in her voice. "You draw me near, and then you push me away to arm's length again, Lily," he had sighed. "You looked at me just now as I have always hoped you would look at me. And then the door closed again. You are two women, Lily, not one. You are determined to fight Hodge McColl by fair means or foul, and at the same time you hate the fighting. There is an unbreakable will in you, and also a shrinking from violence. You will do anything—even marry McColl, I fear—to conquer him, even though it destroys you."

He wheeled his rig to head back down the trail. "What else will I find at Jay Webb's place besides a wounded man whose identity must be kept secret?" he commented dully. "Only outlaws hide their names, Lily. I had feared it would come to this with you. You are hiring gunmen. But this step will lay on your conscience. Your nature is not to walk with lawless men."

"Would you have me marry McColl, then?" Lily asked.

Will had smiled wryly. "Nothing I would say would sway you one way or another in that decision, I fear," he said. "You will decide that for yourself."

9

Lily reluctantly let her thoughts leave Will Overmire and swing back to the present. The trail still remained deserted, and her anger toward Jay Webb returned.

She looked at the banjo clock on the wall. She arose impatiently and began pacing the room.

She returned to the desk, opened the ledger, then the tally book. She closed them just as quickly, for the figures they contained were familiar to her from many hours of inspection in the past.

The books always added up to the same result. Pitchfork was not only losing range to McColl, but was losing brand strength also. The previous year's calf roundup had showed a puzzling drop of more than five per cent. And Al Shepherd had warned her of bigger trouble when the present season's drop was tallied.

Al had said the winter kill was unusually high, but Pooley Moon had told her the past season had been no worse than the average winters through which the she stuff had roughed in good shape.

Lily abruptly left the office, walked to her bedroom and changed from her house dress to her divided riding skirt. She glanced out at the weather, then pulled on long woolen stockings, a woolen shirt, a knitted cardigan and a heavy, sheep-lined brush coat. She drew a tam-o'-shanter over her hair.

Sabrina intercepted her as she was leaving the house by way of the living room. "What in the world . . . ?"

"I'm off for a little ride," Lily said.

"In this weather? My land, it's going to blow and snow. Maybe even a blizzard. Now you listen to me, young . . ."

Sabrina was talking futilely, for Lily was gone. She got her gear, caught up her mare at the corral and rigged it, and fended off Pooley who came hurrying to object to her leaving the ranch in the face of such a day.

"I may stay away overnight," she said. "So don't worry about me."

She rode down the trail, hoping Jay Webb would appear and make the trip unnecessary. But the way ahead remained empty, and this sharpened her determination to bring him to heel.

Five miles from the ranch she passed the hay camp Hodge McColl had built at Eagle Creek. Her father had always cut wild hay there in past years, hauling it to the main ranch and feeder camps, but McColl had moved in with a mowing crew, taking the crop for his own use.

There were other meadows available to Pitchfork, though they were not as convenient, so that the loss of Eagle was not vital. Barney Benton, ill at the time, had not been told about this, and Al Shepherd had failed to make an issue of the matter.

McColl even had the effrontery to build a shack there as quarters for his crew. Erection of the shack, virtually on the doorstep of Yellow House, was final notice that Chain was claiming the meadow permanently and that this was the first step toward full invasion of the upper country.

Sight of the shack brought Lily's temper to a new edge. The shack was a challenge and Pitchfork had not met that challenge.

She pushed the mare faster. Presently, as she passed the side road that led to Frank Spain's place, the wind brought the faint, dank odor of wood smoke. She wondered if Frank had found the courage to return to his ranch in defiance of McColl.

She was half a mile from the junction with the main trail when she caught faint, intangible sounds. They might have been gunshots . . . or might only have been the throb of her own pulse in her ears, for the wind had died temporarily, and a dead calm held the dripping timber.

Then a rain squall, mingled with sleet, came whooping through the trees. She loosened the poncho that was rolled on the saddle, wrapped its clammy protection about her. It was evident the weather was worsening and she sat there for minutes, debating whether to go through with this.

She said aloud, fiercely, "I've got to know." She rode ahead again, and soon reached the junction and turned westward, away from town and toward Jay Webb's ranch.

There were fresh hoof tracks in the mud, water-filled by the squall, showing that a rider had passed down this trail not long before, heading in the direction of Spearhead.

And behind her the wind carried away the last elusive scent of the gunpowder that had been burned there recently.

After Lily had passed out of sight westward Al Shepherd rode out of the brush. He was leading a riderless horse. Shepherd had followed Lily when she left Yellow House. Staying in the timber, he had spotted Dave Hollister's horse stampeding riderless through the brush, and he rounded it up.

Shepherd, bending from the saddle, studied the hoof tracks in the mud. He traced them to the boulder, and found Dave Hollister's body. He did not resume trailing Lily. He was sure she was going to Jay Webb's place, and that was what he wanted to know.

It was mid-afternoon when Lily approached the Slide Creek meadow. She left the trail and rode into the timber, pulling up where she could study the house without being seen.

Smoke haze showed above the chimney. A lean man in dog-eared boots came from the kitchen with a cedar pail. He walked to the creek, swung the sweep, filled the pail and went back into the house. That would be Ben Tracy, leader of the riders, according to descriptions she had read on the reward posters.

She was breathing fast. She told herself she was surely foolish to go through with this, and she was on

106

the point of riding away. Then a voice spoke back of her. "*Buenos tardes,* señorita. You are looking for someone, no?"

Lily whirled. Mario Rodriguez had stepped from brush behind her. She strangled a half-scream. Mario was smiling politely, doffing his hat and bowing graciously.

Lily identified him, also, from descriptions. Mario had his hat in his left hand, and in his right he held a repeating rifle. A six-shooter showed in a holster beneath the open skirt of his short poncho. The thought came to Lily that guns were as much a part of his life as his beating heart, with both being vital to his existence.

She forced herself to straighten, and say, "You are Mario Rodriguez."

Mario was pleased. "At your service, forever. And you must be the Señorita Lily Benton."

"So Jess Steele told you about me?"

"The name," Mario said reprovingly, "is Jay Webb, I believe. You will be kind enough to remember that, señorita."

"Is he here?"

"Here? Why, he left this morning to journey to your ranch, this Green House, I believe it is called."

"Yellow House. But he didn't show up."

Mario frowned. "Come," he said.

He helped her from the saddle, then walked her across the clearing, leading the mare. His eyes were always busy, studying the trees and the brush. Lily understood that he had been posted as a guard to warn against unwanted visitors.

The door opened as they neared and Ben Tracy stood eyeing them with a flat stare. Behind him Lily saw two more men.

"This is the Señorita Benton from Yellow House," Mario said. "She tells me Señor Jay did not appear at her ranch this morning. So she came here to inquire."

Ben Tracy motioned her in. Lily determinedly fought off panic as the door closed behind her. She saw that the other two men were the ones described as Steve Tracy and Tom Faye on the law dodgers.

"Go out and stand watch, Tom," Ben said. "You stay here, Mario."

He studied Lily, a brooding distrust in his eyes. "I guess you know who we are," he said, "seeing as how you're the one who tricked us into coming here."

"I know you," Lily said. "Every one of you."

"Then you're the one who stole a picture from this room, and sent a certain letter to my mother."

"Yes," Lily said.

"Who wrote that letter?"

"That doesn't matter," Lily said. "But he doesn't know exactly why it was written, or who any of you really are. He merely did it as a favor to me."

She waited for Ben to show anger. But his gaunt face remained blank, letting her dangle in suspense.

Through the door she saw the wounded man in the living room. Ward Steele was moaning a little. There was the smell of sickness and a desperate fight against death in this place.

"Jay Webb was to come to Yellow House today," she

said, her voice shaky in spite of herself.

"He left this morning," Ben said. "He said he would go to this town called Spearhead first to buy some grub. Maybe you didn't wait long enough. Maybe you're too impatient, Miss."

"And maybe I don't trust Jay Webb," Lily said.

Ward was mumbling deliriously. Lily walked into the living room. "Did Dr. Overmire come here?" she asked.

"Yesterday," Ben nodded. "He said he'd show up today, but he's failed to keep his word up to now."

Lily slid out of the poncho and saddle coat. She placed a hand on Ward's feverish forehead, pushed back his damp hair. She saw that he was hardly more than her own age.

"I'll do what I can," she said.

"It'll be one more gun for your side if you can pull him through," Ben answered in his hard voice.

"That is correct," Lily said tersely.

She used cold compresses. She found fresh, clean sheets in the bureau, and had the men help while she changed the bed linen.

Ward quieted after a time. He became rational for a few minutes. He gazed up at her wonderingly. "A chestnut . . . or are you a bay?" he muttered. "I asked for a taffy-hair, but you'll more than do, whoever you are."

"Seems like Ward's feeling better," the young, red-haired one she had identified as Steve Tracy said. In his voice was a moving note of hope that surprised Lily. Apparently, even among killers and outlaws, there was a bond of affection.

Lily finally opened the bandage that Will Overmire

had placed on Ward's wound. She shrank at sight of the injury, then set her teeth and made a new dressing.

She smoothed his hair again, for that seemed to soothe him, and presently he drifted into an easier lethargy. She could not help but pity him, no matter what his past.

She had been vaguely aware that flurries of sleet had flailed the cabin occasionally. She was dismayed to realize that the afternoon was far gone. The wind's violence was increasing.

She turned to a window and saw snow driving across the flat. The growing storm was rolling down from the high peaks, and roaring through the timber.

"Dr. Overmire will surely come by tomorrow," she said. "I must be going now. I believe he is a little better. But he is very weak."

"Bad storm," Ben said. "And building up. Nightfall isn't far away."

"I can make it," she said, and began pulling on her coat.

"You could stay here," Ben said.

"I'd feel safer with the storm," Lily said levelly.

"Lady, we're not that kind of men," Ben said, his voice equally sharp.

"I'm not afraid of you," Lily told him. "Don't ever make the mistake of thinking that." Then, something in Ben Tracy's face caused her to relent a little. "I'll be all right. I know the country, and so does my mare. It can't be too tough a storm this late in season.

She moved to the door, and Steve said dubiously, "I'll fetch the mare."

While she waited for the saddled mount to be brought to the door, she glanced toward Ward. "Feed him more broth, if he can take it. The doctor will be here tomorrow, or myself."

The mare protested at facing the storm, but the wind was mainly at their back as they headed down the trail, and once the animal knew there was no refusing it lengthened its stride.

But premature darkness caught them before they had covered half the distance to the fork. The snow became a blinding force. A little panic began to form in Lily, for she began to fear she had missed the Yellow House fork, and she slowed the mare, straining to make out some familiar landmark against the sky-line of storm-tossed timber. She became more and more certain she had overrun the fork, and was about to turn back. Then she came upon it.

Gratefully she turned south toward Yellow House. But the mare was tiring and fighting to drift with the storm off the trail. The panic began to edge back into her mind.

Then a clearing showed ahead, and she saw that she had reached Eagle Creek where McColl had built his hay camp. She realized now it would be folly to attempt the remaining miles to Yellow House, so she left the trail and headed across the flat.

She could not make out the outline of the shack until she was almost upon it. What she first saw was a yellow smudge of light.

Spurring the mare nearer, she saw the shack. Lamp-light from a window was caught by the whirl of the storm. Riding within a few feet of the window she could see the interior of the shack.

Jay Webb stood working over the cookstove. An attractive, tawny-haired young woman in a dark riding habit was holding slim hands to the warmth.

Lily peered, astounded, embarrassed. Then, impatiently, she lifted her voice and hailed the place. She watched Jay straighten. Then he strode to the door and opened it.

Lily slid from the saddle, moved into the light. "I'd like to come in and hug that stove for a while," she said. She added, with edged politeness, "That is, if I'm not intruding."

10

Jay motioned her in, and closed the door. "At least I can sleep inside now with a clear conscience," he said. "We have a chaperon."

"That puts me on my good behavior," Lily said. "I've never been classed as so sedate before."

"Miss Benton, Miss Dallas Carver," Jay said, making the introductions. "Miss Carver is Frank Spain's fiancée. She arrived in Spearhead today from Missouri. Unfortunately, Frank was unable to meet her."

"A pleasure, Miss Carver," Lily said, moving to the stove and stripping off her poncho and gloves.

"How do you do, Miss Benton," Dallas said calmly. "Is it Miss Lily Benton?"

"Yes," Lily said, glancing at Jay. "I'm flattered that you have heard of me. Was it Mr. Webb who mentioned me?"

"No," Dallas smiled. "Mrs. Monday."

"That does mean that I must be on my very best behavior," Lily sighed. "Ma's opinion of me is even worse, no doubt, than Mr. Webb's."

"It is unfortunate we cannot offer you more comfortable quarters for the night, Miss Benton," Dallas said.

"Right now," Lily said, "I'll settle for a cigarette."

Frowning, Jay handed her his tobacco sack and wheat-straws. He saw Dallas' eyebrows arch a little as Lily Benton rolled a neat cigarette with practiced speed.

"I hope you're not shocked," Lily said, and Jay saw mockery in her eyes.

Jay changed the subject. "Did you happen to try Frank Spain's place first, for shelter?"

"No."

"It's gone. Burned. Miss Carver had intended to stay there until Frank returned. We had to come here instead."

"I regret you received such an inhospitable welcome to our range, Miss Carver," Lily said. "You'll discover that the Wardrum country has its better face if you stay."

"I'm sure it has," Dallas said. "And I intend to stay. Mr. Webb has been very kind to me. I fear he has gone to too much trouble to look out for me."

"Apparently some of the trouble had fists," Lily

113

observed, gazing at the court plaster on Jay's face. "Was it Sam Leathers again? And did you turn the other cheek this time?"

"Mr. Webb fought a man in Spearhead today," Dallas explained before Jay could speak, and he could see an icy formality growing in her manner toward Lily Benton. "I believe the person's name was Leathers."

"Who won?"

"Mr. Webb," Dallas said. "But if you don't mind, I would prefer not to go into details. I fear I was the cause of the trouble."

"Now you really have me all agog," Lily sighed.

Jay led Lily's mare to the dugout. He returned, carrying the gunny sack. Lily was adding fresh fuel to the stove, which was making little headway against the rigid chill in the shack. She had rustled up a rusty iron skillet and a blackened coffee pot, and was melting snow to clean them.

Jay opened the bottle of brandy. "A little fire inside us will help," he said. "It'll have to be roundup style. No glasses handy."

Lily Benton lifted the bottle, took a gulp. She gagged a little, and shuddered. "My father used to say Mort Skelly sold the worst brandy in the territory," she said.

Dallas refused the bottle. "I'm warm enough," she said.

Jay emptied the gunny sack on the table, and began selecting food. He unrolled the gun belt, and hung the holstered weapon on a bunk post.

He saw Lily's head lift as she looked at the gun, sleek and black and sinister in its waxed holster. The faint mockery faded from her eyes, leaving a gravity.

Jay sliced bacon while Lily scoured the coffee pot. He covertly studied her, trying to see beneath the frothy front she had shown Dallas. He was thinking of Dave Hollister. If she had sent Hollister to kill him she was accomplished at hiding her emotions.

"Another pound," Lily said as they began eating. "I never can resist flapjacks and bacon. But I'll make up for it tomorrow."

"It's always so easy to let our faults take care of themselves tomorrow," Dallas smiled.

"Yes," Lilly said. She looked at Jay. "That reminds me that you were going to take over as my range boss today. I trust you won't disappoint me again tomorrow."

Their eyes met and their wills locked for a moment, with neither yielding. "I can't refuse, of course," Jay said.

Lily turned to Dallas. "I hope you will make Yellow House your headquarters until you decide your future plans. Yellow House is where I live."

"You're very kind," Dallas said. "I'll be only too grateful to take advantage of your offer until Frank can rebuild his ranch house."

Jay and Lily glanced at each other. "There is a possibility Frank may want to leave this range," Jay said reluctantly. "He may not want to rebuild."

"Then I will rebuild the house myself," Dallas said quietly.

She watched their expressions, and added, "I'm not going to let any man—or woman—drive me out of this country now that I am here."

"As far as the man goes," Lily said, "you and I see eye to eye. His name is Hodge McColl."

"Ma Monday told me about McColl," Dallas said. "Now, if you don't mind, I'll try to get some sleep. I'm very tired."

Jay drew the table nearer the stove, and Dallas curled up on its top, wrapping herself in her coat and Jay's slicker.

Lily tested the rawhide-slung bunks and said wryly, "They say the West was built of rawhide, but it seems to me they could have drawn the line somewhere. A few featherbeds would have helped."

She finally selected one. Jay pulled off his boots, and occupied a bunk across the room. He arose occasionally to replenish the stove. Dallas seemed to be sleeping well. She lay like a tired child, her head cuddled on an arm, her hair coppery gold in the glow from the stove.

Lily Benton lay huddled beneath her poncho, though she awoke at times and murmured complainingly that her back was cold.

Toward morning the blizzard blew out and the battering of the wind faded. Red dawn aroused Jay from full sleep, and he arose, stiff and numbed. The stove had guttered out. Through the window he saw that the sky was clear.

As he rekindled the stove Lily awakened. "By noon the sun will be ripping away the last of this snow, and we'll be wading in mud," Jay predicted. "There's less than six inches on the level. Let's hope this was winter's last bender. In a couple of weeks there will be new grass as far as the toe of Big Drum, and fresh-dropped calves will be bawling on the range. Cowboys are going to have work to do, beginning soon."

Dallas aroused, and said sleepily, "Good morning."

They ate a repeat of their night meal. Dallas said she had slept well, and she looked it. She had color in her slender cheeks, and her eyes were almost violet in this light.

Lily kept gazing out at the rising sun, and Jay could see that her thoughts were remote. Softening snow was already beginning to cascade from the tips of the firs. Lily, he surmised, was facing the realization that this was spring at last, and that the coming summer would spell the fate of Pitchfork.

He saddled and led the horses to the door. He helped Dallas into the sidesaddle, but Lily mounted swiftly, impatiently turning from assistance.

They rode across the flat, turned up the trail toward Yellow House. Jay glanced back and pulled up with an exclamation.

Smoke was spurting through the shake-roof of the hay shack. Then a tongue of flame flickered from a window as heat broke the glass pane. Jay swung his horse around, but pulled up again, realizing it was useless. The fire was building up inside the shack now that it had the draft from the broken window to feed upon.

The shack was going up in flames. At least it would

burn out and cave in under the weight of its snow-soaked roof.

He glanced involuntarily at Lily Benton. That fire had gained too swift a start to be accidental. Someone must have either scattered the remains from the stove's fire, or used the last of the oil from the lamp inside the room before leaving. Perhaps both.

Lily and Dallas had been outside, waiting, when he had brought up the horses from the dugout, and the door had been closed. He had no way of knowing which had been the last to leave the shack, but he had no doubt but that Lily was the one.

He said, "Hodge McColl will have to build a new hay shack—if he wants one."

They rode in silence. Dallas kept her eyes straight ahead, her face carefully expressionless. Lily Benton wore her faint, ironical smile.

Burning the shack, Jay reflected was a futile, petty gesture. It could easily be rebuilt. But, considering it further, he realized it had a deeper meaning. There was a feline quality in that blow at Hodge McColl that indicated ruthlessness in a fight, a capacity for taking advantage of any means at hand.

The silence held during the trip to Yellow House. The snow was melting rapidly now, and the roofs of the ranch buildings were steaming in the warming sun as they rode into the muddy yard.

Pooley Moon came to help with the horses. He nodded crustily to Jay.

Lily introduced Pooley to Dallas, then led her to the house. She motioned Jay to follow. He obeyed, and that compliance to her command drove home the realization that he was no longer his own master.

Sabrina Moon met the girls at the door. She gave Jay a glare, and uttered a disparaging snort.

"Wait in the office," Lily told Jay, pointing.

He crossed the long living room, which had Indian rugs on the waxed cedar floor, easy chairs and a settee, and entered the room Lily had indicated. He found himself in the ranch office, with the framed picture of Barney Benton and his wife looking down at him.

He waited, hearing the indistinct chatter of women's voices somewhere in the house as they were getting Dallas settled.

Presently Lily returned, still wearing her cardigan, flounced riding skirt and saddle boots.

"First, I want to shove over to my place," Jay said. "I—"

"I saw your brother yesterday afternoon," she interrupted. "He is in bad shape, but was still hanging on."

"Did Overmire show up?"

"Not up to the time I had left. But he will be there unless he's seriously delayed by some other patient. Will Overmire keeps his promises."

"You seem sure of him," Jay said.

"Will is the only one I am absolutely sure of, excepting Sabrina and Pooley and Yancey Tolliver," she said. "I'll see to it that your brother is well cared for. I will send Sabrina and Pooley to your place today to look after him."

To keep Ward prisoner so they can hold him as a club over me and Ben and the others, Jay reflected.

"I want the other four riders to come here," Lily went on. "I'll sign them on the payroll at regular wages and will give you the additional money I mentioned to hand over to them. They'll use assumed names, of course."

"How many riders do you carry now?"

"Fourteen. Ten are at the east camps. We usually put on eight or ten more during the summer."

"McColl must have twice that many on his payroll right now."

"He hires every drifter who comes into the country, provided the drifter carries a gun and knows how to use it. Three of our regular riders quit during the winter. McColl's men keep forcing trouble on my crew. That's where we are at a disadvantage. We've never hired gunfighters."

"Until now," Jay said.

She nodded. "Until now. I have to fight fire with fire."

"So I noticed this morning."

A rush of color stained her cheeks. Then she bit back whatever retort she had intended. "I want you to see that McColl's riders quit terrorizing my men," she said. "I want you to put the fear of wrath in them. I want to keep all the range that properly belongs to us, and I want Hodge McColl to be taught that he must stay within his own limits. I'm no grass hog, nor was my father. We never objected to any man using range that Pitchfork did not use. But we intend to hold what we have. And I want to know why we are losing calves."

Jay had to concede that she had justice on her side, as far as range rights were concerned. Pitchfork had never objected to other brands as neighbors. Barney Benton had voluntarily pooled the upper benches and winter range with small outfits that operated off homesteads. Though Jay and Frank Spain had never entered the pool, they had never been molested by Pitchfork.

"One other thing," she said. "As you know, the Cheyenne reserve will be opened sooner or later. This country south of the river is open to homesteading, and even that is a mistake, for farming is a losing business at this altitude. Even the government is realizing that, and the reservation undoubtedly will be limited to grazing entry."

She stood gazing out the window for a time. "We want our fair share of that new range when it is opened," she went on. "Now that the railroad has reached Castle Bend, more homesteaders are moving in. They'll fail eventually, but they'll cut us up. It is difficult to operate a big brand in a checkerboard area, as you know. If and when the reserve is opened, the outfit that locates its cattle first will have priority. McColl must be well aware of the situation also, and will move in a hurry when the time comes. In fact I'm sure the reason McColl came into this country was because he had the reservation in mind for expanding."

"Does Al Shepherd know I'm taking over as range boss?" Jay asked.

"Yes. I told him after my talk with you the day

before yesterday."

"Did he fur up?"

"Well, he wasn't happy about it," she admitted.

"Did he quit?"

"No. But he's sulking. I assured him he would continue as foreman, and have general charge. But I also made it clear that you have entire authority over the crew and the cattle."

"That makes him a hell of a foreman. All he can do is boss himself under that setup."

"That's the size of it," she said.

"And after we do the rough work Shepherd will take over again."

"Perhaps."

"Do you carry a rider on the payroll named Dave Hollister?" Jay asked abruptly. He watched intently for any sign of guilt, but if the question disturbed her she did not permit it to show.

"Why, yes," she said.

"Seen him lately?"

She thought for a minute. "He's been riding out of the home ranch. I saw him yesterday morning. Why do you ask?"

Jay did not answer that. He was about ready to admit one thing. Lily Benton knew nothing about that attempt to ambush him. No one could conceal such knowledge so completely.

"You have no confidence in Al Shepherd, have you?" he asked abruptly.

She studied that a moment. "Al hasn't been too eager to oppose McColl," she admitted. "But he's growing old, and perhaps too cautious."

"You mentioned you were losing cattle. Where, and in what way?"

"Calves," she said. "We were off five per cent on the average drop last year. Al says we've had a heavy winter kill among the she stuff, and that our increase will be down even more this season."

"My stuff roughed through in good shape, even up in the higher benches," Jay said. "Why would Pitchfork be hit harder than other brands?"

"That is what Pooley Moon keeps asking me," she said wearily.

"These riders of yours? How do they stack up? Will they stick with you—or me—in a fight?"

"I've asked Pooley the same question. He knows them better than I. Pooley believed the majority of them are loyal and honest."

"The majority? What about the minority?"

"The fact is," she said, "Pooley believes some of our trouble is right inside our own crew. There have been some fist fights among our own riders. Evidently you must have heard about it, for you asked me a few minutes ago about Dave Hollister. He was mixed up in the trouble. And those three riders who left us last winter didn't quit, as I said. They were fired by Al Shepherd. Al blamed them for the fights, but Pooley says those men were reliable hands who had been with Dad for several years."

"This job you're handing me seems to fit the salary," Jay observed. "You're fighting Hodge McColl, and your own buckaroos are fighting among themselves.

What else do you have up your sleeve?"

"Only a derringer to protect myself if I need it," she said, and there was a wan hue on her lips. "I'm never forgetting that I'm dealing with outlaws and that I know too much about them for their own safety. And I warn you never to forget that letter I mentioned."

"You speak of devils, and another one pops up," Jay said, nodding toward the window. "Here comes Hodge McColl, riding his single-footer, and wearing an ice cream hat, a fancy shirt with bull's-eye buttons, and forty-dollar boots. That's a man's courting clothes. Hodge never lets business interfere with plea-sure if there's a pretty girl involved."

Lily arose hastily, tucking at her hair and smoothing her skirt.

"You better spruce up some more," Jay remarked. "You're a sight after a night in a shack."

She gave him an inscrutable look, then walked out of the room, across the living room and to the gallery.

11

McColl dismounted at the gallery steps. He was shaved and barbered and smelled of bay rum. He swept off his big hat, and said, "Hi-yu, Lily."

Lily was smiling brightly. Watching her, Jay decided she really was pleased. There was something inside a woman that responded to masculine attention, no matter what reservation she might have in her mind. And Jay wondered if Lily Benton actually held any

124

reservations in regard to McColl's courting.

McColl took the hand she had offered, and was patting it familiarly. "I believe you know Jay Webb," she said. "I've just hired him as range boss at Pitchfork."

McColl now saw Jay standing in the open door beyond Lily. He slowly released her hand. "Range boss?" he repeated, a wary edge entering his voice. He stood gazing at Jay, and though the smile remained fixed on his fleshy, brown face, it was entirely without depth.

Jay moved out into the sunlight, stepped off the gallery steps. "Your hay shack at Eagle Creek burned down this morning, Hodge," he said.

"So I noticed, so I noticed," McColl exclaimed. "I came by there. Well, no matter. We'll throw up another shack when haytime comes."

"Don't bother, Hodge," Jay said. "If you put another hay crew in that flat, I'll build a fire under them hotter than the one that burned the shack. That's Pitchfork hay from now on."

McColl turned to Lily, aggrieved. "I come here to make a social call, and Webb gets wringy about a little hay," he protested. "If you want that flat, Lily, all you had to do was say the word. I'd be the last man in the world to horn in. There're plenty of other meadows to cut hay. I figured you wasn't needing Eagle, and it was handy to the road for me to wagon it over to Chain."

"Thirty miles isn't handy," Jay said.

"You're not going to let a little thing like this cause trouble between us, are you Lily?" McColl asked.

125

"A hay meadow is hardly worth fighting about, is it?" Lily answered.

McColl laughed—too heartily. "Well, that's settled. Eagle is all yours, Lily. Is that satisfactory?"

"Very," Lily said. "Come in and sit a while."

"I sure will. I . . ."

Dallas Carver had stepped on the gallery. She wore a neat house dress, whose straight lines set off the grace of her slim figure. She had the combed, fresh-scrubbed aura of a woman always meticulously careful of her appearance.

Lily introduced them. There was a faint irony in her voice as she added, "Miss Carver is Frank Spain's fiancée. She arrived yesterday to marry Frank, but he was absent on urgent business. Dallas is my guest until Frank returns."

"Frank is a lucky man," McColl said silkily.

"That remains to be seen, I'm afraid," Dallas said. "I intend to try to be a good wife to him."

Then Lily led them into the house and their voices faded off into indistinction.

McColl, Jay reflected, was going to be a hard man to pin down. On the one hand he was playing the role of an affable, neighborly rancher, while with the other he was persistently working to smash Pitchfork. He was gunning for Frank Spain, and a married woman was involved in the feud, and at the same time he was courting Lily Benton with a strict regard for convention.

McColl was showing a good face to the majority of the people of the Wardrums, knowing this was all

126

many of them would ever see. His other face was reserved for the half-light of the deep timber, and the remoteness of the canyons and line camps. It was a time-tried method of laying the basis for future respectability.

Jay walked to his horse. He intended to ride to his place at once, for Ward's condition was weighing on his thoughts, and he knew that Ben and the others would be on edge because of his prolonged absence.

He paused as he reached for a stirrup. Will Overmire's rig was coming up the trail. Al Shepherd followed it, saddleback, leading a riderless cowpony which carried a saddle with empty stirrups lashed.

Overmire pulled up his team at the saddle shed, and Jay saw the tarp-covered outline of a body in the buckboard, with death-stiffened, booted legs projecting over the tail.

Lily moved out on the gallery, shading her eyes against the sun. She stiffened, and Jay saw the breath rush soundlessly out of her.

Then she came hurrying. Dallas and Hodge McColl followed, but Dallas stopped when she saw what was in the doctor's buckboard, and remained at a distance, a pallor coming into her face.

"It's Dave Hollister," Al Shepherd said as he slid from the saddle. "His horse showed up, empty-saddled, before the storm set in yesterday. I backtracked until the blizzard sent me to cover at Sealover's ranch. I finally located Dave this mornin'. Found him dead in the brush at the fork of the Spearhead trail. Doc Overmire was the first to come along, so we brought Dave here. Somebody had bushwhacked him, shot him through the head."

Pooley Moon came hurrying to join the group, and Yancey Tolliver quit schooling his colts and rode in.

"Go back in the house, Lily," Will Overmire said gently. "And this other young lady also. I'll call an inquest as soon as possible. I have coroner's powers. I'll notify the deputy marshal."

"Was . . . was there any evidence as to who killed him?" Lily asked. Her face was ashen.

Shepherd shook his head. "The storm had wiped out everything in the way of tracks."

Jay kept an eye on Hodge McColl. But McColl was showing only a puzzled interest in this, as were the others.

Lily joined Dallas, and they walked back to the house. Hollister's body was carried into the bunkhouse and placed on planks that Pooley Moon laid across sawhorses.

"Apparently it was murder," Will Overmire said. "Hollister didn't seem to have a gun on him."

Jay now saw that Hollister's gun belt was missing from his body.

Al Shepherd walked to a bunk, lifted a holster and belt that hung on a peg. "This is Dave's gun," he said. "He wasn't much of a man for packing hardware."

Shepherd flipped open the gate, rolled the cylinder. "Five good ones and a safety empty," he said. "Barrel's clean."

He passed the gun around to the others. When it was handed to Jay he glanced at the cylinder, peered down the bore, and returned it to Shepherd. He was certain it was the same gun Hollister had used in trying to kill him. Evidently someone had located Hollister's body, taken the gun, cleaned and reloaded it, and placed it here in the bunkhouse.

"We'll need three or four more citizens to make up a coroner's jury," Will Overmire said. "Pooley, see if you can round up somebody on the trail."

Presently Jay found a chance to speak to Overmire alone. "Got anything to tell me, Doc?" he asked.

"I stopped at your place this morning," Overmire said curtly. "I was on my way back to Spearhead when I ran into this other matter. Your brother is holding his own. He may pull through, but it is far from sure as yet."

"That's hopeful news, at least," Jay said. "The first I've heard in some time."

Overmire turned and walked to the house. Lily was waiting on the gallery. She took the tall doctor's arm with that confidence a woman shows only to a man whose heart she knows, and led him inside.

Jay found Al Shepherd waiting to speak to him. Shepherd rubbed his palms along the seams of his pants, and said, "Lily told me yesterday she was puttin' you on as range ramrod, Webb."

Jay nodded, waiting. Shepherd smiled a trifle grimly. "I ain't goin' to be mealy-mouthed enough to tell you I'm happy about it. I figured I was doin' the best job possible here."

"Does that mean you don't intend to co-operate with me?"

"It's just the other way around," Shepherd said. "I think Lily's makin' a mistake. I don't savvy this deal, but I owe it to Barney Benton's memory to stick with her and see to it that she gets a fair shake. I'll back your play as long as I think it's fair for the good of Pitchfork. But I'll be watching every move you make."

"I like a man to tell me just where he stands," Jay nodded.

"As range boss you're entitled to move into the foreman's house with me. There's plenty of room."

"So you can keep a closer eye on me?" Jay smiled.

"Could be."

"Thanks, but I'll hang up in the crewhouse. I'll be on the move a lot anyway."

Jay walked again toward his horse, which Pooley had stripped of saddle, but left tied at the corral. Pooley was rigging a horse, preparatory to riding to find jurymen. When Jay started looking around for his own saddle, Pooley said from a corner of his mouth, "Lily says to wait 'til after dark. Then me an' my wife, Sabrina, will go with you."

Jay paused. "Seems like there's a fellow over at your place that dropped his gun by accident an' shot hisself," Pooley murmured. "Lily says for Sabrina to take care of him, an' for me to look after your stock. She said you might want to see this wounded fellow tonight."

Jay met Pooley's wise eyes. Pooley's glance was mild, neutral. A tough, knotty, hoop-legged man with a wrinkled neck and a ragged, graying mustache,

Pooley wore a disreputable, old, weathered hat with a rawhide drawstring through the brim to take up the sag. He had boots two sizes big to favor his bunions.

"How's your wife for keeping gossip to herself?" Jay asked.

"Sabrina's got a sharp tongue," Pooley remarked. "But once she makes up her mind not to talk that's the end o' it."

Pooley leaned back on the cinch and said to the horse, "Exhale, cuss you, Brutus!" He laced the latigo, reached for a stirrup. He paused, speaking softly over his shoulder. "Dave Hollister was packin' that gun when he rode away from here yesterday mornin'. Fact is, I never seen Dave without a weapon. Figgered, sometimes, he must keep it belted on even when he was sleepin'."

The old cowboy rode away then. At least, Jay reflected, Pooley Moon was withholding judgment on him. And Pooley had voluntarily contradicted Al Shepherd's statement that Hollister had not been carrying a gun the previous day. That meant Pooley didn't see eye to eye with Shepherd.

Sabrina clanked the dinner bell and called, "Grub on the table!"

She singled out Jay and pointed disdainfully toward the cookhouse. She served only Jay and Yancey Tolliver there, bringing the food from the house kitchen. Al Shepherd ate in the main house with Lily and her guests.

Sabrina displayed only a frosty tolerance of Jay. Tolliver ate in silence and in haste, then picked up his hat and was on his way, saying, "I gotta git back to them colts."

All Pitchfork was waiting, wondering which way the wind blew. It was apparent none of them understood Lily's motives in bringing in Jay as range boss.

Later, as he was smoking his after-meal cigarette, heelsitting against the bunkhouse wall, Dallas came to the Yellow House gallery, looked around and then located him.

She walked to him with her straight, sure stride, then stood a moment with him, deciding in her mind what to say. She smiled a trifle wanly. "Have you any idea where Frank could be found?" she asked.

"Any of twenty places, and all likely to be wrong."

"I could possibly forgive a man for an affair with another woman. I might even forgive him if he shot another man in an honest fight. But I wonder if I can forgive him for being a coward."

"That's being rough," Jay said. "It isn't only Hodge McColl that Frank is avoiding. It's Sam Leathers and Buck Clay and others of McColl's outfit. They've all got their orders, I imagine. After all, a man can't fight everybody."

"McColl is the only one who counts in a situation like this," she said. "If Frank faced McColl and had it out with him that would settle it one way or another."

She added, with a sudden, fierce blaze of that fury he had sensed in her before, "Hasn't Frank any pride? Hasn't he any respect for me?"

"When a man is lucky enough to have the chance of marrying a person like you he doesn't like to think of getting killed. He would lose more than his own life. You've got to take that into account, Dallas."

She let the fury die. "Talking to you is like hitting a featherbed. I get nowhere. You are a strange man, Jay Webb."

Then, after a moment, she said, "I'll need a tent to live in and something to sleep on and a stove. I can buy these in Spearhead, I imagine. But I also need a carpenter who knows how to build a good house. I have a little money."

"You still intend to rebuild Frank's place?"

"Yes. And I want to start at once."

"McColl won't like the idea."

"That is one reason I propose to go through with it," she said. "A minor reason, however."

"Ask for Gus Nielson in town," Jay said. "There are other carpenters, but he's the best of the lot."

She looked at him. "Do I understand you are actually approving of my decision to stay in this range?"

"Yes," Jay said abruptly.

She had been smiling, and now it faded into something deeper and more thoughtful. They stood silent for a moment and Jay felt the compelling knowledge of her beauty move through him. He knew she was aware of this.

"You give me strength to go on," she finally murmured. "And I needed it, Jay. I do need help."

"I have a little money, if you want it," Jay said. "And I'll drop by at every opportunity."

"To protect me from McColl?" she asked mischievously.

133

"That," Jay said, "is only a minor reason with me also."

"Then we're allies as well as . . . as friends," she said softly. She extended a hand. Her fingers were warm and compliant in his palm. She finally drew them slowly away. She gave him a grave and understanding smile, then walked back to the house, the breeze whipping her skirt against her body.

12

Pooley Moon returned at mid-afternoon with four freighters he had prevailed on to serve as jurymen.

Jay stayed out of sight during the brief inquest that Will Overmire held, for it would have been awkward if the doctor asked him to serve.

Al Shepherd was the only witness. The verdict was that Hollister had been killed by a party or parties unknown.

Then Hollister's body was placed in a freighter's wagon, which headed for Spearhead for burial. Al Shepherd accompanied the wagon.

Hodge McColl rode away soon afterwards, and Will Overmire presently climbed into his buckboard also. Lily followed Overmire from the house, and stood at wheelside talking. Then she took the medical man's arm, pulled him closer, and stretched on her toes and kissed him.

At dusk Pooley harnessed a team to the light wagon and loaded in his wife's metal trunk. Sabrina, her jaw clamped in a reproving thrust, came from the house rigidly garbed in her black Sunday dress and fascinator and cape and bonnet and settled herself on the seat.

Jay saddled, and discovered that Lily was accompanying them also, riding a roan gelding.

They rode in silence over a trail muddy with thaw. Jay's place was dark when they came into the Slide Creek flat, but when he called out the door opened, letting out light, and Ben Tracy stepped out. The windows had been blanketed.

Mario, Steve and Tom appeared a minute later, stamping into their boots. "So," Mario said, peering at the court plaster on Jay's face, "you have been fighting again, no? While we cool our spurs, and sit up worrying that you have been killed, you are only having all the fun. It is unfair."

"The fun is just starting," Jay said. "How's Ward?"

"About the same," Ben said. He dubiously eyed the rig in the background. "Seems like we got company."

"A nurse for Ward," Jay said.

Ward was conscious, but in obvious pain. "That damned sawbones," he told Jay, his voice taut with agony, "did something to me that hurt like hell. And it never has quit hurting."

Lily joined them. "What he did was to give you a chance to live," she said. "You were too far gone to feel pain when he first saw you. But now you're gaining."

Ward stared. "The chestnut filly!" he marveled. "So you're real after all. I figured I had only dreamed it

135

that other time—a year ago it must have been. But you're flesh and blood! You're staying this time, aren't you? With you nursing me I could stretch out this little illness for a couple of months."

"My housekeeper, Sabrina Moon, will take care of you," Lily said.

"Housekeeper?" Ward asked suspiciously. "How old is she?"

Lily brought Sabrina into the house. Sabrina glared belligerently at the men, and held her skirts clutched tightly about her, as though fearing contamination. She stood over Ward, looking at him challengingly.

Ward peered, then closed his eyes and groaned, "I thought so. Can't you just let me die in my own happy way?"

"Young man," Sabrina said in her nasal voice. "I'll have you understand I'm not here of my own choosing. But as long as I am here you will do what I say."

She peered scornfully around the house, which, in Jay's opinion, was orderly and well swept. "First," Sabrina snapped, stabbing a finger at Steve Tracy, "you get a scrub bucket, and mop that kitchen. The rest of you rascals pitch in and help. This place is like a pigsty."

It was nearly an hour before Sabrina grudgingly was satisfied with their labors. The men were only too glad to escape outside away from her sharp tongue. They gathered in the starlight, rolling cigarettes.

"Shall we go?" Lily asked pointedly. "It's nearly

midnight. Sabrina and Pooley will take care of things here."

They debated it in their minds, rebelling at this dominance she was drawing over them like the harness on a horse. Then, grimly, they got their warbags and bedrolls in the house, went to the shed and saddled their horses.

Lily led the way down the trail, riding a few rods ahead.

"Ward won't ever forgive us for leavin' him with that old catawampus," Steve said. "It's a lowdown trick."

"What's the layout?" Ben whispered.

"The same as before," Jay murmured. "Play along with Lily Benton until Ward can travel. Then we'll make long tracks."

Keeping his voice low so that the girl could not hear he told them about the bushwhacking attempt and Dave Hollister's death. They thought it over in sober silence.

"It could have been this Hodge McColl's work," Ben said reflectively. "He likely don't cotton to the idea of you range bossin' at Pitchfork."

"McColl didn't even know until today that Lily Benton had hired me," Jay pointed out. "I was present when she told him. I'm sure it was the first he knew about it. If he sent Hollister to kill me it wasn't because Lily Benton had hired me."

Jay went on to tell of meeting Dallas Carver and the fight with Sam Leathers and the burning of the hay shack. "Everybody is hitting below the belt," he concluded. "We'll follow the same rules."

"This Señorita Carver," Mario questioned hopefully, "she is attractive, yes?"

"Yes," Jay said shortly. "Very."

Something in his voice caused Mario to peer closely in the darkness. "I see," Mario sighed regretfully. "Beautiful, but pure."

"Damn it, Mario!" Jay snapped. "She's engaged to Frank Spain. Keep that in mind."

"Apparently," Mario said, "you are the one who must remember that, amigo."

Lily Benton spoke ironically from ahead. "Either speak loud enough for me to hear, or low enough to avoid arousing my curiosity. And if you men are beginning to quarrel among yourselves, you can stop it right now. That is an order."

They rode the rest of the way to Yellow House in silence, turned their horses into the corral and carried their war sacks into the bunkhouse.

"Make yourselves at home," Lily said, and left them.

Steve tossed his sack under a bunk. "I figured I always wanted to die in Texas," he said. "This north range must get mighty cold in winter on a man sleepin' in the ground. You got the makin's, Je—Jay?"

Jay tossed him a tobacco bag. "You still haven't learned to carry your own," he complained.

"I've had to for six years," Steve said. "Ever since you left us."

A sudden gravity and a remembering touched them. Jay glanced toward Yancey Tolliver, who had awakened in his bunk, and was regarding these strangers with wonder. He motioned, and they filed outside.

"I've been waiting for you men to ask me if I shot Mason and Vince Lomack that night in Concho," Jay said quietly.

"We know better than that," Steve said.

Ben spoke. "Who killed them, Jess?"

Jay shook his head. "I heard someone running after the shots were fired. But the building was between us. Then I had to ride or be burned down."

"Sid Ferris was in town that night," Ben said. "Did you know that Sid is now Wyatt Lomack's partner in the Double Arrow? He won half the ranch from Wyatt in a poker game—at least that's what Wyatt says."

Jay stood gazing at Ben. "I didn't know that," he said.

There was little cheer among them as they turned in for the night.

They slept until mid-morning. With Sabrina gone and the cook still in town, Lily cooked breakfast for them, serving the meal in the cookhouse. She moved with a sure efficiency. "Señorita," Mario said, offering her his most winning smile, "never have I eaten such delicious food. You have won my heart. I trust you will do me the honor of becoming my bride."

"Wait for a better offer, ma'am," Steve said hastily. "He beats his wives. Every durn one of 'em. Now me, I'm gentle an' halter-broke. And I don't sleep with my spurs on, like Mario does. Those Spanish spurs would be right uncomfortable on a cold night."

In spite of herself Lily found herself warming to

139

them. "Well," she said. "I can hardly marry both of you. What are we to do?"

"It's one of these cussed triangles," Steve complained. "How about another stack of flapjacks while I do my planning?"

"You perceive, señorita," Mario said, "that he is a very crude person. He talks of flapjacks now, while my heart is broken. He has no conception of the finer things of life. I warn you there is no filling him up with these flapjacks. It was in Del Rio that a cook tried to satisfy his appetite one day. I speak truly, when I tell you the cook became demented after my friend had consumed thirty-one, and—"

"That's a lie," Steve said. "The fella ran out of batter."

Jay said, "Cook him one more stack, then close up shop."

Lily noticed that Ben Tracy's gaunt grimness had eased, and there was a lax pleasure and a remembering in his eyes as he listened to this banter. Tom Faye, the silent one, was smiling too, through the smoke of his cigarette, with the expression of a man hearing an old, familiar song.

Something inside Lily responded to the mood of these men, and she recalled what Will Overmire had said about a lawlessness in her.

Afterwards Jay and his four men picked a saddle string from the remuda that Yancey Tolliver had hazed into the corral. They roped out mounts for the day, and saddled up, and loaded a pack horse with bedrolls and grub sacks.

"We'll be gone two, three days, maybe," Jay told Lily. "We'll take a swing through the line camps to size up the situation. In the meantime hire any riders who come along, if you figure they're worth their salt."

Dallas came to the gallery, and waved to Jay as they rode away. Lily stood silently, watching them go.

Winter range extended some fifty miles from the Shoshone Buttes on the south to Pipestone Creek. Pitchfork had once grazed north of Pipestone, but McColl held that range now as far as the Ox Bow River.

The remaining winter range was cut by two main streams, Antelope and Wagon Creeks. The creeks later, under the blaze of summer, would dwindle to trickles, but now they were rising, feeling the first run-off from the mountains.

Because of their late start they camped overnight, resuming their journey again at sunrise, heading for Pipestone Creek. Line camps had been established by both Pitchfork and Chain on Pipestone, and it was the main duty of the riders to throw back cattle from the opposing brands at the creek.

But, as they rode deeper into the flat country, they saw that Chain cattle were south of Pipestone in considerable numbers.

It was mid-morning when they rode up to the Pitchfork camp. It was a pole-built shack with a stovepipe fingering through the shaggy sod roof. Two cowhands appeared, eyeing them questioningly as they dismounted.

Jay knew them. He glanced at their riding strings in the pole corral, then walked to the door and eyed the dog-eared poker deck that was spread on the table.

"Day off, boys?" he asked.

Cal Jenkins, the taller of the two, lifted an eyebrow. His companion, Bob Allen, was a round-faced tow-head of nineteen.

"Howdy, Webb," Cal Jenkins said uneasily. "What brings you down here? Them Rockin' J's of yours drift this fur?"

"I'm working for Miss Benton now," Jay said. "And so are the men with me. I've hired out to Miss Benton as range boss. What kind of work did you hire out for?"

They both flushed. "How long since you two rode up the stream?" Jay asked. "How long has it been since you've turned back any Chain stuff from this side?"

"Now look!" Jenkins protested. "How do we know you're range boss? How do . . ."

"I just told you," Jay said. "Now you tell me why you two are taking it easy here, with the south side alive with Chain stock."

"Hell!" Jenkins snapped petulantly. "What do you expect a man to do for thirty a month? We ain't paid to git beat up an' shot through the guts. I told Al Shepherd long ago that we needed more men. McColl keeps four or five tough hands at his camp a couple miles from here. What can two of us do ag'in that many? We did our best at first, but they throw the cattle across the crick twice as fast as we can line it back, an' they're spoilin' to knock our teeth out if we look slaunchwise at 'em. So we give up."

"Draw yourselves a couple of horses," Jay said. "We'll go down to this Chain camp for a medicine talk."

Jenkins and Bob Allen looked a little scared, and a little hopeful too. They roped horses, saddled nervously, and mounted. Cal Jenkins eyed the five men who were waiting. "Maybe we got ourselves some help after all, Bob," he said.

They forded the creek, rode through scattered brush for two miles, then came upon a sod shack, flanked by a saddling corral.

Two roughly garbed men were sunning themselves before the shack. Then three more appeared. All were armed.

Jay and his crew dismounted. "Which one acts as ramrod of this camp" Jay asked.

"I do," said an unshaven, squatty man. "Who's asking?"

"Webb's the name. Range boss of Pitchfork. What handle do you go by?"

The man hooked a thumb in his belt just above his gun, and his hard eyes roved carefully over Jay and the others. "Gossard," he said surlily. "Pete Gossard."

"Seems like you and your crew haven't been earning your keep," Jay said. "Suppose you begin. You can shove some of your Chain stuff back where it belongs before dark. And more tomorrow and the day after until the job's cleaned up."

Gossard glanced at his own men. They had shifted

slightly, drifting warily apart. "Shove 'em yourself, if you're of a mind, mister," Gossard said. "We've done our ridin' for the day. We . . . ."

Jay and the four long riders moved in unison. Jay was upon Gossard in two swift strides. He slashed down with the heel of his left hand as Gossard drew, knocking the gun from the man's hand. In the same motion he smashed his right to the jaw, knocking Gossard reeling against the wall of the shack.

Tom Faye, chopping down with the barrel of his gun, halted the draw of a second man, then rammed the muzzle of his gun in his quarry's stomach, holding him frozen. Mario Rodriguez, who had the steel-spring speed of a cat under his languid pose, had moved in with a butting tackle, wrapping his arms around a third man. Mario drove ahead, crashing his victim against the shack, his head slamming into the stomach with an impact that brought a strangled wheeze of agony.

The fourth man, with Ben Tracy's lean, hard bulk coming at him, managed to clear his gun and fire a shot, but the bullet went into the ground at his feet, kicking up a burst of dust. Then Ben buffaloed him across the temple with a gun barrel, and the man staggered and fell on his hip pockets.

The fifth Chain rider, a young, thick-lipped redhead with a weak chin, had made a blundering gesture toward his gun, then had halted in frenzied fear, for Steve Tracy had him covered and was telling him to raise his arms.

Jay gathered up their guns. Pete Gossard got to his

144

feet. He wiped blood from a gashed jaw. "Wait'll Hodge McColl hears about this," he said thickly.

"Give Hodge my regards," Jay said.

Ben brought a water pail from the shack and sloshed the contents over the other dazed men until they revived. Finally all five were on their feet, sullen and unconvinced.

"We're wasting time," Jay said. "Roll your spurs."

He prodded them toward the corral, and they ragingly rigged horses. Under the domination of their guards they crossed Pipestone Creek and began drifting Chain cattle north.

Jay kept them at it until sundown. They had made only a small impression on the task, for hundreds of McColl's cattle were scattered miles south of the stream.

"Stay with it until you've cleaned up," Jay told them. "I want to see results the next time we ride by this way."

Pete Gossard fingered his bruised jaw. "After they bury you, Mister," he said thickly, "you'll stay here a long time. Ever think of that?"

"Tell Hodge I'm holding him personally responsible for any more cattle that drift south of Pipestone," Jay said.

"I'll tell him," Gossard said. "I'll sure tell him."

Jay ordered everyone to bed down in the brush away from the Pitchfork line camp that night. "Gossard and his pals might brave up enough to shoot up the place," he said.

But the night passed without retaliation. As they ate

145

breakfast Jay studied Cal Jenkins and young Bob Allen. Finally he asked, "Want to draw your time?"

They pondered it a while. At last Jenkins said, "Hell, we wouldn't leave no widows anyway."

Bob Allen nodded, and grinned weakly. "I got a hunch they'll think hard an' long before they try to crowd us ag'in," he said. "You men was mighty rough."

Jay and his four companions saddled up, and headed away southward. But, after half a mile, Jay pulled up. "Ben," he said. "You and Mario and Tom better hang around here for a day or two. Jenkins and Allen seem to be loyal to Pitchfork, and now that they figure they've got some backing they'll start pulling their weight. But they deserve protection too in case Gossard and his crowd try to haze them."

Ben eyed him quizzically. "Seems like you're doing a lot of worrying about Lily Benton's cattle and her crew, Jess," he observed.

Jay rubbed his chin, annoyed at first. Then he smiled wryly. "I guess it's McColl's methods that rub my hair the wrong way," he admitted.

"We'll keep an eye on things here," Ben said. "How about you?"

"Steve and I will take a look at the other camps and meet you at Yellow House in a couple of days," Jay said.

It was good to ride with Steve again. He always had been one to see the beauty of the country. Steve liked the wind in his face. Occasional sight of an elk track, or the flash of an antelope rump in the distance,

146

aroused the old, pleasurable speculation between them, and the urge to follow, and brought reminiscences of other days. And the silences that fell between them were comfortable.

It was mid-afternoon when they pulled into Pitchfork's east drift camp near the brakes of Sand Creek. This camp, Lily had explained to Jay, was manned by riders named Mack Kessler and Luther Smith. They had to wait until sundown before the pair showed up.

Jay's announcement that he had been appointed range boss obviously aroused a surge of excited speculation in their minds, but they remained outwardly noncommittal.

"I hear you've had a big winter kill in these flats," Jay remarked.

"Yeah," Kessler said remotely. "Hard season. Lots of she stuff gone."

"I don't see any hides," Jay said.

"Reckon the carcasses got mudded over when the thaw come. We didn't find much worth skinnin'."

"Got anything else to tell me?"

"I reckon not," Kessler said.

Jay wasn't sure about them as he and Steve pulled out the next morning. It was certain they knew more than they would tell, but whether their reticence was due to personal guilt or a refusal to take sides in a matter they figured didn't concern them, Jay was unable to decide.

The next camp was near Smoke Butte twenty miles south. The two men here were home. Lily had told Jay that Bill Suggs and Jim Lightfoot were long-time

Pitchfork riders, and that she was sure of their loyalty. Suggs was better known in the Wardrums as Calico Bill.

Jay questioned them about the loss of cows, but they were evasive. However, as he and Steve prepared to ride on, Calico Bill followed them to their horses. "You fellas like huntin'?" he asked casually.

"Could be," Jay said, and waited.

"I got a hunch there's game in the big malpais beyond Split Butte," Calico said, choosing his words carefully. "Me'n Jim, bein' past middle age an' stove up, ain't never felt quite up to goin' that fur into bad country to take a look. It's on to fifty miles from here an' that malpais is mighty rough travelin', they say. Some men have gone in there an' never come out."

Jay and Steve glanced at each other. "What kind of game would a man be likely to find in the malpais?" Jay asked.

Calico Bill shifted his cud of tobacco. "Slow elk, maybe," he said.

Slow elk! In range country that meant rustled beef. Jay stood a moment, gazing off across the sweep of the flats. Then he said, "We'll borrow fresh ponies from your strings."

"If them slow elk are there they'll be mighty spooky," Calico Bill warned.

Jay and Steve caught up new horses, shifted rigs, and mounted. "Much obliged," Jay said to Calico Bill.

Then he and Steve headed northeast, deeper into the plains. Steve slid his rifle from the saddle boot, made sure the magazine was filled, then shoved the gun back in place. "This is like old times, amigo," he said. "You an' me together."

13

Dallas Carver stood in the foot tub, bathing, in the Sibley tent that had been pitched on the clearing where Frank Spain's burned cabin had stood. It was sundown, and the air was balmy with the first real warmth of the onrushing spring.

She dipped lukewarm, water from a pan on the apron of the stove, let it flow deliciously down over her shoulders and body. The physical weariness she felt gave her a great sense of personal satisfaction, a knowledge of accomplishment and progress toward her purpose.

This was Saturday evening, and Gus Nielson, the crusty Danish carpenter, had gone to town over Sunday. She had hired him in Spearhead, and had bought the tent there, along with food and tools, and a slow-footed harness horse and a second-hand top buggy.

She smiled a little in rueful despair as she viewed her fingernails. She had raked ashes, savaging what she could from the rubble of Frank's cabin, and she had helped Gus to the best of her ability as he began leveling ground for the foundation of the new structure.

She had selected a new site, higher on the sloping clearing, where the west windows would offer a picture view of the Wardrums.

Over Gus's violent opposition she was planning a thirty-by-twenty main room, with a lean-to kitchen.

"You vill freeze in such a blace in winter," Gus had protested repeatedly. "A fifteen-voot ceiling is no goot in vorty below zero."

"We'll build it my way, and put in a false ceiling temporarily, if necessary," she decided.

What Gus did not know was that this room was but the nucleus of her plans. Some day, she visioned, it would only be the showplace. Later, with the years, would come additions and wings; quarters for everyday living, bedrooms and galleries. It was all clear in her mind.

She paused now, listening to the scuff of a horse's hooves coming nearer. Frowning as she became conscious of her situation—naked, with only canvas walls to shield her—she looked at the .44 revolver which lay in sight on a trunk, and felt reassured.

A man hailed the tent. "Anybody home?"

She recognized Hodge McColl's heavy voice. She said, "You'll have to wait. I'm in the tub."

"Few women would dare make a statement like that," McColl chuckled. "It proves that my first impression of you was correct, Miss Carver. You are an unusual person, and not as conventional as school-marms are supposed to be. I'll wait, and it will be a pleasure."

Dallas toweled herself and dressed. She selected a jade green skirt and a cool, white waist that she knew was becoming, and worked with her hair until she was satisfied with what the mirror told her.

Dusk, colored by the afterglow from the peaks, held the flat as she stepped out. The warm breeze had died, and the hoarse bickering of a jay echoed in the stillness of the timber.

The sharpening attention in McColl's eyes told her it had been worthwhile to take her time.

"Again I say Frank Spain is a lucky man," he remarked.

She glanced toward the scattered ashes of the original cabin. "A man without a roof over his head would hardly consider himself blessed with good fortune."

"Houses can be rebuilt," McColl shrugged, "as you are demonstrating. But other things are harder to come by. That takes real luck. When do you and Frank plan to be married?"

"You did not ride all this distance to ask me that," Dallas said.

McColl turned that over in his mind. "No."

"What you really want to know is whether I've been in touch with Frank. Isn't that the truth?"

"You know," McColl said, "in addition to being a beautiful woman you are also very intelligent, and practical."

"Why are you so intent on killing Frank?"

"Killing him? You're being harsh."

"No man would run away from me—even Frank—unless his life was at stake," Dallas said calmly. "I have that much confidence in my attractiveness, at least."

McColl tried to change the subject. "Gus Nielson

tells me you're planning to build the damnedest place. A barn, Gus calls it. He says . . ."

"Everyone believes this trouble between you and Frank is over a woman," Dallas interrupted. "I have a different opinion."

McColl's heavy smile was unchanged. He waited.

"Neither of you would value a woman to the extent of trying to kill each other," Dallas said. "I know Frank, and my judgment of you is that you look at such things the same way Frank does. Whoever this woman is, she is only an excuse for the real reason why Frank is hiding for his life from you and your gunmen."

"Gunmen?" McColl acted shocked, but she saw that he was inwardly all irony and arrogance. "You insist on being rough on me. I hire only honest, hard-working cowhands."

"The same kind Lily Benton is hiring, evidently."

"Meaning Jay Webb?"

"Perhaps. But there are others now."

"Others?" McColl demanded sharply. "How many?"

Dallas laughed. "You respect Jay Webb, don't you? I mean the kind of respect that is synonymous with fear."

McColl laughed back at her. "If you're trying to prod me into pawing the ground and beating my chest and telling you how tough I am, it won't work. You want me to give head to things I'll wish later on I hadn't said."

"And so neither of us have learned much from each

other, have we?" Dallas said lightly.

"I'm beginning to respect you more and more," McColl said. "And admire you." He gazed at her with frank speculation. "There is always a dance in town on Saturday night. What if . . . ?"

He let it ride. Dallas hesitated, just the smallest instant, then shook her head. "No. Good night, Mr. McColl."

He had not missed the significance of that hesitation. He drew a cigar from his breast pocket, removed the band while he tried to estimate just what it had meant. He flicked a match into flame, touched it to the cigar and savored the tobacco a moment.

"Another time, then," he finally said. "I'll be back—often."

Dallas did not answer that, and he turned to his horse, suddenly sure of himself, and elated. "You must be lonely here," he added as he mounted. "That will be remedied."

Dallas remained motionless for a time after the sound of his horse had faded into the deepening dusk. Then she went into the tent, lighted an oil lamp. She moved to the dresser and again consulted the mirror.

Then she placed a flat iron on the stove, and got out her sewing basket. She had never found pleasure in such homely routine tasks, but there was no monotony in them now, for the excitement of McColl's visit held her thoughts.

She had been at these tasks more than half an hour when a voice spoke cautiously outside the tent. "Dallas!"

It was Frank Spain. She pushed open the flap. He was standing back, where the fan of lamplight would not touch him. "I'd rather talk out here," he said.

The first glow of a rising moon showed above the trees. She walked out into the darkness, and Frank drew her farther away from the tent and the light. His arms went around her, and he said huskily, "Dallas, something told me I'd find you here, so I took the chance."

She stood rigid, and turned so that his mouth found only her cheek. She was sharply aware of the rough grating of his stubble of dark beard. His saddle coat hung limp from his shoulders, and his clothes looked like they had been slept in.

He acknowledged her coldness by letting his hands slip slowly away from her. "I couldn't get here sooner," he said apologetically.

She was conscious of the edged way he scanned the surroundings. The band of the cigar Hodge McColl had lighted lay on the ground in the light from the tent. Frank saw it. "Someone has been here," he said sharply.

"Mr. Webb," Dallas said. "He left nearly an hour ago."

Frank drew her still farther away from the glow of the tent, and she saw by the easier ride of his voice that he felt safer now. "Then Je—Jay met you when you arrived at Spearhead?" he said. "He promised he would. Did he tell you why I was called away?"

"Frank," she said, "I could perhaps overlook this matter of the other woman, but I can't overlook the way you ran from Hodge McColl. That was craven."

"So that's the story Jay Webb told you," Frank said, a quick anger thinning his voice.

"Everyone in Spearhead knows," Dallas said. "That's why it is so humiliating. They actually pitied me. Pity! I'll never forgive them for that."

"Is that why you're living here in a tent?" Frank asked contritely.

"I could not endure staying in Spearhead. Jay Webb brought me here that same day. We arrived after dark in a howling blizzard, and found your place burned."

"That must have been rough."

"We found shelter until morning at a place they call the Eagle Creek hay camp."

"You stayed there with him alone." The quick resentment had returned to his tone.

"You are a weak man, Frank," she said evenly, "and inclined to judge others by your own standards."

"You're bitter, Dallas."

"Yes. And with reason. I accepted the hospitality of Lily Benton at Yellow House for a day or two until I could make arrangements to begin rebuilding here at your place."

"Rebuild? That's hopeless, Dallas. You don't savvy. I—we've got to pull out of this range."

"Surely you're not afraid of one man, Frank?"

"One man?" Frank scoffed. "McColl has half a dozen on his payroll who will kill me on sight."

"Then it wasn't about a woman, was it, Frank?" she said quickly. "This feud is over something else?"

Frank believed she was offering him a chance to win forgiveness. And he was in a mood to unburden his soul. "Amelia Haskell doesn't mean a thing to me, Dallas," he said, in a gust of confession. "You're the only one who does. You know that. We'll go to California . . . Oregon . . . somewhere a long ways from here, and be married. We'll get us another ranch somewhere, and . . ."

Dallas had made a mental note of that name. Amelia Haskell! She said pushingly, "If it wasn't Amelia Haskell, then what was it, Frank?"

He hesitated. "McColl has been running a high blaze on Lily Benton," he finally said. "He started it while Barney Benton was alive, but bedridden. What I mean is that McColl has Lily's foreman, Al Shepherd, in cahoots with him along with three or four more Pitchfork riders. They're pulling a stunt called sleepering calves. Doing it on a big scale. I stumbled onto it one day when I was hunting antelope down in a badlands a long ways east of here."

Dallas waited. "And so McColl wants to make sure I keep my mouth shut permanently," Frank finished lamely.

"How did McColl learn you had found out about his scheme?"

"I guess some of his outfit saw me down there in the malpais, and knew I had seen something."

"The truth is," Dallas said quietly, "that you went to McColl and asked to throw in with him. Either that or a bribe to keep you quiet. Instead, McColl, being a ruthless man, intends to kill you in order to silence

156

you. That's the real story, isn't it, Frank?"

"Damn it, Dallas!" Frank protested. "You're being—"

"I'm facing facts," Dallas broke him off impatiently. "You know too much for your own safety. It's too late to reveal the real reason McColl is out to kill you, isn't it, Frank? You're tarred with the same brush. Everyone would guess why you kept quiet instead of going to Lily Benton with your story. Even your friend Jay Webb would turn against you."

"Jay Webb?" Frank exploded. "Do you have to keep comparing him to me? Why would he give a hoot about Lily Benton's cattle?"

"He's range boss of Pitchfork now. My guess is that Lily Benton is paying him to do her fighting for her— and her hanging, if necessary."

"Jess—Jay Webb—working for Pitchfork?" Frank exclaimed, astounded. "What's become of Al Shepherd?"

"Shepherd still seems to be foreman, but without much authority. Jay Webb apparently is in charge. And he has brought with him at least four new riders who look like fighting men. Or outlaws, perhaps."

"I don't savvy that," Frank muttered.

"You called Jay Webb by the name of Jess a moment ago," Dallas said casually. "Is that his real name?"

She saw Frank stiffen. "You must have misunderstood," he said, and abruptly changed the subject. "You can't stay here, Dallas. We could be out of this range by daybreak, and on our way to new country."

"You really mean you'd abandon your ranch?"

"A measly, two-bit spread," he scoffed. "A hundred head of stock."

"From what I understand, Pitchfork and Chain are at each other's throats," Dallas pointed out. "A small outfit can grow, if the others wear themselves out in this fight."

Frank sighed. "The truth is, Dallas, I don't even own my own land, or my brand. It was mortgaged when I took it over from a fellow who couldn't make a go of it, and I haven't been able even to meet the interest. The bank is the real owner of the Rafter S, and always has been."

"How big a mortgage?"

"Three thousand dollars, plus nearly three years' compound interest. You see, Dallas, it's hopeless."

"Jay Webb is fighting McColl," she said. "He isn't running."

"You seem to know a lot about Jay Webb," Frank snapped.

Dallas said nothing. The weak shallows of Frank's nature came to the surface. "So that's it?" he raged. "You've fallen for him? That's why he was here tonight."

Still Dallas remained silent, and Frank took that as a confession. "I'm not good enough for you," he panted, the words tumbling out in petty spite. "You prefer a man wanted for murder!"

"Murder? Frank, what are you saying?"

"Ever hear of Jess Steele and the Fence Cutters of Texas?" Frank frothed. "Ever hear of Wyatt Lomack, owner of the Double Arrow outfit in the Concho country down there? Wyatt Lomack will give ten thousand dollars to any man who delivers Jess Steele into his hands alive. Jess Steele murdered Wyatt's father and brother. Wyatt will . . ."

Frank's outburst faded. When he spoke again his voice was dead, shamed.

"I didn't mean that, Dallas," he almost whispered. "What am I saying? Jess is my friend, and I never believed he murdered the Lomacks. I rode with Jess in Texas. I was a Fence Cutter too. If anything happened to him because of me, I'd be a Judas. I've made my mistakes, but I'm not that low."

"I've already forgotten everything you said," Dallas assured him. She brushed his unshaven cheek with her lips. "Frank, things are mixed up. I've got to have time to think. You understand that, don't you?"

He pulled her again into his arms. "Then you do still love me?" he implored.

He held her tighter. "Oh, Frank," she said, chidingly, and pushed him away.

She added placatingly, "I—I don't know. I just don't know. You must give me time. You've hurt me terribly. Surely you realize that?"

He stood for a moment, a gaunt shape in the darkness. "All right," he said dispiritedly. "But I'll keep coming back—each night."

He went away reluctantly. Presently she heard the faint scuff of hooves in the timber. The sound died.

She walked back into the tent, picked up the flat iron, absently tested it with a dampened finger. She mechanically finished pressing a petticoat. Then she hung the garment away, and put aside her sewing basket.

She merely sat for a time, thinking, her fingers laced together in her lap. Moonlight lay full on the tent now, burnishing the canvas above her to a golden hue. The mountain night was vastly silent. Yet there was no loneliness in her, only an aching restlessness and a longing and a knowledge of unfulfilled ambition.

It had always been this way with her on such nights. Born in a small town, her father had been a bookkeeper, and she had seen him drudge away his life in obscurity. Her parents were dead now, and they had made sacrifices to educate her for school-teaching. But teaching had held no more appeal for her than needlework or home tasks. There was no patience in her for routine, and no respect for men—or women—who followed the beaten paths made by others.

She had been courted by young and solid men, even been twice engaged to marry, but always the restlessness and the impatience had driven her to end these affairs.

She had moved westward into Missouri, drawn by a need for fresher country. But Missouri was only another Illinois, already settling into its unbreakable mold. Then Frank Spain had come along, and now she was in the Wardrums, and upon her was the burning belief that she had at last reached her destination. She felt a wild and passionate kinship for this mountain country.

She could hear the drive of her own pulse in the stillness. She was breathing fast. It was as though she was being wooed by an invisible presence whose touch was irresistible—and also terrifying.

Names tolled in her mind. Jess Steele—Wyatt Lomack—Concho. She had heard vaguely of the Fence Cutters war in Texas. It had been a sensation in its day, but so remote from her life it had meant nothing to her. Now, she tried to recall details, but they eluded her.

But she was carried now by a frightening exhilaration, a knowledge of secret power that brought both a dread and a new and dazzling horizon ahead of her.

Finally she went to her trunk, brought out an atlas, which was among the few books she had thought worth saving from her teaching career. Turning to the map of Texas she located a town named Concho.

Ten thousand dollars reward. She kept hearing Frank's words. She abruptly snapped the book shut, thrust it deep into the trunk. She met her reflection in the mirror, and turned away swiftly, angrily, as though she had found something there that she did not want to face.

Presently she went to bed and lay for hours watching the slow march of the moon shadows across the tent.

14

Beneath that same moon Jay and Steve Tracy rode into the malpais. Split Butte pushed splintered fingers into the night sky to their left, towering above the torn waste of eroded ridges and brushy coulees. This badlands, long a refuge for maverick cattle and maverick men, stretched some thirty miles northeastward, enclosed by the swing of the Ox Bow River.

"No use telling you that you don't have to go in," Jay said. "You always were knuckle-headed."

"That makes a pair of us," Steve grunted. "After all, they're not your cattle. Just because the Benton girl is paying you three hundred a month is no reason you have to try to earn it. It's slave labor anyway."

"Maybe I'm just curious," Jay said.

"This curiosity can be fatal," Steve said soberly. "If we find what I think we're going to find, there'll likely be men who won't want us to tell about it."

Two days of patient riding had revealed a few, faint puzzling signs of cattle having crossed the plains in the direction of the malpais, but weather had blurred the trails.

They had been about to give it up when the wind had brought the taint of decaying flesh. Tracing that into the malpais they had found a dead Pitchfork cow that had been shot after it had broken a leg. The animal evidently had lain there all winter, and now the thaw was revealing its presence.

Quartering the area, they eventually came upon a trail that had been much used by cattle in the past, and showed evidence of occasional recent use.

"They ran the stuff in small bunches down the country last summer by different routes so as to leave no plain sign in the open," Jay said. "But all of them finally funneled into this draw. And riders have been over this trail lately."

They had holed up until dark before following the trail farther.

Now, keenly conscious of the disadvantage of their position, they rode slowly, the rattle of their mounts' hooves loud in their ears. Occasionally they pulled up to listen.

The draw narrowed, mounted and faded out, and they emerged in the full moon glare on a bald ridge. From there the trail led them again into the shadows of a wider draw beyond.

After some three miles they found themselves following a small stream. Cottonwood, alder and quaking aspen fringed the creek, and thickets of bullberry brush matted the flanks of the ridges.

They pulled up abruptly, hearing the far, dismal echo of a cow bawling. They looked at each other.

"All right," Jay murmured.

They dismounted, tethering their horses to an aspen. Carrying their rifles they moved ahead. The moon had climbed, shortening the shadows. As they advanced, the ridges flattened and receded into the moonlight.

They halted as a bedded cow lurched to its feet from bed in brush ahead, and moved off at a lumbering gallop. Her bulk showed she was in calf, and Jay caught the plain shadow of the brand as she turned. Another of Lily Benton's Pitchforks.

Now a large basin opened before them, studded with islands of quakie thickets and rock outcrops and boulders that were tombstone white in the moonlight. The creek coiled through the center, and the scent of new grass was a fragrance. And amid that rode the indefinite tang of stale wood smoke.

Jay peered, making out the shapes of more cattle in the foreground. "Sleepering job," he murmured. "They hold 'em here until the drop is weaned, brand the calves in their own iron, then turn the cows out on open range again. No telling how many are here. Plenty though."

He added, "Let's backtrack. We'll come back another day with more help. That wood smoke says there's a camp somewhere. That means a crew of some kind."

They followed the run of the brush shadows as they headed back toward their horses. Their pace quickened as they sighted the animals, and they stepped into the open to cross a small clearing beyond which the animals stood tethered.

"Looks like our medicine was strong tonight," Steve breathed. "I've got goose pimples the size of . . ."

Then a man's voice yelled, "That ain't Al! Burn 'em down!"

Jay was hitting the ground as guns opened up. Two rifles were bearing upon them from a grove of quakies to the left of where the horses stood.

A bullet whipped gravel into Jay's face. He rolled, hearing the heavy smash of another slug into the soil. He then got his own rifle going. Steve, a few yards to his right, opened up also. They laid their fire on the nearest flash of gunflame.

They drove that opponent down, but the second rifle was pumping at them from the aspens a hundred feet farther to the left.

Jay heard the tearing impact of a bullet in flesh, heard Steve's breath suddenly rasp harshly in his throat.

He knew both of them were done for if they remained there in the open moonlight. He arose, racing crouched toward the aspen.

Both guns were turned on him, but missed as he veered, taking advantage of clumps of brush and small boulders. They emptied out, and the next deeper slam showed they had changed to six-shooters.

But he reached the quakies unhit. These aspen, at this lower altitude, had sprung into half-leaf, and here the moonlight was shattered into a fantastic pattern of shadows.

Jay had his opponents flanked. He drove ahead, zigzagging among the white boles of the aspen. The nearest man's nerve broke, and he reared from cover as he tried to shift to meet this charge.

In doing so he outlined himself against the filtered moonlight. Jay had his six-shooter in his hand now. He fired twice as he ran forward. He saw his man reel back under the punch of the slugs, and up-end over a deadfall.

Jay ran past and upon the second opponent's position. He had the advantage of initiative and momentum, and he was yelling and crashing brush.

It was too much for his quarry. The man, shooting frenziedly, made the mistake of rising into view also, and attempting to retreat. Jay fired a belly shot, and the man went down.

Jay dug in his heels, halting instantly. He crouched down, silencing his breathing, saving his last shells. The shells were not needed.

He finally inched ahead until he reached the twisted figure which lay face down in the moonlight. This man was dead. Jay turned him over and peered close. It was Buck Clay, who had been with Hodge McColl and Sam Leathers the day they pursued Frank Spain up the Fort Relief trail.

Jay moved back through the brush, pushing fresh shells into his gun. He found the first man. This one was alive. He was groaning, and seemed to be hard hit, but he still had the strength to swear. He was a stranger to Jay.

Jay turned, ran out of the brush. "Steve!"

Steve was still breathing when Jay reached his side in the moonlight. Steve gasped, "Get out of this, Jess. There'll be more of 'em. Tell Ben . . . tell him . . . so long . . ."

Then Steve was gone. Jay crouched, gray-faced, over him. "Steve! Steve! Damn it, Steve. . . ."

But Steve could not answer. Jay refused to accept that for minutes. At last he numbly became aware of the far rumor of sound. Riders were coming. Evidently the two he and Steve had encountered had been out-guards. Now the shooting had aroused the main camp.

He lifted Steve, carried him to the horses, which had calmed after their terror during the shooting.

He laid Steve across the saddle. Steve's body was as limp as old rags. This was all a man amounted to after the life and the spirit was gone. A slack residue of flesh and bones that would never again know the beauty or the pain of life.

Jay lashed Steve to the saddle, hating the ludicrous position in which he lay, remembering the proud way he had always sat a horse.

He mounted, seizing up the whale line, and headed over their backtrail, leading the burdened horse. The stir of sound had resolved into the steady clap of hooves. But sound carried far in this stillness, and Jay still had nearly a mile advantage.

That was enough. It was pale dawn when he cleared the last rough opposition of the malpais and rode out into the open plains. After a time he bushed up on a rise where he had his backtrail under observation. But no pursuit appeared from the malpais.

Presently he mounted and rode on again, leading the weary horse.

15

It was mid-morning when he reached the Pipestone Creek line camp. Bob Allen and Cal Jenkins were absent. He borrowed fresh horses from their strings, leaving a note of explanation.

It was long after dark when the lights of Yellow House showed ahead. As he rode into the yard Ben Tracy arose from his heel squat by the bunkhouse and flipped away a cigarette. Mario and Tom Faye were with him.

Lily appeared from the cookhouse and stood in the lamplight, peering anxiously.

Jay knew that this was the way it must have been with them the past days—waiting and listening for him and Steve to return.

Jay remained in the saddle. He watched the strides of the three men shorten as they made out the lumped shape on the lead horse.

"It's Steve, Ben," Jay said.

Ben came to a stop, and all the drive faded out of his long length.

Jay slid to the ground, leaning against his horse. Exhaustion was a dead weight upon him. "Steve's gone, Ben," he said. "I led him to his death."

The lamplight from the bunkhouse window revealed the empty desolation of Ben's thoughts. Mario crossed himself, and Tom Faye said forlornly, "Oh, no."

Then Mario and Tom wordlessly, gently, freed the

lashings and lifted Steve's body from the saddle. The grotesque, jackknifed position into which death had frozen Steve was the final, terrible indignity.

Lily Benton came across the yard, step by step, forcing herself by sheer will.

Jay looked at her, and said, "He earned his hundred a month."

She drew a shaken, smothering breath. Then she moved to Ben Tracy, touched his arm in an appealing, comforting gesture. Ben pulled away from her, slowly, bitterly, without looking at her.

Four more men had come from the bunkhouse, and were clumped uneasily in the background. Yancey Tolliver was among them. These were the last of the Pitchfork headquarters crew, assembling for the season's work.

Jay now watched Al Shepherd appear. Shepherd pushed through the circle, looked at Steve, then at Jay. "How did it happen?" he asked, his voice jarringly sharp.

Jay did not answer. Tom and Mario had turned to carry Steve into the bunkhouse, but Lily said, "No. Take him to the house . . . please!"

They hesitated, but Jay nodded, so they carried their burden to the main house. Lily hurried ahead, brought a soft, rich eiderdown quilt from her bedroom and spread it on the settee. "Lay him there," she said.

Ben still stood in the yard. Jay went to him. "The blame is mine, Ben," he said lifelessly.

"Who killed him?" Ben's voice was a monotone.

"We'll talk it over in the house," Jay said.

He steered Ben to the house, and Ben paused for a time in the living room to look down at his brother. Then he moved with Jay and the others into the office.

Jay motioned Lily to a chair. He preferred to stand, and so did Tom and Mario, but Ben sagged into a chair.

Jay told them the story. Lily sat, her fingers locked rigidly on the desk, as she listened. She wore a gingham apron over a short-sleeved dress. A fine powder of flour dusted her arms, for she had been helping Lem Riddle with the baking.

Jay finished and let a silence fall. He had withheld one detail in the account.

"Hodge McColl engineered the steal," Lily finally broke the silence. "The fact Buck Clay was involved proves that, if any proof was needed. The calves were to be branded in the Chainlink iron, no doubt. The same thing must have happened last year also. That's why our increase was off."

"But McColl had help from your own outfit," Jay said.

"Who . . . ?" she began, but let it trail off, as though shrinking from the answer.

Jay addressed Ben directly. "There's one thing I didn't tell you, Ben. Buck Clay and his pal let us go into the basin without challenging us because they evidently weren't sure who we were. They waited until they got a good look at us at close range before they started to cut us down. Then one of them yelled, 'That ain't Al!'"

Lily drew a slow, resigned sigh. Jay nodded. "That's

the way it is," he said. "And it tells why Dave Hollister tried to ambush me that day on the Spearhead trail."

Her eyes came up to his, wide with dismay. "Hollister? Hollister tried to kill you?"

Jay said evenly, "Yes."

"Then . . . then it was you who . . . who killed him?"

"He missed with his first shot when he tried to rub me out," Jay said. "I was luckier. I couldn't understand why Hollister was in that bushwhack for me until last night in the basin. Then it became clear. You had told Shepherd the previous day that you had hired me to take over. Is that right?"

"Yes," Lily said dully.

"Shepherd knew a new range boss meant exposure for him. As foreman, he'd hired what men he needed to help spot cattle where McColl's men could run them into the malpais.

Some of your honest riders had a hunch what was going on, but were afraid to talk."

Ben Tracy got to his feet, and moved toward the door. There was a flat, deadly set to his face. He was wearing his gun.

"I'll go with you, Ben," Jay said.

"I need no help."

Lily sprang up, tried to bar Ben's path, tried to push him back. "No!" she choked desperately. "No more killing!"

Ben set her aside and walked out of the office, and across the living room to the gallery. But at that moment the quick rush of hooves arose from the direction of the corral. Ben broke into a run and Jay followed him out of the house.

A horse, hard-spurred, was beyond the corral, heading for the timber. It was hidden from sight by the intervening wagon shed.

The group of riders still stood near the bunkhouse. "Who was it?" Jay asked as he and Ben ran up.

"Al Shepherd," Yancey Tolliver said. "He saddled up an' lit a shuck as though the devil was on his trail."

Ben took two long, raging strides toward the corral. The impulse was to saddle and pursue his quarry.

"No use, Ben," Jay said gently. "He's got too much of a start in the darkness."

Ben pulled up, stood there while the deadly thirst for vengeance tore at him. Finally he said harshly, "Another time then. He guessed I'd come after him to make him answer for Steve. He must have got the hunch that it happened in the malpais, and that we were onto him."

Lily had followed them. "Let's talk this over," she said pleadingly.

She led them back into the house. She stood at the desk, looking down unseeingly for a time. She was pale, but her voice was steady when she spoke. "I'm calling off our bargain. I made a mistake when I brought you men into this affair."

"You mean in hiring killers to fight killers?" Jay asked stonily.

"If you want to put it that way, yes. I had hoped a mere show of force would cause McColl to back off, and that we would come to an agreement that would avoid bloodshed. But the bloodshed has already started. Two men have already been killed. It must be stopped. Killings lead to more killings. You men should know that better than anyone alive."

She watched them a moment, trying to see into their thoughts. "I am aware of your problem, Jay Webb," she went on. "I understand that you do not trust me. You will feel safer if you leave this range. That means giving up your ranch. I will pay you a fair price for your outfit."

Jay was surprised. He studied her, seeking to read her purpose. The offer did not fit his estimate of her character. As long as she had Ward under her control she held the whip hand over them. She surely knew this. And she could hardly be in a financial position to take on additional range without further weakening her own resources.

Yet it came to him that she meant what she said. He saw in her a woman's pity and sorrow for Steve . . . and a woman's deep and grieving self-blame for his death. He realized now that she had sincerely believed her troubles could be solved without this waste of lives.

Now she was seeing that she had been wrong, and she wanted to quit the fight—along this line at least.

"How's Ward?" Jay asked abruptly.

"Better . . . slightly. I was over there yesterday. Will Overmire says your brother is gaining and believes he will pull through now."

"What about a certain letter you wrote?" Jay asked.

Her eyes, dark and brooding in this light, searched

him. Finally she said, "That letter will stay in a safe place . . . for my own protection." Then she added, ". . . Until I'm sure . . ."

"Sure of what?"

"Of several things," she said tersely.

"You must know that McColl isn't the kind to be bluffed into making a deal," Jay said. "Violence is the only argument he understands. He can be busted physically, but not with words. It's whole hog or nothing with a man like that."

"There must be other ways," she said wearily.

"Marrying him, for instance," Jay said.

Her chin lifted. Her gaze met his squarely. She did not answer that.

"But I've already told you that Hodge isn't the marrying kind," Jay went on relentlessly.

Her stare became cold, scornful. Then she turned to her desk. "What value do you place on your cattle and range rights, Jess Steele?"

She spoke his true name with a deliberate and bitter emphasis.

"Don't you understand that all this is out of your hands now?" Jay asked, the roughness gone from his voice.

Her eyes lifted, then swung to Ben, then to Mario and Tom Faye. She saw something in their expressions that silenced her.

"It's too late to call off any bargains," Jay explained. "We thought a lot of Steve."

"It is the truth, señorita," Mario said apologetically. "We have, what you call it, the obligation to Steve. We would not feel right if we ran away now, leaving him here after they have killed him in such a manner. We have learned to shoot back when men shoot at us."

"You've grabbed a tiger by the tail," Jay told her.

16

They buried Steve the next morning on a knoll overlooking the ranch, not far from where the graves of Lily's father and mother were marked by chiseled boulders.

Lily had suggested that location without explanation. There were two other graves on the knoll, and Yancey Tolliver told Jay they held the coffins of old-time Pitchfork riders who had died in Barney Benton's service.

Tom Faye read the Lord's Prayer in his steady, careful voice. Lily attended the service. She was the only one who wept.

Afterwards Jay singled out Tom Faye and Yancey Tolliver. "Strip the line camps," he said. "Tom can do that alone. Have them report at the Pipestone Creek camp tomorrow—armed. Yancey, you visit every man who runs cattle in the pool. Tell them the situation. Have them report here before morning. Tonight, if possible."

"Can't we leave the little outfits out of this?" Lily protested. "There are only five of them, and the majority of the owners are married men with children."

"It's time for you to count your friends," Jay said.

Then he saddled up and rode away. He headed toward his own place, for he wanted to see Ward. But he turned off at Frank Spain's road, and was conscious of an eagerness as he neared the Latigo Creek flat where Gus Nielson's saw was whining.

Dallas straightened from some task around the site of the new house, whose foundation was taking form. She waved, and came to meet him, smiling.

She had a bandanna over her hair, and wore a cotton shirt and a calico skirt, shortened to clear the dust. Her ankles were slim, graceful. She took both his hands as he dismounted. "I was beginning to fear you had forgotten all about me, Jay."

Jay eyed the construction. "Looks like you're building solid, Gus."

"I yust follow orders," Gus said gloomily. "A castle I am building, not a house."

Jay waited until they had moved out of Gus's range. "Heard or seen anything of Frank?" he asked.

Dallas' animation faded. "No," she finally said. Jay frowned. "Maybe I better take a ride over into the Brule for a look," he said.

"I imagine I'll hear from Frank . . . if he thinks it is safe."

"Don't condemn a man until you hear his side of the story," Jay said. "Frank probably doesn't know you are here. Otherwise he wouldn't stay away. You're not the kind of a woman that men stay away from, Dallas."

She smiled dubiously. "I wonder! I've been consulting my mirror lately, and counting my wrinkles."

"That mirror must be warped," Jay grinned.

She laughed, gaily linked arm with him. "That sort of talk is good for my morale. I'm past twenty-four, you know. That's a frightening age for a woman to remain unmarried. But I'm forgetting my manners. You're hungry, no doubt. I'll get something ready."

"Next time," Jay said. "I've got to make tracks."

She came to stand at his stirrup as he mounted. "I'd prefer that you stay away from Brule Basin," she said. "Frank will learn where I am and come to me—that is, if he thinks it is worth the risk. If not . . ."

She left it unfinished, and stood there as Jay wheeled his horse and rode away.

It was noon when Jay rode up to his cabin on Slide Creek. Pooley Moon was absent, but Sabrina opened the door. "So it's you," she sniffed.

Ward was thin, his tan bleached out, the marks of suffering around his mouth, but he could grin now, and the grin extended to his eyes.

He appraised Jay. "You've been hitting the saddle right regular lately," he remarked. "You've lost your winter's tallow." Then he added slowly, "You look like you did six years ago. Remember?"

"I'm working as range boss at Pitchfork."

"Yeah. I know."

"How much do you know?" Jay asked.

"Lily Benton told me a few things," Ward said. "She's been here a couple of times with Doc Overmire. She is a gal who calls a spade by its right name." He leaned closer to Jay so that Sabrina could not hear.

"I'll be able to set a horse in a week," he murmured. "I'll be ready whenever you say the word."

"Maybe," Jay said "Keep your shirt on."

It was evident Ward was getting the best of care. The sheets were spotless, the house pin-neat. But it was also evident that he would not be in shape to ride in a week. A month, perhaps.

Leaving his place Jay rode to Spearhead. He needed shirts, socks, tobacco and other items to carry him through the spring work, and this likely would be his last chance.

It was late afternoon when he racked his horse at the tie rail before Mort Skelly's store and went in to make his purchases. Emerging, he was lacing the bag of purchases on his saddle, when he paused.

The night stage for Castle Bend was loading mail and passengers at the station platform half a block away, and on the opposite side of the street Mort Skelly, who was also postmaster at Spearhead, came hurrying from the store with the last thin bag of mail.

Hodge McColl came from Pat Slattery's saloon beyond the stage station, accompanied by two men. McColl wore saddle garb, but his companions had on town clothes over spurless half boots.

Jay's glance struck at these across the notch of his saddle. Then he turned from his horse, walked back inside the store. "Forgot to buy me a neckerchief," he told Hugh Parker, the clerk.

He stood back in the cool, deep shadows of the store, watching McColl's companions walk to the stage. They had not seen him. He was sure of that.

They shook hands with McColl, then climbed aboard the stage.

It had been six years since Jay had laid eyes on either of them. One had changed so that Jay might not have recognized him at a casual glance. But the other was the type that was ageless. This second man was Sid Ferris, gunman, who had been ramrod of the Lomack fighting men in the war against the Fence Cutters. Gray-templed, gray-faced, always wearing a loose, dark sack coat and a flat-brimmed black hat, and a stiff white collar and black string tie, Sid Ferris had the inevitable long stogie in his left hand.

With Ferris was Wyatt Lomack, who was eager to pay $10,000 for the pleasure of hanging Jay to a tree. Lomack was in his early thirties. Six years had put a diamond on his finger and another in his necktie, dressed him in broadcloth and white linen. It had added a bulge of fat above his belt, given him the sure strut of arrogance and power. For, even though he shared the profits of the Double Arrow with Ferris, he was now a very wealthy cattleman.

Jay remained in the store while Hank Cass mounted the box, spread the ribbons and kicked off the brake. The six horses whipped the stage out of town with a creak of thoroughbraces.

McColl lingered on the sidewalk for a moment, looking after the departing stage, a wry and thoughtful glint in his brown face. Then he spat with distaste, and walked back to Slattery's.

Jay debated it for the time it required to roll and light a cigarette. A wire-taut tension thrummed in him, while at the same time, he was aware of a deadening disappointment.

His first thought was that Lily Benton had betrayed him after all for the sake of that $10,000 reward.

Yet, if Ferris and Lomack had come here looking for him, why had they showed themselves so openly? And what was their connection with Hodge McColl? And why had they pulled out for Castle Bend?

He had to know. He walked out of the store, crossed the street, and entered Slattery's.

McColl stood at the bar alone, tossing off a drink with the abstracted air of a man who had a new and dubious problem on his mind.

Sam Leathers sat at a table playing euchre with two more Pitchfork riders. Leathers laid his cards down when he saw Jay, shoved his chair back slightly, and sat canted forward, his legs braced for quick movement. Jay moved to the near end of the bar, placing himself in McColl's line of vision. McColl saw him now, and snatched his thoughts back from a distance.

For the briefest space McColl measured Jay, waiting. When Jay said nothing, McColl forced a bland smile and spoke, "Howdy, Webb."

It was the guarded, careful reaction of a man who had measured an opponent and found him strong. McColl surely must have learned of what had happened in the malpais, and that Jay was aware of his connection with the sleepered cows. But McColl also knew there was no actual proof.

But that was all that showed in McColl's small eyes. There was none of the mockery of a man who had found a surprising and fatal weakness in his antagonist. McColl was not deep enough to conceal such knowledge entirely. If Lomack and Ferris had come to Spearhead looking for Jess Steele they had not confided in him. He did not know that Jay Webb was Jess Steele, wanted for murder.

Jay slid a coin on the bar, and said, "A beer is my limit today, Pat. Hello, McColl."

He drank the beer and walked out, carrying with him the memory of the way Sam Leathers had relaxed from his readiness to go for his gun.

Jay rode out of town. It was nearly midnight when he unsaddled at the Yellow House corral and stamped the stiffness out of his legs.

The bunkhouse was asleep, but a light showed in Lily Benton's bedroom in Yellow House.

He walked to the house, heavy with his weariness, and tapped on the main door. Lily's voice responded instantly, "In a minute."

When she opened the door she held an oil lamp with a china shade in her hand. She wore a quilted dressing gown, caught at the waist with a braided cord, and beneath that were slippers. Her thick, chestnut hair was brushed to a gloss, showing that she had not gone to bed. Jay saw the signs of nerves, and of thinking that went in circles, and of worry and indecision. This, he reflected, was the price of responsibility.

She had been waiting his arrival. He perceived that now. She lifted the lamp so that the light struck across his face. She searched his features anxiously for some new sign of trouble. This, he realized, was what he meant to her now. Bloodshed, violence!

"I just came from Spearhead," he said. "I saw Sid Ferris and Wyatt Lomack there."

He had hit her with it roughly, for he wanted to watch her reaction.

She didn't understand for an instant. Then it registered. She backed off a pace, a fearful question in her eyes. Her glance swung to his gun, then returned to his face.

"No," Jay said. "There was no shooting. They didn't see me."

Now she understood what he meant. She slowly stiffened. "You think I sent for them," she said.

Their eyes clashed, and she waited, offering no other denial. After a time Jay shook his head. "I did at first," he said. "But now I see that I misjudged you. I'm still worth more than $10,000 to you alive."

She said levelly, "Perhaps."

"Lomack and Ferris were with Hodge McColl," Jay said. "They shook hands with Hodge, then took the night stage out. Hodge acted like he had swallowed bad medicine. That's all I know. Does it mean anything to you?"

She stood troubled, thoughtful. "No."

Jay gazed at her, suddenly conscious of her shapely allure. She saw this thought in him, and they looked at each other, almost with shock, disturbed by a new and unexpected awareness of each other.

Jay's voice gentled. "You're losing too much sleep, Lily. Try counting sheep instead of dead men. Good night."

"Good night," she said, and slowly closed the door.

Jay, as he turned in for the night, carried with him the memory of that surprise in her eyes. He conceded a grudging admiration for her. She had started this snowball downhill, and now she was caught in it. But she was asking no favors, and was making no attempt to avoid responsibility.

His mind swung to Dallas Carver and Frank Spain. The ease went out of him suddenly, and he slept fitfully.

17

Jay awakened at dawn. Of the five small brand owners in the pool, four had arrived at Yellow House during the night, armed and ready to ride. Doug McDonald, Mike Cavanaugh, Trent Craig and Andy Cummings were solid, dependable men.

The fifth man, Bill Sealover, was missing. Yancey Tolliver said that Sealover's patch-saddle ranch looked like it had been suddenly abandoned.

When Jay counted noses at the final assembly at the Pipestone Creek line camp late in the afternoon, four of Lily's Pitchfork riders were missing also. Among the absent ones were Hutch Kessler and Luther Smith.

The following morning Jay led fifteen men into the malpais. The disloyal had read the handwriting on the wall, and had followed Al Shepherd's example by clearing out of the Wardrums.

They reached the basin and found more than 400

Pitchfork cows, nearly all in calf, with the drop already started. But they found no humans there. Buck Clay's body and the wounded man were gone, and the bloodstains and boot tracks had been carefully blotted out.

They found the ashes of a burned shack, and the wreckage of corrals and branding chutes back in the draws. But McColl's men had taken pains to remove any evidence that would connect Chain with the sleepering job.

Jay now discovered that Lily was present. She had followed them into the basin. Dust of the long ride lay on her saddle garb, and shaded her eyelashes.

"When McColl began stealing he went first class," Jay commented to her. "This is quite a holdout. And it's pretty much of an airtight scheme. He only branded calves. It's hard to pin anything on him."

"I seem to have got back my ten thousand dollars' worth already," she said.

Then she turned and rode away. Jay did not see her again, and Yancey Tolliver told him, when he inquired about her, that she had pulled out for Yellow House.

They drifted the sleepered cows out of the malpais to open range, a slow process, for the calf drop was in full swing now.

New grass was coming with a rush, and the middle and upper country was opening; the last, weather-soiled snowdrifts in the timber were evaporating. Granite ribs were showing on the flanks of the Wardrums, though the rims were still unsullied.

Jay spread the crew from Pipestone to the Shoshone

Buttes. The weather turned hot, and the cattle were on the move, drifting up into the timbered benches, following the new grass.

This was the eternal cycle of the cattle country. This was the rebirth of the range after winter's bleakness. Always cattle and men followed the new grass with a new hope.

Within a fortnight the lower range was deserted, and in another week the cattle were working in the middle benches in the vicinity of the headquarters ranch.

Jay was in the range the greater part of the time, directing the scattered riders, whose numbers were augmented by four new men whom Lily had hired for the summer. He took time out to ride to Slide Creek twice to see Ward, who was plainly gaining. And he saw Dallas Carver each time at the Latigo Creek flat, where her new ranch house was taking shape.

Yancey Tolliver found Jay one afternoon at one of the range camps, and told him Lily Benton wanted to discuss a business matter with him.

He rode into Yellow House at dusk, accompanied by Ben Tracy. Lily came from the house to meet them at the corral.

Jay was surprised to see Sabrina Moon appear at the door of the house.

Lily answered the question in his eyes. "Your brother is here," she said. "We moved him from your place two days ago. Will Overmire said it would be all right. It's more convenient. Also safer. Yancey will look after your cattle."

They had settled Ward in a bedroom. He was able to

185

sit up now, and was strengthening slowly.

"It won't be long until I'll be able to put on my own pants when there're no females around," he told Jay.

Lily waited until they had finished their talk, then led Jay and Ben to the office.

"I think I've learned why Wyatt Lomack and Sid Ferris were in Spearhead that day," she said, keeping her voice down. "I had Pooley Moon make inquiries. Pooley first talked to Hank Cass, the stage driver. Hank said he had been told by cowboys at Castle Bend that Wyatt Lomack is looking for northern range. Like most big Texas outfits they want to branch out.

"Lomack and Ferris sent a herd of three thousand head of mixed she stuff and young cattle up from the Concho country late last summer and wintered them in western Kansas. Hank says, from gossip among trail men, that Lomack intends to put another herd of the same size on the trail this year also. But he hadn't found range for his stuff yet."

She let them think that over. "Hank also says that Wyatt Lomack and Hodge McColl are shirttail relatives," she added. "Second cousins. McColl came from Texas originally, you know."

Jay was frowning. "Have you heard anything lately about whether the Cheyenne reserve is likely to be opened soon?" he asked.

"I had the same thought," she nodded. "Lomack and Ferris probably are hoping to move in there, when and if the opening comes. They must have made that trip

186

to Spearhead to talk over the situation with Hedge McColl."

"Maybe that explains why Hedge acted like he had found a worm in the apple," Jay commented. "He wouldn't cotton to the idea of having Wyatt and Sid Ferris as neighbors. If he's a relative of Wyatt he knows what kind of a neighbor Wyatt would be."

"I received a letter from our Senator a few days ago," Lily said. "Amos Dean. He was a friend of Dad's, and he has been keeping me informed. He says there is every chance the reserve will be opened any day, and that homesteading will be excluded. He promised he would wire me the instant the news came. The message would be sent by way of the telegraph office at Castle Bend. I've sent Pooley to the Bend with orders to rush the word to us if it ever comes.

"How's the river?" Jay asked quickly.

Lily shook her head. "Bad. Still rising. I sent Yancey there this morning to take a look. The run-off hasn't reached its peak yet."

"We better start moving stock in that direction so as to be in a position to cross into the reserve if the word comes," Jay said.

"Yancey says it's already too late. He says the river is too wild all the way from the gorge to the flats to ford cattle. And McColl evidently knows as much as we do about what is going on back in Washington. Yancey learned that McColl is holding a steer herd of about one thousand head on winter range near the river. He'll have a better chance of fording Ox Bow

187

down there, and can drive into the Cheyenne reserve by way of Flint Basin. It's a hundred miles out of his way, but if we are blocked by high water up here he'll be first on the ground."

"You've got to cross up here if you cross at all," Jay said. "McColl claims all that range down there along a river, and he'd like nothing better than an excuse to stampede you if you tried to drive Ox Bow across his graze. It would be useless anyway. It would cost you a week's time to get a herd back down there."

"I know," Lily said, worried. "All I can do is hope the opening is delayed until the melt slows and the river is down. Whoever gets on the reserve first with cattle will have priority claim on the top graze. It's always that way in land openings."

She paused, then went on, her voice a trifle uncertain. "I've been trying to find another man to take over as range boss, but with no success thus far. Working for me doesn't seem to have much appeal for the average man these days."

Jay said nothing, waiting.

"Now that Wyatt Lomack and Sid Ferris are likely to become permanent fixtures in this range I'm taking it for granted that you will want to pull out at once," she explained, choosing her words carefully. "I understand how you feel about Steve's death, but Al Shepherd has evidently left the country, and you've already had a measure of vengeance on McColl to pay for Steve. You killed one of them, wounded another and broke up McColl's calf-stealing scheme after he had put a lot of time and money into it."

She watched Jay's face. Finding nothing readable there, she added, "And . . . and you've taught McColl a lesson. He's quit crowding us. His men are even turning back cattle along Pipestone. He's staying on his own graze. That's all I ever asked of him. He's welcome to what he has."

"You've won a skirmish, not a war," Jay said. "McColl will come at you again. You know that. And if he gets control of the reserve he'll be too big to stop. You know that too."

A fury that puzzled Jay showed in her voice. "Lomack will have you hanged. Or Sid Ferris will kill you. Hodge McColl is an oily schemer who will fight only when the odds are in his favor, but Sid Ferris is another matter. His business is killing. How much chance would you stand against him?"

"Ferris is fast," Jay conceded.

"Then why risk it? You're free to go. Ward can join you later, after he is able to travel."

Jay said nothing, but stood looking at her.

"If . . . if it's that letter you're thinking about, I will destroy it," she said, her voice trembling.

"Why are you so anxious suddenly to get rid of me?" Jay demanded. "First you force me into this fight, now you want me to turn tail and run."

She kept her eyes on the desk. "I have my own reasons. I want you to understand you are under no obligation to me. You have already fulfilled your share of the bargain in stopping McColl."

Ben Tracy, who had been listening quietly, spoke now. "If it's Sid Ferris you're worrying about, ma'am,

I want to point out that Ferris never went out of his way durin' the trouble down in the Concho country to pick a fight with Jess Steele. Fast guns shoot both ways, you know."

"That's exactly what I want to avoid," Lily almost sobbed. "Even grass isn't worth—"

The sound of hoof beats of a heavy-footed horse, lashed to a lope, drifted from the darkness, halting her. A voice hailed the house.

It was Gus Nielson, riding a blanket pad on his swaybacked harness horse. "Frank Spain iss dead," Gus panted as they came hurrying. "It vas a gunvight. Hodge McColl, he kill Frank this night at Frank's blace."

Gus slid from the horse. He said in a helpless, raging voice, "I knew it vould habben. Dot damned woman!"

Lily said, "Sabrina, get Gus a drink." She added in a lower voice that only Jay could hear, "Perhaps at least one cause that keeps you in this range isn't hopeless for you now."

18

Dallas Carver's fingers were ice cold as she used a hair-curler which she kept reheating at the stove.

Outside, darkness had come. The tent held the day's residue of heat, reinforced by the stove, but none of this seemed to touch her. Her cheeks were pale, dry, and there was a gripping chill within her.

She could hear the distant, brittle reports as Gus

Nielson broke dry limbs to feed his cook fire. Gus had moved his camp wagon a quarter of a mile farther away to a new location off the flat and well beyond sight of the tent. He had said that he liked that site better, but Dallas knew he was disassociating himself from anything that went on at her tent.

For Gus, no doubt, was aware that Frank Spain was showing up every night. And Hodge McColl, though he had confined his visits to daylight, was visiting the flat with increasing frequency. Gus's conversations with Dallas were now strictly limited to matters concerning the carpentry.

Dallas finally finished with the curler. She pulled on a new print dress over her chemise. She drew on black silk stockings, a luxury for her limited purse, and donned new slippers.

A dance was to be held at Turner's Hall in Spearhead on this night, and Hodge McColl soon would be arriving to act as her escort to the affair.

She had returned to the tent the previous night after several days' absence. When she had pulled out, driving her buggy horse, she had told Gus not to worry about her because she had some special shopping to do, and might have to go to Castle Bend to find what she wanted.

She had left the rig at Charlie Beal's livery in Spearhead, and had taken the night stage to Castle Bend. She had spent a day at the Bend, returning the following day. She had bought the print dress, and the stockings and slippers and other items, but the real reason she had made that long trip was to mail a letter.

She had not wanted Mort Skelly, who was postmaster as well as storekeeper at Spearhead, to know about that letter.

It was addressed to Wyatt Lomack, Double Arrow ranch, Concho, Texas.

Its contents were brief:

"If you are interested in the whereabouts of one Jess Steele, get in touch with the undersigned, personally."

She had used a pencil, and had printed the characters crudely to disguise the handwriting. She had signed Frank Spain's name to the message, also in printed letters, along with directions to his ranch on Latigo Creek out of Spearhead.

When she had dropped the envelope through the slot in the Castle Bend post office there was no turning back for her. It had been the climax of weeks of tension and wavering resolution and sleepless, tossing nights.

During that time she had drawn from Frank Spain, little by little, the full story of Jess Steele. Frank, who came each night to renew his plea that she leave with him to start life over again somewhere else, had grown increasingly resentful of her interest in the man known in this range as Jay Webb. She had used his jealousy to loosen his tongue and goad him into talking.

And, from Frank, she had also learned much about Amelia Haskell.

Frank was hiding at one of the pool ranches, and he

knew about the holdout of sleepered stock in the malpais, and the gunfight in which Steve Tracy had been killed.

"But that's only the start," Frank had predicted. "McColl will pretend to pull in his horns, maybe, but he'll try again. He's bent on being top man in this range. And Lily Benton is like her father. She'll fight him with her last dollar. Some people think she's trying to marry Hodge. I don't believe that. And I don't think Hodge believes it either. All that hand-patting is only on the surface. Underneath they're fighting each other to a finish and they both know it. Chances are both of them will go broke before it's over with."

Dallas shared that opinion. She and Lily visited occasionally, and she had come to know Lily's nature. She believed there was opportunity here for someone who was strong to step in and seize control of the Wardrum country if Pitchfork and Chain came to the point of exhaustion.

Frank's place was a start. His location controlled the headwaters of Latigo Creek, and a considerable watershed of mountain range. If Pitchfork weakened, the small ranchers in the pool would be glad to sell out for a song, no doubt. Then there was Webb's Rockin J on Slide Creek.

If all these small ranches, with their control of streams, could be consolidated, Lily Benton and Hodge McColl would find that a new factor had entered the struggle for supremacy in the Wardrums. What Dallas lacked was money. She had brought some $500 with her, but the most of that was gone now, and she was buying lumber on credit at Herdman's mill, and owed Gus Nielson two weeks' pay.

On her return to Spearhead from Castle Bend, she had called on Otis Haskell at the bank.

"I understand you hold the mortgage on Frank's land and on his cattle, Mr. Haskell," she had said, after she introduced herself. "I would like to arrange to buy it from you."

Otis was surprised. She saw in his eyes a kindly sympathy and pity for her. That kindled a contemptuous resentment in her.

"I would advise you not to be hasty, Miss Carver," Otis had said. "I wonder if you understand the real situation?"

She knew what he meant. Otis wanted to tell her that Frank Spain was not strong enough to stand against Hodge McColl. He believed she was only being blindly loyal, fighting a hopeless fight to put Frank back on his feet.

"I understand the situation," she said. "Do you?"

"I—I hear that Hodge McColl and Frank have had trouble," Otis admitted reluctantly. "Serious trouble. I fear McColl is the kind of a man who doesn't forgive easily."

"Do you know what the trouble was about?" she asked, wondering just how much he really knew about Amelia.

"No," Otis said crisply. "It's best to stay clear of things that are happening in this range."

Dallas' impersonal scorn for this little, colorless man increased. For he was the one who was being blindly loyal. If he suspected that Amelia was involved in the feud he was determined to ignore it.

"Exactly what is the amount of the mortgage?" she asked.

Otis consulted a file, made a calculation on a scratch pad. "Frank has paid no interest on the paper," he said. "However, if you are seriously considering buying the mortgage, Miss Carver, I'll relinquish at face value . . . three thousand dollars. The bank will take the loss in view of the circumstances."

Dallas arose. "You'll hear from me soon, Mr. Haskell."

Leaving the bank she got her rig from the livery and drove out of town by way of the west trail. Once she was beyond sight of Spearhead, she circled the town by side roads and drove to Otis Haskell's residence, which stood alone beyond the east fringe of town, overlooking the Castle Bend road.

Otis had built for his bride an imposing, two-story house. There were many gables and bay windows and ginger-bread scrollwork and colored window lights, and a deep veranda. The house was painted white, with green shutters, and stood enclosed by a white picket fence and a slope of natural lawn, broken by fir trees.

Carrying her knitting bag, Dallas mounted the veranda and rang the bell. It was Amelia who opened the door. She seemed to be alone in the house.

Amelia stood gazing at Dallas, both a challenge and

a fear in her dark, revealing eyes.

"May I come in?" Dallas asked.

Amelia hesitated, then led the way into the parlor, which was furnished to the bursting point with bandy-legged, tapestry-covered chairs and settees, marble-topped stands and bric-a-brac shelves.

"Expensive, isn't it?" Dallas commented, glancing around. Amelia stood tense, waiting.

"You know who I am, of course, even though this is our first face-to-face meeting," Dallas said.

Amelia nodded. She wore a full-sleeved, tight-bodiced dress of a better fashion than either Mort Skelly or any store in Castle Bend offered. "I know who you are," she said, her voice low, husky.

Dallas said bluntly, "I am in need of a little money. Three thousand dollars. I want you to loan it to me."

"Three thousand dollars? Where would I get that much money?"

Dallas let her eyes travel over the room. "Otis seems to be very generous with you. I'm sure you've held out money for yourself from time to time as a nest egg for the day when you leave him."

The last of the color ebbed from Amelia's thin face. She moved behind a chair, placing it between them as though needing a shield.

"You do intend to desert him, don't you?" Dallas went on coldly. "Otis is too sedate for your tastes. You are in love with Frank Spain, aren't you?"

"Where is Frank?" Amelia asked shakily.

"He's alive."

"You've seen him?"

"Of course."

"You don't love Frank Spain," Amelia said, a sudden, fierce accusation in her voice.

"I'm engaged to marry him," Dallas said icily.

"But you don't love him!"

"I want to help him," Dallas said sharply. "And you can help him also by loaning me the money."

"And if I do not loan it to you, you will go to my husband and tell him I am the woman Frank and Hodge McColl were fighting over?" Amelia's voice was steady now—and scornful.

"Yes."

Amelia gazed at her a long time. "You surely know that Frank must leave this range," she finally said. "Hodge McColl is a relentless man and intends to kill him."

"That would be awkward for you, wouldn't it?" Dallas said. "His blood would be on your head."

A bitter pride straightened Amelia, giving her dignity. "I love Frank," she said slowly. "I admit it. I only flirted with Hodge McColl, but I fell in love with Frank. I know I am only a passing fancy with him. I admit that too. But I could not bear to be the cause of his death. Therefore I'll let you blackmail me, Miss Carver—but on one condition."

"Blackmail is a harsh word," Dallas snapped.

"There's no other word for it. I do have three thousand dollars here in the house. I'll give you the money, provided you promise to leave this range with Frank."

"Your consideration for my fiancé is touching," Dallas said.

Amelia gazed at her a long time, trying to guess her thoughts. "You will prevail on Frank to leave, won't you?" she asked pleadingly.

"Of course," Dallas said lightly.

Amelia hesitated, then left the room. When she returned she carried a weighted metal keepsake box. She placed the box on the table, unlocked it, and from its contents counted out $3,000. There were some greenbacks, but the bulk of the money was in gold coin.

Dallas recounted the money, and slid it into her knitting bag. "Exactly right," she said.

Amelia's dark eyes were tragic. "Be a good wife to him, won't you, Miss Carver?"

"A better one, I hope, than you've been to Otis," Dallas said, and brushed past her, walked to the door and out of the house, carrying the sagging knitting bag.

She drove back into Spearhead and to the bank. Otis Haskell was surprised by her return. And he was more than surprised when she aced the money before him.

"I'll buy the mortgage now, if you don't mind," Dallas said. "You can transfer it to my name."

Otis sat gazing at that collection of gold and bills, a hopeless and aged defeat in his face. Dallas surmised that he suspected its source.

Then he said heavily, "I'll take care of recording it in your name on my next trip to Castle Bend next week. That is the county seat."

It was nearing sundown when Dallas left town. Driving homeward she encountered Hodge McColl on the trail, riding toward Spearhead. "This is luck," he said. "I just came from your place. Gus Nielson said you were away. I trust that your shopping trip was successful."

"Very," Dallas said gaily. "I have a new dress, and it's a dream. And other adornments."

"A new dress needs to be displayed," McColl said. "There's a dance in town tomorrow night as usual. Don't refuse me again. A pretty girl can't stay buried forever in the tules."

She sat considering that, a sudden remoteness in her eyes that puzzled him. Then she brought her thoughts back, dropped her eyes and said demurely, "I shouldn't. You know that. But I'm too weak of will to think of sitting in that tent tomorrow night when people are dancing."

McColl drew a long sigh of triumph, and his grin became intimate. "I'll call for you about this time tomorrow," he said. "With my hair greased and my boots shined."

"That will be too early," she said. "I intend to keep Gus working until dark, for he's probably been loafing, without me to prod him. I'll want time to get ready. Don't call for me until after dark."

And now this was the tomorrow that McColl had mentioned. No, there was no turning back for her.

She moved the lamp nearer, turned the wick higher while she added a faint touch of color to her cheeks.

She was aware of the increasing tautness in her body. Her mind kept forcing herself to believe it was only because she was listening for McColl's arrival.

But she was also straining tensely to hear something else.

Gus's woodchopping had ended now, and the pines were silent in the windless lull of early nightfall.

Then Frank's voice spoke softly outside the tent and even though this was what she had expected, she uttered a little, gasping, strangled sound, which she mastered after a moment.

She drew the tent flap aside, peered out. But she could not see him in the darkness. "You are as soft-footed as an Indian, Frank," she said. "I never hear you approach. Come into the tent."

He emerged from the darkness. She saw him gazing around as he always did, sifting the night for any hint of danger.

"There's no one, Frank," she said impatiently. "And if there was, isn't this your own place? Your home?"

He moved toward her then. She had never before asked him to enter the tent. Always she had met him in the open, keeping him at arm's length.

Now he felt that she was relenting, for he came into the lighted tent with a lift in his stride. And when she dropped the flap, shutting them in together, he said exultantly, "Dallas, you've made up your mind. You're going away with me?"

"I've decided to discuss it at least, Frank," she said.

He had shaved, but his black hair curled heavily over the collar of his flannel shirt, and his boots seemed too big for him. He had thinned, and his eyes were set deeper in his face.

"I've been thinking it over also, Dallas," he said.

"And you are right about this being my place. I've decided to stay here. We'll be married tomorrow."

She realized quickly the blankness in her eyes, and turned away from the light. "What made you change your mind, Frank?"

"I've spent a lot of time since you went away, looking at a fellow," he said. "I was looking at a man named Frank Spain, who wasn't worth a damn. Least of all was he worth the love of a girl like you. You could never be happy with a coward. Even if you went away with me that knowledge would always be in our hearts, and we'd never ever be really close. You could never respect me. So I'm going to stay here and face it, no matter what comes."

He watched her anxiously. "That's how I spent these past days," he said. "I came here every night, and when I found this tent black and cold and vacant each time, I began judging Frank Spain as he should be judged."

As he talked Dallas heard the far rumor of hoofs and wheels. Frank heard it also, for he went silent, and turned, giving this all of his brooding attention.

But the sound had died. "It was Gus Nielson," Dallas said. "He is driving to town. It's Saturday, you know."

As she spoke she saw that Frank's shadow against the lamplight was a clear, black etching on the canvas wall.

Frank moved toward her, and she watched his shadow move with him. He drew her into his arms, kissed her. "I was a long ways down the wrong trail,

Dallas," he said humbly. "But I'm back now, and I'll never run again from anything."

His voice was a boy's voice, eager, rejuvenated by the rebirth of his pride. She remained passive in his arms for a moment, then drew slowly away. "Frank, you are hard to resist," she said. "You had better go."

"I'll come back tomorrow," he said jubilantly. "At sunup. We'll ride to Spearhead and be married."

"That's not giving me much time, Frank."

"Name the day."

"Oh, Frank, give me a chance to think. Don't touch me again. It's sinful . . . just the two of us alone here."

She pushed him to the door and through the flap into the darkness.

She dropped the flap and grasped the tent pole for support, seized by a terrible faintness that was a sickness.

For, over Frank's shoulder, she had seen the bulky shadow of Hodge McColl standing a dozen paces from the tent in the soft darkness.

She heard it all. McColl spoke, and his voice was metallic. "Hello, Frank."

Then came the violent, overlapping roar of guns. Beneath that were sounds that were like the copping strokes of Gus Nielson's ax. For a moment Dallas did not comprehend. She now heard the whistling, stricken gush of breath from lungs, and the groan of a man.

She knew then that those sharp impacts had been the smash of bullets into flesh.

The shooting ended, and the echoes raced off

202

through the timber. The silence moved back. Then Hodge McColl said in a strained voice, "You should have known better than to try to shake down a man like me, Frank. If you had lived you would have talked some day. It was not in you to hold your tongue."

McColl's voice strengthened. "The rig is waiting, Dallas," he said. "You don't want to be late for the dance, do you?"

She said in a choked, wild voice, "Go away!"

"Frank also should have known better than to let you stand him between a lamp and a tent wall," McColl said. "That was his last mistake. I'll come back another day, Dallas."

Then he walked away. Presently she heard the retreat of the rented buggy he had left at a distance when he had seen that shadow on the canvas.

Dallas sank to the floor, still clinging to the tent pole. She was there when Gus Nielson came at a run.

Gus pushed aside the flap, letting the lamplight stream out. A shapeless form lay ten feet from the tent. One arm was extended, a six-shooter grasped in the hand.

"It's Frank!" she moaned. "Hodge McColl killed him!"

Gus bent over Frank's body for a time, then straightened. "Yes," he said. "Frank iss dead."

He stood, gazing down broodingly at Frank. "I vill ride to Yellow House and bring help," he decided.

"To Yellow House? And leave me here . . . alone with a dead man?"

She saw the stony, condemning set of Gus's seamy face. His glance traveled from her hair down over her dress to her slippers. "Yah," he said. "It iss a leetle late to be afraid of death. You should have thought of it bevore you asked McColl to come here ven you knew Frank vould be here too."

Then he added in the same flinty voice, ". . . Or berhaps you did think of it."

Gus brought a quilt from her cot, spread it over Frank's body, and went away without giving her another glance. Presently she heard him ride away.

She stood in the tent door, looking off into the darkness in the direction Gus had gone while a cold and bitter rage tore at her. Then she dropped the flap. What Gus Nielson thought of her hardly mattered.

She pulled off her dress and donned a dark waist and a plain skirt, and changed to cotton stockings and shoes. Pouring water in the basin she scrubbed the color from her cheeks and lips.

She was still sitting in the tent when, after an endless wait, she heard horses coming.

Jay rode out of the darkness. With him was the lean, graying, inscrutable man whom Frank had told her must be Ben Tracy. And Lily Benton accompanied them, riding astride.

Jay dismounted before the tent, lifted the flap, and looked at Dallas' pale face. "Gus came to Yellow House and told us, Dallas," he said quietly.

He turned, lifted a corner of the quilt, and gazed at Frank for a time. "How did it happen?" he asked.

Dallas began to sob. "I don't know. Frank came here

to talk to me. I had been urging him to leave this range, for I was afraid McColl would kill him sooner or later. McColl must have trailed him here, or been watching me in the hope of finding Frank. Frank left the tent to ride away. I heard McColl say, 'Hello, Frank.' Then they both started shooting."

Lily had dismounted. Dallas moved to her and leaned her head against Lily's breast. "It was awful," she choked.

Jay watched the way Lily stood rigid, unyielding, letting Dallas cling to her, but offering no comfort of her own.

Jay bent, loosened the gun from Frank's fingers. He flipped open the gate. "Three empty shells," he said. "One a hammer safety, and the others fresh fired. Frank shot twice."

"That's enough to make it self-defense as far as McColl is concerned," Ben Tracy shrugged. "There were no actual eyewitnesses. Miss Carver says she was in the tent. McColl can claim that Frank drew first. An' maybe he did. There's no way of telling. McColl is the only one who knows."

Gus Nielson arrived on his weary harness horse which had been outdistanced on the return trip from Yellow House. In the old man's attitude Jay saw the same granite indifference toward Dallas that he sensed in Lily.

"We'll take Frank into Spearhead for decent burial in the town plot, if that is all right with you, Dallas," he said. "Will Overmire will have to be notified, and an inquest held."

"Yes," Dallas said faintly.

"You can't stay here," Jay said. "You must go to Yellow House."

"We'll go in your rig, Dallas," Lily said levelly.

There was still that aloofness in Lily as she climbed into the buggy after Jay and Ben had harnessed. Taking the reins, with Dallas sitting slumped beside her, she drove away down the trail into the darkness of the timber, leaving the men to take care of Frank Spain.

Resentment raked Jay. There seemed to be no charity or pity in Lily Benton.

19

The inquest was held the next morning in Spearhead. Will Overmire impaneled a jury to hear the evidence and Hodge McColl and Dallas were the only witnesses. McColl testified that he had happened by to pay a neighborly call on Dallas and that he had encountered Frank, and that Frank had fired first.

Dallas' evidence did not shake that story. The verdict was that McColl had fired in self-defense.

They buried Frank in the afternoon in the Spearhead cemetery. The season's first sultry day brought a thunderstorm as the funeral cortege moved toward the burial place, and the circuit-riding minister stood clad in rubber boots and slicker as he consecrated Frank's body to the muddy earth.

Will Overmire had brought Dallas and Lily Benton

to the funeral in his rig. He shielded them with an umbrella as Dallas stood, a kerchief to her eyes, while Jay, Ben Tracy, Mario and Tom Faye handled the straps that lowered the pine coffin.

Only half a dozen others attended . . . cowboys and townspeople who felt obligated to pay respects to the dead.

But, as the dismal rite ended, and Jay took Dallas' arm to lead her away, he saw Otis Haskell's top-buggy in the background. The storm curtains were up, but he glimpsed Amelia Haskell's dark eyes, tragic and tear-bright, at the small isinglass window. Amelia was alone in the buggy.

Then Amelia drove away.

Jay handed Dallas and Lily into Overmire's buck-board, got his own saddle horse and followed them into town. They pulled up before Ma Monday's eating house. "Coffee will warm us all," Jay said.

As the two girls alighted from the buckboard and stood shaking out their skirts, a rider on a weary, mud-streaked horse came into the head of the street off the Castle Bend trail.

It was Pooley Moon, soggy with saddle weariness. Pooley spotted them, and swerved his horse, pulling up before them. He drew a wrinkled scrap of paper from a pocket.

"Lily!" Pooley croaked. "It's come! The telegram from Amos Dean. The Cheyenne country is open. Injun Bureau issued the proclamation yesterday."

Lily read the telegram, passed it along to Jay. Her hands dropped limply to her sides. "We're in a hopeless position," she said wearily. "This rain will only increase the run-off. We can't cross the Ox Bow with cattle for weeks."

"Hodge McColl had a rider waitin' at Castle Bend too, an' he got a message also," Pooley said. "I reckon it brought the same word thet Amos Dean sent to us."

Ben Tracy had arrived from the cemetery now, along with Mario and Tom. They were watching Jay. "Shove back to the ranch," Jay said to them. "Start dragging the benches north of Blue Coulee. No use bothering with anything south of Blue. Too far away. We ought to pick up a thousand head or more north of Blue without much trouble. Steers is what we want. Big stuff, and strong, that can stand a fast drive. Pick up every man. Bring in the drift riders south of Blue."

"You still think you can cross the river?" Lily asked dubiously.

"No telling," Jay said. "But we can try. First, we've got to get a herd shaped up. We'll worry about getting it across later."

"A man can lose every head of stock, tryin' to drive Ox Bow in the high country at this time o' year," Pooley warned. "You ever seen the river when she's on the boom?"

"I've seen it," Jay said. "I know what we're up against. I've been studying this over for some time, figuring on what to do in case we get caught as we're caught now. I've got a half-baked idea in mind that we might try if there's no other way. First, I'll head up the river for a look-see. There might still be a chance somewhere to ford strong cattle."

He mounted his horse. "You get a long sleep, Pooley, before you do any more riding," he said. "You'll need it. After that I want you to keep an eye on Chain. McColl will be driving for the river down in the flat country as fast as he can shape up his herd. Let me know when, and if, he crosses."

He looked at Dallas. "Don't rake through memories that can't be changed, Dallas," he said.

She said gravely, "I know. And thank you."

Jay's glance veered briefly to Lily, who stood beside Dallas, but aloof from her. Again he felt the puzzled stir of resentment.

"I'll be back no later than tomorrow night," he said. "By that time I'll know one way or another."

He rode out of town. He headed first to the river bridge, and rode out on the wooden plankway. The structure spanned the Ox Bow at a point where it narrowed and deepened between high clay banks.

The river was beginning to lose its wildness here. Even so it was an ugly proposition. Driftwood was coming down from the mountains, and the stream was picking up the mud from the first run of the flats. Eddies and boils of foam roiled its surface.

No herd could cross without heavy loss and Jay guessed that McColl would have his troubles even miles farther east where the river spread out still more and slowed and shallowed. But westward . . . in the high country . . .

Jay rode upstream, hoping he might find some point where a crossing would be possible. But it was wasted time. A mile west of town he came to a rapids where the river made its last jump from the mountains. The situation was the same or worse in the rougher country upstream.

He finally gave it up and left the river. He reached his own place on Slide Creek long after nightfall. He slept there, and at daybreak was in the saddle again.

He headed for the high country. Two hours of steady climbing brought him to Middle Park, a high meadow near timber line. Snowbanks still held out here in the lee of boulders and in the deep thickets, and directly before him soared the bulk of Big Drum Mountain, whose massive flanks were still winterbound.

The day was turning hot and clear again, and he heard a distant deep murmur from the mountains. A slide. The big snowfields on Big Drum were beginning to loosen.

Ox Bow River was born in this snow country. Its channel cut across this high peak. It emerged from a gorge a mile above, dropped in a series of rapids, coursing here for half a mile in a wide, rocky bed before beginning its next plunge downward.

In late summer, the river, in its passage through Middle Park, was a beautiful trout stream, fed by beaver-dammed tributaries. Now it was a savage force, milk white and fifty yards wide, sweeping with the speed a horse could gallop. Here and there it fought boulders, piling up in foam and spray, recoiling into eddies that would carry a steer or rider to his death, then driving ahead with the increasing weight of the run-off pushing it relentlessly.

Jay studied the river, then set his horse up the mountain again. A mile carried them into deep snow and Jay finally left the horse and climbed on foot.

The crust supported him, and he worked his way higher until he was above the gorge. He reached the crest of a small reef of exposed rock, and before him lay a massive mountainside, blanketed in snow.

This snowfield pitched a thousand feet downward into the notch of a canyon, and in the depths was the river, black and swift against its white background. To his right and below his position the river entered the gorge between buttresses of granite that rose a sheer five hundred feet above the stream.

He moved from the security of the rock reef out onto this snowfield, and watched a small slide slice from the lower fringe on the opposite canyon flank and dissolve into the river. It left a new, raw expanse of exposed mountainside above the margin of the stream.

The surface on which he stood seemed suddenly insecure and rubbery beneath him. He broke into a wild run back to the safety of the rock outcrop.

Once he had reached the reef he pulled up, grinning thinly at the way he had stampeded. But he still heard the quick thud of his heart. He would have to go back out on that poised, ponderous snowfield again—and soon.

He descended to his horse and mounted. Crossing Middle Park he angled southeasterly down the mountain. He crossed the head of Slide Creek, and by noon he was not far above Frank Spain's place on Latigo. Wood smoke spiraled above the timber in the direction of the flat, and he turned, following the creek downwards, even though it was off his direct route to Yellow House.

When he rode into the flat Dallas was cooking a meal in the tent, and had the flaps and walls furled for ventilation, for the midday heat was that of full summer.

She came from the tent to meet him, walking with her straight, poised grace.

"You should not have come back here alone so soon," Jay said chidingly.

"I didn't want to impose on Miss Benton. She has been kind, but she is also a busy person."

Jay said slowly, "I see." He looked around. "Where is Gus Nielson?"

"He has quit," Dallas said resignedly. "I'll have to find another carpenter."

"Dallas, do you really intend to go ahead with this now that Frank is gone?" Jay asked, looking at the partially built house.

"Yes."

"But how about title to this place? You may be building on a homestead that . . ."

"Frank had mortgaged everything," she said. "When I found that out I bought the mortgage from Otis Haskell. I had some money of my own. Eventually I'll own the place by foreclosure after the estate is settled. Mr. Haskell is taking care of the legal arrangements."

"Don't start anything you can't handle," Jay admonished. "What do you know about cattle?"

"Well, they've got four legs and big, sad eyes. But I intend to go deeper into the subject. I imagine I'll learn by trial and error. That's the way it's usually done, I believe."

"Mostly by error. Mixed with sweet and peppered with cussing.

He took one of her hands, stood looking at it, seeing its slender perfection and its strength. "I can't say I want to talk you out of this," he admitted.

"It's comforting to know I have at least one friend in this range," she said. "There are others who are not as helpful."

"You mean Lily Benton?"

Dallas shrugged. "I'm afraid she resents my being here. I presume she wanted Frank's place to add to Pitchfork range.

She was silent a moment. "Lily Benton is a strange person, Jay. There is a ruthless side to her nature. I have a belief that she knows something about you that she should not know. It's only my intuition, but I can't help but fear that she means great harm to you. I've . . . well, I've watched the way she looks at you. I can't exactly describe it, but it is as though you were some object valuable to her only as long as she needs you . . . but no longer than that."

"And how do you look at me?" Jay asked abruptly.

She let her hand lie in his. "Not the way Lily Benton does," she said.

Jay touched her hair with his other hand. "It's as soft as I thought it would be," he said. "And cool."

Then he released her hand. "Frank lost more than his life, Dallas," he said. "He lost you. But you must not let his death destroy your own happiness."

"I had known for some time before that . . . that night that I could never marry Frank," she said. "I realized that I did not really love him."

Then she turned. "Our talk is too sober. This time you can't refuse to dine with me. I am tired of eating alone."

They ate in the tent, and Dallas was almost gay. When Jay rose to leave she walked with him to his horse, and said, "I'm happy that I told you how I really felt about Frank. I had not admitted it even to myself until that moment. But I had known it in my heart, and I realized that you should know also."

Then she moved against him, kissed him on the lips. She stepped back and said, breathlessly, "Don't let Lily Benton destroy you, Jay. She is an ambitious woman. Whatever power she holds over you she will always use for her own purposes."

"Lily told me I was staying in this range because of you," Jay said. "Maybe she was right."

He mounted then and rode away, carrying with him a strange sense of futility. He had momentarily grasped a sunbeam, held it in his hand, and its warmth was still with him in the memory of the pressure of Dallas' lips on his. And then it had escaped from his grasp with the mention of Lily Benton's name.

Dallas stood there a long time after Jay had gone from sight, triumph in her eyes. She had always sensed a puzzling constraint between Jay and Lily Benton, an armed watchfulness that colored every word they spoke, every look they gave each other. Frank Spain's betrayal of the secret of Jay's past had given her the possible key to the answer.

Now she was certain. She had made those accusations against Lily with a double purpose, and had watched Jay's reaction closely. The fact that he had not pursued the subject further had clinched it. Lily Benton knew that Jay Webb and Jess Steele were one and the same, and she was using that knowledge to force him to act as gun boss at Pitchfork.

Pleased with her own acumen, Dallas turned to walk back to the tent. Then the little half-smile faded from her lips, and she halted, staring at the man who stood there.

It was Hodge McColl. He must have come out of the timber beyond the tent. He looked in the direction Jay had gone, and said, "You're not even a promised grass widow yet, Dallas. Grass can't grow on Frank's grave in a day. And already you're having your way with another man."

A three-day stubble of wiry beard blackened McColl's wide jaws. He wore bullhide chaps, caked with dried mud and dust, a flannel shirt, and a hat ripped and shapeless from much saddlework in the brush.

He carried a rifle slung in his arm. He had been riding steadily for days with his crew, and the work had hardened him, grooved the lines deeper around his small eyes.

"Jay Webb is beginning to get in my way too much," he said.

Dallas looked at the rifle. "You fool!" she exclaimed frenziedly. "Don't even think of such a thing."

215

Hodge's smile widened. "I can see your viewpoint. Another shooting here at your tent would be very embarrassing."

"Why did you come here?"

"Your attitude seems to have changed," McColl said dryly. "We had a date to go to a dance, remember? I don't understand you, my dear."

"You murderer!"

"Executioner is the proper word," McColl said, his stony grin unchanged. "At least I took my chances, fair and square. In fact Frank almost got me. One of his bullets missed me by an eyelash. He was faster than I expected."

He added, his grin suddenly gone. "But you didn't take any chance at all. You set Frank up for me, kept him in the tent where I would see his shadow the minute I drove in sight. You knew what would happen. You brought me here that night for one purpose."

Dallas was gray-faced. "How dare you say that!"

"And before that you had arranged to grab possession of Frank's place," McColl went on. "And you wanted him out of the way so that you would have a clear path. I asked Otis Haskell about that mortgage, and he told me you had bought it. Three thousand dollars. That's quite a pokeful for a schoolmarm who came into the frontier to marry a man she didn't give a damn about."

"I won't listen to . . ."

"Then I guessed where you had raised the money, Dallas. I think Otis Haskell knows it too. I called on

Amelia. She tried to shoot me, but I took the gun away from her. She's pretty much broken up about Frank's death. Women are strange critters. I never thought Amelia was serious about Frank, or about me either, for that matter. Anyway, she's in a bad mental state. She called you a murderer, among other things. She mentioned the three thousand dollars you had black-mailed her out of in her own home. I'd steer clear of her if I were you. She might take a shot at you. She seems to blame you for Frank's death more than she blames me."

"Amelia lies," Dallas almost screamed.

McColl stood his rifle against the tent. He seized her in his arms, kissed her roughly. Dallas wrested a hand free and raked sharp fingernails down his face, laying a grid of red gouges down his unshaven cheek.

He caught her arm, imprisoning it again. And again he kissed her.

"If you're planning on throwing in with Jay Webb against me, forget it," he said. "He might believe you're pure and innocent, but I know different. You and me look at things eye to eye. And don't ever try to put me in a deadfall like you put Frank Spain."

Their eyes clashed. Dallas was the first to waver. Slowly she let the opposition slack out of her body.

McColl picked her up in his arms, carried her to the tent. "From now on," he said, "you belong to me."

20

Ben Tracy had thrown every Pitchfork and pool rider into the middle range north of Blue Coulee by the time Jay arrived on the scene.

The crew was working in the brush and timber, picking up big steers and barren cows, and shoving them into a holdout herd that was forming in a clearing.

Lem Riddle, the cook, had brought up the chuck wagon and Yancey Tolliver had supplied a remuda of a hundred horses.

Lily Benton was working with the men. Jay didn't recognize her at first glance as she came out of the timber, rope-ending lumbering steers. She was riding circle, along with Mario Rodriguez and Tom Faye.

She had abandoned her divided skirt in favor of breeches and a heavy brush jacket and a man's hat. Chousing cattle in the brushy slants was rough, dangerous work. One sleeve of her jacket was ripped to the elbow, and she had used safety pins to repair damage to her breeches. Her face bore brush marks.

She sighted Jay, and came riding up at a lope. "Did you . . . ?" she began anxiously.

"Circle riding is no job for a woman!" Jay snapped. "Do you want to break your neck?"

Mario had ridden up also. "I have implored, I have pleaded," he said wearily. "But she is the stubborn one. We will have to take severe measures, I fear. I advise tying her up bodily. That is the way to treat refractory females who . . ."

"It's my neck, and also my cattle," Lily said. "I don't intend to stay at the ranch tatting doilies, or whatever they do to doilies. But did you go to the river, Jay? How is it there?"

"Roaring, and hell for leather," Jay said.

"But . . ."

"There's one chance. We might be able to cork it above the gorge and drop the level at Middle Park long enough to run the herd across. Is there any dynamite at the ranch, Lily?"

"Dynamite? I hardly think so."

Jay turned to Mario. "Get Yancey Tolliver and head for town," he said. "Mort Skelly sells dynamite. I'll take black powder, if necessary, but prefer the stick stuff. A case will be enough. A hundred and fifty feet of fuse and caps. Write an order, Lily, authorizing them to charge it to Pitchfork. Mort knows Yancey and will honor it."

He answered the question in their eyes. "I'm going to try to blast an avalanche down into the river above the gorge, hoping we can block the stream long enough to cross the herd below."

Ben Tracy had come up now to listen. "I always said there's two ways of skinnin' a bear," he commented, "but we always seem to pick the hard one. Assumin' you do manage to plug the river, she won't stay plugged long. What if she breaks down your dam while we've got the herd in midstream below the gorge?"

"That's the chance we'll have to take," Jay said. "It'll be up to Lily whether we take it. They're her cattle."

"We'll decide that after we see whether we can plug the river," she said.

They began drifting the holdout herd northward and higher up the benches, and its strength was steadily augmented as the circle crews continued to throw additional cattle into line.

At noon the second day Jay halted the circle riders. The herd numbered more than 1,000 head on snap tally now. The entire crew, which included the four small brand owners in the pool, began pushing the cattle at a steady pace. The distance to the river was twenty miles, but the route they followed across the face of the mountain was rough and timbered, and progress was slow.

Mario and Yancey Tolliver overtook the drive late in the afternoon, leading a pack horse carrying the dynamite and tools.

And, after dark, as the crew was camped, with the herd on bedground, Pooley Moon rode into the firelight, slid lumpily from his horse, and massaged his stiffened knee joints.

Pooley brought news of the Chain drive. "They got twelve hundred head o' big steers across the river," he said as he swigged coffee, "but they had a hell of a time. Even down thar where she flattens out the Ox Bow ain't no millstream. Took McColl an' his outfit two days. Had to swim 'em in small bunches. They must have lost thirty, forty head. Lost one rider too.

Drowned. I laid up in the brush, watchin' them work."

"Where did they make the crossing?" Jay asked.

"Way down. Just above where Pipestone Crick comes in."

"They've got a tired herd on their hands, and more than a hundred miles of driving through rough country before they can get up on the best graze in the reservation," Jay estimated. "If we can cross at all it will be the day after tomorrow. That ought to put us on the reserve well ahead of them."

They prodded the herd off bedground at daybreak, and drifted them steadily, but without undue haste. Jay did not want a sullen herd to contend with when it came time to try the crossing.

The bulk of the drive was composed of Pitchfork cattle, but Lily had given orders that every brand in the pool must be represented. Mike Cavanaugh, Andy Cummings, Trent Craig and Doug McDonald, each had nearly two score of their steers in the herd.

For, small though their numbers were, priority of cattle in the new graze would be a valuable asset. A brand already located would be certain to emerge from any adjustment later with advantage.

Jay had taken this factor into account while he was riding circle to help finish off the herd. Some of Frank Spain's Rafter S cattle had shown up in the brush while the area near Latigo Creek was being worked. Other riders had thrown them back, but Jay had made a point of bringing them in, and turning them in with the drive. There were nearly a score of Rafter S steers in the herd.

He knew Lily was aware of what he had done. She had seen him bring in Rafter S stock, and turn them into the drive. She had looked at him, her face strangely blank. Then she had ridden away without comment.

Later he discovered that some of his own Rocking J cattle were also in the line. He had scrupulously been turning back any of his own stock that he came upon, but, apparently, Ben and Mario and Tom were doing him this favor.

He appreciated their loyalty, but there was an unyielding pride in him that rebelled at being placed in the position of accepting a favor from Lily Benton.

He rode to where Ben was on swing with the herd. "We seem to have picked up some stray Rocking J's," he said.

"Yeah. 'Bout thirty head, I'd say."

"Pass the word to cut them back into the brush whenever they show up within reach."

"Lily Benton gave different orders," Ben said. "She said to make sure them J's stay with the drive. Fact is she brought quite a few of 'em in herself."

Ben let the trace of a smile crease his face. "She seems to want to give you a fair shake, Jess," he added.

"Or maybe she wants to keep me tied to her chariot," Jay said. "Offering a watchdog a picked bone, so he'll hang around and keep the wolves away from the banquet table."

"She told me an' Tom an' Mario that we could draw our ridin' pay in cattle instead of money if we wanted," Ben said. "Said we could take delivery after we crossed the river, if we preferred, an' that the steers would be vented into whatever brand we chose."

"So she's tying all of us to the chariot," Jay said.

"Even a picked bone on that Cheyenne reserve is goin' to have a lot of fat on it in years to come, from what they tell me," Ben observed mildly. "It's a mighty big country, and room for plenty of brands if they work together."

Jay tried to glare Ben down. It wouldn't work. He began to grin wryly. "You know it just isn't human nature to throw away a chance like this," he admitted. "I could refuse, but you know I won't."

He added, "Tied to the chariot by a golden rope. That's tougher to break than the other one. Lily Benton is like a spider wrapping up a man thread by thread in her web. She's making us partners in this deal. We'll never get out from under her thumb."

"There's a spider in this range," Ben said, "but it ain't Lily Benton. An' you know what happens when a spider gets hungry."

"Maybe I'm the one that's getting hungry," Jay said. "There comes a time when a man decides not to run from trouble any longer."

"Yeah," Ben said gravely. "I knew you had made up your mind about that some time ago. But I wasn't thinkin' of Hodge McColl when I referred to spiders. McColl is more of a hog than he is a spider."

Then Ben rode away, and Jay sat staring after him, a cold and shocked anger working through him.

They bedded the herd at sundown in Middle Park,

two miles from the river.

Before daybreak the next morning Jay pulled out, leading the pack horse that carried the dynamite and tools. He was accompanied by Tom Faye, who was wiry and fast on his feet, and also had experience with explosives.

Later, the day would turn hot, but at this altitude frost now whitened the grass, and new shell ice crackled in the shallows of the small streams they crossed. A razor-thin cold worked through their saddle coats.

By the time they had reached the snow line and tied up the horses the sky was pink overhead, golden rose in the east. Packing a posthole digger, shovels, and the dynamite and fuse and capbox, they climbed on foot, supported by the newly frozen crust. Their breathing painted long streamers of vapor in the brittle, thin air.

They reached the low rock reef overlooking the big snowfield as the sun cleared the horizon. The river was a blue-black ribbon in the depths, and they could hear its lonely droning; a bleak drift of air struck at them.

They moved out on the slant, Jay shoveling and punching holes through the snow to rockbottom, while Tom followed, laying the dynamite. They worked against time, racing the rising sun which soon would be softening the surface.

Occasionally they would pause, feeling their stomachs constrict sickly. For now and then a deep tremor communicated itself to them from the vast, tenuous surface on which they stood.

Then they would grin at each other from stiff lips, and begin working faster.

"If a man sneezed a little too hard this whole mountainside might let go," Tom commented.

The sun cleared the rim of the plains, striking rainbow tints from the white peaks above them. Sounds carried far in this morning stillness, and from below drifted the far, occasional bawl of cattle, and the "hiyah" of riders.

That would be the crew shoving the herd off bedground in Middle Park down the mountain. Meanwhile, Pooley Moon, under Jay's instructions, would be riding to Spearhead to warn town folk to stay clear of the bridge during the day. Elsewhere there was little chance that anyone would be in the vicinity of the river.

Looking up from his task Jay discovered Lily standing on the rock roof that marked the safety line, watching them anxiously. She was still laboring for breath after her climb. The sun was delivering its warmth now, and she had hung her hat on her back from the loosened chin-string, and had unfrogged her canvas brush jacket. Her hair was a rich, coppery hue in this light. Even in the rough saddle garb she was entirely feminine, a full and ripe young woman.

Jay helped Tom tamp the last charge in place. They had mined the snowfield on a line about a thousand feet out from the rock reef. The fuses were cut to varying lengths so that the touch-off would go simultaneously.

They retraced their steps to safety at a fast pace,

beset by the sinking emptiness in their stomachs as the snowfield shuddered again beneath them.

Lily handed them a canteen, wrapped in a towel, which held hot coffee spiked with brandy. They drank gratefully, the tension easing out of them as the warmth touched their blood.

Lily gazed downward at the river, and at the notch where the torrent swept into the gorge. "Will it work?"

"It's a fifty-fifty chance," Jay said. "We'll wait until nearly noon. The snow will soften by that time, but the melt doesn't really start until afternoon, and the volume of the river won't be much greater than it is now. Snow alone won't do the job. We've got to get rock and timber. There's a reef of boulders down there where you see that hump in the snow. Just below that is a stand of spruce and some quakies. If the slide is big enough it should pick up enough heavy stuff to add consistency when the avalanche piles up in the river. But nothing will plug the stream for long. I'm hoping for thirty minutes, but it might be less."

They descended to the herd, which was on graze in loose formation. Jay and Ben rode to the river and picked a spot where there were no cutbanks, and with the approach fairly free of timber. The crew now crowded the herd into a solid mass, and walked it to the approach, halting it there.

The animals were objecting to the handling, and beginning to wring their tails. "Keep 'em in the notion of stampeding, but don't let it happen until we want 'em to run," Jay said. "And when they jump, make sure they head for the river."

Jay rode up the mountain again to touch off the dynamite. Lily followed him.

"Stay with the cattle," Jay commanded.

"No. Someone should be there to help you, if anything goes wrong . . . if there's any possibility of helping you."

She added slowly, "This is another payment on that ten thousand dollars."

"This one," Jay said levelly, "is on me. I've got a stake in this game myself now. And so have Ben and the others."

Panting, they reached the rock reef. Jay waited to catch his breath. Then he said, "All right," and moved out on the snowfield.

He had a dreadful sensation of height and insecurity on this slanting white mass. The snowfield seemed to tremble beneath him. The sun had softened the crust, and he broke through occasionally.

He worked his way to the fuse farthest from safety. He had brought a chimneyless oil lamp from the chuck wagon, and now he touched a match to the wick, adjusted it until it burned steadily. Using this as a torch he ignited the first fuse.

He floundered to the next explosive and repeated the operation. Trying to hurry in this softening surface brought the nightmare sensation of maddening sluggishness.

Five fuses sputtering. He was sweating now—a cold, nauseous sweat, and the fear was lumping in his stomach. It seemed to him that the first fuses would surely go before he could reach the end of the line.

He heard Lily's frantic call, "Quit it! Quit it!"

But Tom Faye had told him he would have time. He stayed with the task, crouching over each fuse. The wind was rising now, tearing at the flame on the wick, forcing him to huddle with cupped hands for agonizing moments until the fuse sputtered, moments that he felt were ticking his life away. Then he would race to the next set.

He touched off the ninth fuse and fought his way to the last one fifty yards from the ledge. It sputtered into life, and he raced toward the safety of the rock wall.

Then the surface gave way when he was still rods from the ledge, and he went through to his armpits. It was like quicksand. He saw Lily's ashen face staring at him. The veins stood out in his face as he floundered.

He escaped that trap, made a few yards and broke through again. He saw Lily descend from the rock outcrop to help him, but then she broke through also and was floundering to her waist in the soft snow.

Jay, with his last strength, rolled over and over. He reached her just as a solid concussion shook the mountain. The snow field heaved and recoiled beneath them. It was slipping!

Jay clamped an arm around Lily and rolled desperately the remaining yards to the rock ledge. He picked her up bodily and jammed her into a crevice beneath an overhanging rock slab, then fell into the shelter on top of her, shielding her with his body. For up-flung frozen snow and small rocks were beginning to rain down around them. Pebbles pounded Jay's exposed back, and a sizeable rock ricocheted from the slab, grazing his shoulder.

Tom Faye had judged his fuses well, for the succession of explosions had been spaced over a matter of seconds.

Silence came for the space of a dozen heartbeats. Lily's pale face was twisted around toward him, and their eyes looked into each other's as they lay with Jay's arm still clamped around her. He saw in her gaze a wild gladness that he was still alive.

Then a new sound took form. It started as a sigh, grew with incredible speed to a deep thunder. Jay arose, and pulled Lily to her feet. They peered.

The snowfield was moving. Great fissures were opening across its face. Then the entire surface broke into chaotic motion.

The avalanche gained speed. Jay saw the rocky ridge vanish down the mountain; the timber below was wiped out. Then the slide was past, and the rocky outcrop and the timber were gone.

The gigantic mass cascaded into the river. The first impact sent a solid wave racing up the opposite canyon wall. The avalanche itself climbed a hundred feet up that flank. The river was buried, the scene fogged by drifting foam and snow spume.

The jar of the slide loosened a second and sizeable avalanche on the opposite canyon flank, and its thunderous descent came as a full and deep echo.

Lily clung frenziedly to Jay's arm. They watched tensely for minutes until the haze cleared above the mass that blocked the river.

Jay said hoarsely, "That might have done it."

For more than a thousand feet above the gorge the river was choked by the avalanche.

They raced to their horses and rode headlong to the park. Ben and the crew already had the herd in motion. Riders were whooping and swinging rope ends, stirring the cattle into a run. Yancey Tolliver and two others led the way with the remuda.

"You corked it!" Ben yelled at Jay. "River's dropping fast. Push 'em boys. Make 'em run."

Jay joined the drag riders. The herd broke into a full run. But it was a controlled stampede. Point and swing men kept the cattle headed unyieldingly toward the river.

Jay rose in the stirrups, peering. Now he could see the river. Its volume had dropped amazingly. It was fordable—momentarily at least.

21

The remuda hit the crossing, and the point of the herd followed at a dead run, with riders refusing to let them veer. Spray flew as the cattle, following the horses, floundered over wet, newly exposed boulders. There was some swimming water, but for the main part the cattle found footing.

The swing followed the leaders into the river without breaking pace. Men were listening now as they worked with the cattle, darting gray-faced glances upstream, where a juggernaut was poised above them.

The horses lurched ashore and Jay saw that Lily had accompanied them, and was safely clear. The cattle followed in a close packed, wet brown blanket.

The main body of the herd was across and mounting the rocky bank and scattering into the timber and brush when Mario Rodriguez, who had reached the north bank, raised a yell.

"Mira! Mira! Andale! Andale!"

Jay and Calico Bill Suggs were still in the river, quirting the drag cattle. The bellowing of the animals and their splashing drowned out all other sounds, but Jay saw Lily waving frantically and pointing upstream, and shouting.

Some forty or fifty cattle were still in the river, and were scattered downstream.

"Get clear, Calico!" Jay shouted.

Now he heard it also. A heart-freezing rumble that was like the roar of the avalanche he had created, and of which this was the harvest. The river was free again!

Calico, nearer shore, spurred his horse frantically to safety. Jay followed. Then his horse stumbled, went to its knees in the water. Jay heard Lily scream despairingly.

He looked upstream and saw a monstrous thing tearing through the brush. It was a wall of water, twenty feet high, the color of dirty slate, and it bore uprooted trees on its face.

Jay's horse recovered and buck-jumped the boulders toward shore, its ears pinned back in terror. But they had drifted downstream so that the bank at this point

231

rose abruptly in a thirty-foot rocky cutbank.

Lay was quirting her horse toward that point. Then Ben Tracy raced in ahead of her, his throw rope ready. The oncoming wall of water seemed to tower over Jay as Ben made his cast. The throw was true, and Jay caught the small loop.

Ben's horse pivoted and Jay was jerked from the saddle, and up the rocky bank. He felt the chill air blast driven ahead of the racing flood, and then he was blinded by spray. A savage force snatched at his body from the waist down. But he clung to the rope with the desperation of death, and then he rolled over the rim of the high cutbank and was clear. But his horse was gone.

He got shakily to his feet, dripping, his hands rope-burned. Behind him the river was buried in a seething millrace of spurring water and debris.

"One thing is for sure," Ben Tracy said. "You wasn't born to die by water, fella." Then he wheeled and rode to help the riders with the scattering cattle.

Lily came riding up, her eyes still big with fright. Jay poured water from his boots, and looked at the flood. "It ought to lose its push and spread out before it hits the bridge at Spearhead," he said. "Otherwise you'll have a bridge to pay for. How many head did we lose?"

"Twenty, maybe thirty," she said, her voice high-pitched. "I wasn't exactly counting cattle at that moment. Well, you saved some of them by staying there too long."

"All right," Jay said. "I cut it too thin."

"That's putting it mildly." Again a hot and puzzling fury was pushing color into her throat.

"Another payment on that ten thousand," Jay said.

The anger died. She drew swiftly into herself. "I hoped I had made it clear that I had got my full value out of you before today," she said. "You are no longer under bondage to me. You do not have to fight Pitchfork's battles any longer. You are safe from me."

Jay remembered the warning Dallas Carver had voiced against trusting Lily. "You're telling me you are no longer to be blamed for anything that happens to me," he said. "Is that a sop to your conscience?"

"Wyatt Lomack is on his way to this range with that Double Arrow herd he wintered in Kansas," she said. "The drive passed Ogalalla a week ago. Sid Ferris is with Lomack."

Jay straightened. "How do you know this?"

"I've had the Double Arrow herd watched ever since I learned the reason why Lomack and Ferris were in Spearhead. I hired Homer Ring, a former cattle association detective, and sent him to Dodge to keep tab on Lomack. Yancey Tolliver brought a letter from Homer Ring. It was among the ranch mail that he picked up in town when he bought the dynamite. It had been mailed from Ogalalla a week ago."

"Yancey came to the wagon the night before last with that letter," Jay said.

"Yes, but . . ." Then she understood his meaning, and she stiffened and sat waiting.

"You delayed telling me my time was growing short until I got your cattle across the river," Jay said.

233

"Money does mean something to you."

"At least I've warned you now, before it is too late," she said, a dreary futility in her voice. "They'll kill you. Ferris will kill you, or Lomack will see that the law hangs you."

"And so, if I leave this range, your purification will be complete," Jay said. "Every time you look at me you are reminded of your sin. You put a man in bondage. Now he is your guilty conscience. So you want to offer him his life in return. The blot on your soul will be charged off."

"Must we always end up this way?" she burst out, sudden tears in her eyes. "Must there always be this bitterness?"

Jay rode to where Yancey Tolliver was holding the remuda, and cut a fresh mount from his string. Lily followed, and watched him shift rig.

"Then you are staying?" she asked wearily.

"I'm staying. I've run from phantoms too long. Phantoms always overtake a man. It's got to end one way or another here, if the cards fall that way. I've come to realize in the past few weeks that there will always be a Lomack or a Sid Ferris to haunt me wherever I go. At—"

"Or a Lily Benton," she said huskily.

"Or a Lily Benton. At first I intended to accept your fighting money only until Ward was able to ride, then pull out, even though it meant giving up my ranch. Now I see things different. Maybe a man never really gets his roots into a country until the blood of a man like Steve Tracy is mixed with the earth."

"More than Steve's blood is holding you here," she said, and now the futility was vast in her tone. "There is a woman too. Dallas Carver."

Jay laced the latigo and looked up at her. "Is that to my discredit?"

"Anything . . . anyone who holds you here now is wrong for you. For it may mean your death. You know that. Your loyalty is your biggest weakness."

Yancey Tolliver came riding up. He brought Jay's saddle which he had recovered from Jay's drowned horse which had lodged in brush downstream.

"I'm sure hopin' I didn't cause no trouble by forgittin' I had that letter in my pocket, Miss Lily," Yancey said as an afterthought.

"Never mind," Lily said wheeling her horse.

"What letter?" Jay snapped.

"One I brung out from a ranch after Sabrina Moon had sorted the mail I picked up in town. Sabrina said it might be important, but danged if I didn't forgit it, what with the excitement of the drive. I recollected it only this mornin'. Miss Lily took a quick look at it after she had got acrost the river, an' before the flood started down. She cussed me out big for forgettin'. Used hide-peelin' language like her Paw used to when he got on the prod. Real cuss words."

Jay turned, stared after Lily. He had been wrong in accusing her of holding back the knowledge that Wyatt Lomack and Sid Ferris were near at hand. And she had scorned to defend herself. "She wins another round," Jay said aloud.

• • •

They drove the herd out of the rough country north of the river the next morning, and the virgin sweep of the Cheyenne reserve opened before them, spreading northward into the distance. Veined by streams and beaver-dammed parks, broken by islands of lodgepole and fir and spruce and quakies, it awaited them, fresh, untrammeled, a grazing paradise.

Ben Tracy gazed at it and sighed. "A long grass country," he said. "And grazed by nothing but buffalo and elk and deer and antelope until now. This is something I never expected to see again in my lifetime."

Jay rode down into it, accompanied by Lily and the small brand owners. They studied the streams and the run of the country until they had the picture clear in their minds. Tepee Creek, the white man's name for the northern fork of Ox Bow River, was the heart of this range, its life artery. Control of the headwaters of Tepee meant control of miles of graze.

At mid-afternoon they began locating cattle, throwing them into the graze along Tepee and pup creeks in small bunches.

Lily Benton was a wealthy girl—if she could hold what had been won. And every man who owned a brand in the herd now found himself facing opportunity. There was more than room enough here for them all.

"You'll not keep all of this," Jay told Lily. "There's graze here for more cattle than all of us will ever need. Other men will come in. Even McColl will find the leavings pretty fat. But you have first claim to the cream of it."

She said listlessly, "You have range rights too, and so does Dallas Carver. Many brands are represented here. And other honest cattlemen are welcome to their fair share of this grass."

"Even McColl?"

"I will always oppose McColl's methods, just as you have. If he tries to crowd us again I'll fight him—just as you will."

"You seem to have me all catalogued," Jay observed.

"Not all of you, I'm afraid," she said.

Jay watched her ride away up country toward the temporary camp that had been established some five miles up the benches. In this moment of triumph Lily Benton seemed caught only in a dark and inexplicable mood of defeat.

Jay swung his horse to follow her, suddenly wanting to tell her he had learned the truth about the letter Yancey had carried, and to offer amends for that and many things.

Then he ruled against it. Each time he had come out puzzled and uncertain of her in such encounters. There was between them no understanding, no common ground of confidence in each other's motives. Apparently it would always be this way with them. Lily Benton's inner thoughts were a closed book to him, and he suspected he was as much of an enigma to her.

He resumed his task, which was that of drifting half a dozen steers toward a grass park where he meant to locate them. He turned back a steer that wanted to quit the bunch, and headed it at a trot past an outcrop of boulders. He had imagined he was entirely alone. But a harsh, jeering voice aroused him from his thoughts.

"Lift your arms, fellow, then look this way."

Jay, startled, debated it a flashing instant, then slowly raised his hands. He looked over his shoulder. Hodge McColl, a rifle in his hands, sat on a horse among the boulders a dozen yards away, covering him. Then McColl, accompanied by two more riders spurred into the open, bore down on him and surrounded him.

McColl had lost his suave oiliness. "We've been wanting a chance to palaver with you alone, Webb," he said, and a throbbing rage was pushing him. "How far did you figure I'd let you go before I stopped you for keeps?"

Accompanying McColl were Pete Gossard, the man Ben Tracy had rouged at the Pipestone line camp, and Sam Leathers.

Jay saw what this meant. He eased around in the saddle to bring his gun in reach, but Gossard, who had flanked him on the right, had already drawn. Gossard brought the barrel of his six-shooter down in a short, chopping blow that numbed Jay's forearm. Then Gossard snatched Jay's gun from his holster and hurled it into the brush.

Sam Leathers dropped the loop of a catch rope over Jay's head and shoulders and jerked him from the saddle. Jay, his arms pinned by the rope, landed on his back with a jar that drove the breath from his lungs.

Leathers roweled his horse to a lope and dragged Jay for a hundred yards through brush and over rocks. Jay's shirt was torn to shreds, and brush and boulders raked his body. Leathers pulled up, then, and jerked him to his feet.

McColl rode in, loosened a foot from a stirrup, and kicked at Jay's face. But McColl's horse was kettling from the spurring, and the toe of the boot rammed into Jay's chest instead.

"I'll make you regret to your dying moment that you thought up that stunt to get Pitchfork cattle in here ahead of me," McColl panted.

McColl's eyes had the glaze of implacable rage. Sam Leathers, remembering his defeat at Jay's hands, was in the same state of mind, and Gossard also had a score to pay. Jay understood now that they meant to beat him to death.

Leathers struck at him with the loaded butt of a quirt. Jay partly avoided the blow, but the quirt hammered on the point of his shoulder.

But, in coming to close quarters, Leathers had slacked the rope, and Jay tore the loop free and threw it clear.

At the same instant, McColl, still mounted, kicked again, his boot driving into Jay's jaw. Jay caught McColl's leg and hauled him bodily from the saddle. McColl's weight came down on him, and the big man, frothing oaths, sledged both fists at Jay's face as he fell.

Jay rammed a punch into McColl's stomach, and brought up his head, catching McColl beneath the chin. McColl's teeth splintered. Then they hit the ground in a tangle.

McColl wrapped arms and legs around him. Leathers and Gossard left the saddles and joined in. Together they pinned Jay down.

McColl gasped, "Now!" He smashed a fist into Jay's unprotected face. And again.

The crash of a rifleshot came, and Jay heard the nearby, harsh impact of a bullet.

Sam Leathers was driven half upright by the force of the slug, and Jay saw his left arm twitching and dangling grotesquely.

"Get away from him!" That was Lily Benton's voice, shrill, frenzied.

She fired another shot. Jay heard the bullet snap above McColl's head. The grating of a fresh shell being levered into a rifle chamber came as an echo.

McColl crouched above Jay, his fist poised while he searched the surroundings with his eyes. Jay, blinded by blood and dust, glimpsed her dimly now. She was among the boulders fifty yards away.

"Stand clear of him, Hodge," she repeated.

For bitter seconds McColl debated. Sam Leathers was doubled over his knees, grasping his bullet-broken arm and rocking in agony and moaning.

McColl weighed his chances. He finally arose reluctantly and stepped back from Jay. Gossard also released his grip on Jay and edged clear. "She's loco enough to do it," Gossard muttered.

McColl spat broken teeth from his bloody mouth. He mumbled at Jay, "You're lucky."

Then McColl raised his voice. "What do we do now?"

"Get your horses and ride," Lily said.

Jay got to his feet, swept an arm across his face to clear his vision. "Not yet, Hodge," he said. Without turning his head he spoke to Lily. "Keep Gossard off me, Lily."

"Don't . . ." she began, realizing his intention. Then she went silent, knowing that this could not be stopped.

"This time, Hodge," Jay said, "you do your own fighting —and alone."

22

Driven by his unsatiated fury McColl grasped the chance eagerly. He knew he had the advantage in weight. He drove in instantly, clubbing his punches at Jay's stomach. Jay straightened him with a left to the face, but the blow landed on McColl's forehead and Jay felt the grind of jammed knuckles.

McColl sledged heavy fists into Jay's ribs, then wrapped his left arm around Jay's neck and clawed for an eye gouge. That exposed his paunch. Jay drove left and right, felt his fists deep. McColl gave at the middle, and went fish-mouthed. He used his head as a ram, hammering it against Jay's jaw.

Jay smashed him again in the stomach. McColl tried to knee him, but failed. Jay drove the heel of his hand against McColl's chin, and more teeth cracked.

McColl faltered. Jay tore free of his clawing hands, battered him with another right and left.

McColl's knees suddenly folded, and he pitched on his face, twisted over on his back.

Jay moved back and stood bent, propping his hands on his knees for support while he gagged for breath. He looked at Gossard. "You want any part of this?" he asked.

Gossard ran a dry tongue over tobacco-stained lips and said nothing.

McColl finally came out of it, and pulled himself to hands and knees. Sam Leathers, still rocking in agony, said dazedly, "I've got to git to a doctor."

Jay moved to Leathers, tore a sleeve from the man's shirt, twisted a tourniquet in place. "Round up the horses, Gossard," he said. "Take both of them away with you."

He helped Gossard boost Leathers into the saddle. McColl was able to pull himself astride, but he swayed and sagged over the saddlehorn, and his skin was a greenish hue.

"You owe Pitchfork at least three hundred head of year-old stuff, Hodge," Jay said. "We broke up that sleepering job this year, but you got away with it last spring. Pay back, and then stay clear of Pitchfork cattle and Pitchfork graze for the rest of your life. You can turn the three hundred over to Miss Benton at calf roundup. If not we'll take them."

McColl was a beaten man. He turned his horse and rode sickly away with Gossard, who was holding Leathers in the saddle. There was an acknowledgment in his attitude that he would never be back.

Lily was at Jay's side. "I spotted them stalking you after I had climbed higher up," she said. "Thank God I got here in time. They meant to kill you."

She laid aside the rifle and began dabbing at the blood with her neckerchief. She stroked his face with her fingertips in a gesture that was infinitely compassionate.

"Your face! Your poor face!"

Then, moved by that same impulse, she kissed him. Her lips were solacing at first. Then they became warm and full with a woman's promise.

She pulled back, startled, and they looked into each other's eyes questioningly and uneasily as though doubting their own thoughts.

Then Lily said wonderingly, "Now, what started that?"

"You never have had the slightest intention of ever marrying Hodge McColl, have you? Jay said abruptly.

"Never."

She became efficient, businesslike. Bringing a canteen from her saddle, she soaked the neckerchief and cleaned away the blood and dust from Jay's face.

She took Jay's tobacco sack from his shirt pocket, rolled a cigarette, put it in his lips and lighted it. It occurred to Jay that he had not seen her smoke a cigarette since that night at the hay shack.

"Where did you learn to build quirlies?" he asked.

"I used to roll them for Dad," she said. Then she realized what he was driving at. She flushed a little, and looked at him with a faint smile.

So all that sophistication—the smoking and the brandy drinking—had been meaningless.

That thought led onward to the burning of the shack—the pettiness of that blow at McColl. Jay's gaze was remote. He was remembering Dallas' lips on his own and he was thinking of Frank Spain lying dead that night before her tent.

Lily glanced at him queerly as she began working on his injuries again, and the silence held between them.

Presently Mario Rodriguez and Tom Faye arrived, tracing down the rifleshots they had heard at a distance.

"When did the stampede hit you?" Tom exclaimed as they swung down.

Jay grinned from puffed lips. "Hodge McColl was a little put out when he found Pitchfork cattle on this grass ahead of him," he said. "He must have been scouting ahead of his drive, and I bumped into him when he was fizzing."

He rode with them back to camp. He carried a collection of bruises and welts from head to foot. His left shoulder was stiff, his left hand puffed. But no bones were broken. Mario worked him over with liniment and Lily applied court plaster.

They were separated from the chuck wagon, which would have to make the long trip by way of the Spearhead bridge. They made a meal on the jerkie and hardtack that the riders carried in their slicker rolls for emergency.

They siwashed for the night, sleeping on saddle

blankets with their feet to the fire, which the men on night watch kept burning.

Lily slept beneath a slicker, flanked on either hand by Pooley Moon and Ben Tracy. It came to Jay that she seemed to understand Ben fully, and placed the same implicit confidence in him that she gave to Pooley.

She had pointedly treated Jay with her old, cool neutrality since that amazing moment when she had pressed her mouth fiercely against his. He had tried to tell himself that the kiss had been the instinctive reaction of a woman who was only seeking to comfort a hurt thing . . . a gesture born of stress and pity.

But it wouldn't stay that way in his mind. A new, vastly disturbing factor had entered his association with Lily Benton. There had been a sudden surging passion in that kiss for both of them, and the memory of that moment would be with them each time they looked at each other. The question would always be in their minds. Why?

Jay forced his thoughts to swing to Dallas Carver, but he was always vividly aware that Lily Benton lay sleeping across the fire from him.

They turned out in the chill of dawn and breakfasted on the last bait of food. They were roping out their day horses from the remuda when a stranger rode into camp. He was a weathered, blocky man with a drooping, sunburned mustache and pale blue eyes. Lily hurried to meet him, and stood apart with him for minutes, talking to him.

Jay watched her, and saw by her attitude that the

news was bad.

He walked to them. He knew Lily didn't want him there. "I'm Jay Webb, Miss Benton's range boss," he said. "Does your name happen to be Homer Ring?"

He had guessed correctly. Homer Ring glanced at Lily. She nodded. "I told Mr. Webb about you, Homer," she admitted. "And about the Lomack trail herd."

Jay eyed the man questioningly, and he shrugged. "I just told Lily she was in for big trouble," he said. "I hired out as a hand with the Lomack outfit at Ogalalla. Cut my string the night before last without even saying good-bye."

"The night before last!" Jay exclaimed. "You mean they're that close?

"Lomack's drive was bedded north of the Shoshone Buttes when I pulled out."

"That's Pitchfork winter range," Jay said slowly.

Ring nodded. "Lomack is driving for this Cheyenne reserve. He got the word that it is open. He intends to take the shortest route, right across Pitchfork south range to reach the reservation."

Ben and Mario and Tom Faye had now joined them, sensing that trouble was brewing. Jay turned to them. "Lomack hasn't changed his spots," he said. "He intends to operate here the same way the Lomacks operated in Texas. He's putting a big drive of Texas reds into that south range on top of the pool cattle. He probably doesn't know he can't cross Ox Bow. That avalanche stunt won't work a second time. That means he'll hold his cattle on the south range until he

246

can cross. And after he crosses he'll try to browbeat and kill until we get out of his way on this side too. And he will be tougher to stop than McColl. The greed is in the Lomack blood. And he's got Sid Ferris to back his play."

He added, "Call in the men."

"What are you going to do?" Lily demanded.

"Stop Lomack and Ferris."

"How?"

"Stampede them. Pile up their cattle. Run them out of the range before they can get their claws in it."

"That . . . that means fighting . . . gunplay." Her voice was shaky, despairing.

"Yes." Jay looked at the Pitchfork riders and pool men who had been summoned. He explained the situation to them.

"Someone will get hurt," he said. "But it's a matter of pride now. We've whipped McColl. He won't come at us again. Lomack may be tougher. That remains to be seen. The question is, do we let ourselves be shoved out of graze we've fought for and won?"

Mike Cavanaugh, who had a wife and two children at his ranch near Blue Coulee, flipped away a cigarette. "This Lomack ain't ten feet tall, is he?" he said. "How much ground does he cover with his shadow?"

Jay saw that this was the answer for all of them. "One thing," he said. "All of you stay clear of a little, thin, gray man. Always wears a black sack suit and a white shirt and collar. That will be Sid Ferris. I'll do any talking to Ferris that's necessary. And to Wyatt Lomack too."

Afterwards Jay walked to his horse. "I'll meet you at Yellow House tonight," he told them.

He rode away alone, down the range, heading in the direction of Spearhead, where he could cross the river by way of the bridge.

Lily watched him go, a pain deep in her eyes. She knew he was riding to see Dallas Carver before he led Pitchfork against the Double Arrow invasion.

Then, dully, she helped break camp. Mounting, she joined the others as they also rode down the benches over the same route Jay was following a few miles ahead of them.

Mario rode at her side, and was silent for a long time. Finally he reached out, touched her hand and said, "You wear your heart in your eyes, *querido mio*. That is not good. No man is worth such pain."

"He hates me, Mario," she said.

"We all hated you once," Mario smiled. "But now you are one of us. Do you not comprehend that you have given us the chance to become men of honor again? We once fought for the things we believed in, and were beaten. Now you have given us a second opportunity."

Lily could no longer hold back her tears. She leaned from the saddle and kissed Mario on the cheek.

"Your kiss is the sweet kiss of a sister for a brother," Mario sighed. "But there is nothing sisterly in your regard for the one who rides ahead alone to see another girl."

23

Sitting in her tent Dallas finished a third cup of coffee, black and strong. This was her breakfast. She dropped a spoon. In bursting, petulant rage she stamped it flat under foot.

Her temper was growing brittle. Only eight days had passed since she had mailed that letter to Wyatt Lomack. Reason told her it was far too early to expect results. It might be weeks, months. And perhaps never. But the strain of waiting was already wearing her nerves to an edge.

She had hired another carpenter, an ancient, slow, inept man named Emil Voss. He was a putterer, and out of his depth on this job, and she often found herself screaming at him like a fishwife.

He had only one saving grace. He was partially deaf, and age had made him nearsighted. He had set up his own ragged tent back in the timber, and he was totally unaware of the visits that Hodge McColl had been making after dark at Dallas' tent.

McColl had left the previous day to rejoin his drive, which he was moving into the Cheyenne reserve, and he had said he would likely not be back for several days. That was some consolation, at least. His kisses were defiling, but that was a secondary affliction. It was the power he held over her that mattered. He domineered her and stood between her and the goal she had set for herself. She prayed that he would die.

She kicked the ruined spoon into a corner and went out. Emil, working at his bench, said apprehensively, "Good mornin'."

"See to it that you don't ruin any more milled lumber today," she said.

The tension drove her, and she worked Emil like a slave. It was past noon when two riders came up the wagon road, rounding out of the timber into the flat.

One was a well-fed, aggressive-jawed man of about thirty, with a small brown mustache and sideburns. He wore much-used but expensive saddle garb, and rode a Morgan horse.

With him was a little, gray-templed, gray-faced man in a dark suit and dusty white shirt and collar. His garb too was creased and dust-veined by much riding.

Their eyes moved carefully over the scene. They appraised Emil, discounted him, and swung to Dallas, assaying her with a puzzlement, as though she presented a factor they had not expected.

Dallas' breath caught roughly in her throat. She suddenly guessed their identity.

They rode up, and the younger one touched the brim of his hat without removing the cigar he held in his hand. "Howdy ma'am," he said. "Does this happen to be Frank Spain's place?"

"It was," she said, feeling the hammering of her heart. "But Frank Spain is dead."

"Dead?"

"A week ago. I was his fiancée. I own this place now—or will when the legal details are settled. I am Dallas Carver."

They glanced at each other, frowning. Emil Voss had paused in his work, and was blinking, trying to make out the visitors through his steel-rimmed spectacles.

Dallas saw this, and said quickly, "Come in and have coffee. You were friends of Frank, I take it?"

The icy gray eyes of the older one looked right into her. She felt the impact of that inspection. This one, she knew, was Sid Ferris, the gunman who had taken the lives of many human beings. Frank had talked often of Ferris. Here was a man utterly cold, utterly merciless, a precise machine.

Ferris nodded to Wyatt Lomack. They dismounted and followed her into the tent, their boot heels clumping woodenly.

Dallas dropped the flap to shut out Emil's curiosity. "The carpenter is hard of hearing," she said, "but it would be best to keep your voices down. Sometimes he hears what he should miss."

Dallas offered a chair and a trunk, but they remained standing, and so did she.

"How did Frank Spain die?" Wyatt Lomack asked brusquely.

"He was killed in a gunfight with a cattleman named Hodge McColl."

"McColl? Hodge killed him?"

"You seem to know McColl?"

"We know him," Lomack said. "My name is Wyatt Lomack. This is Sid Ferris. We're bringing a stock herd north from our Double Arrow ranch in Texas. We expect to locate in this range."

"In this range?" Dallas was startled.

Lomack smiled thinly. "Yes. Sid and I were up here not long ago, looking over the situation. We talked to Hodge McColl. He's a second cousin of mine. He didn't like the idea of us as neighbors any better than you apparently do. But that's beside the point. A certain letter, signed with Frank Spain's name, was delivered to me at Ogalalla. The letter had been mailed at Castle Bend. It was addressed to our headquarters ranch at Concho, Texas, but the postmaster at Castle Bend knew I would be passing through Ogalalla, and he directed it there by way of General Delivery. I received it a little more than a week ago."

"That explains your quick appearance," Dallas said. "Then you know about that letter?"

"Yes."

Sid Ferris spoke for the first time. His voice had the same chill quality as his eyes. "You wrote that letter, didn't you, Miss Carver?"

"Yes. I wrote it."

"Damned if you weren't right, Sid!" Lomack exclaimed. "You said from the start that it looked like a woman had written that thing."

"Where is Jess Steele?" Ferris asked.

"I believe there is an offer of ten thousand dollars for that information," Dallas said.

They inspected her with a new care, and now they understood fully her strength and her purpose.

Lomack said slowly, cautiously, "All right. That's my offer."

Dallas smiled and said nothing.

"I don't carry money of that amount in my pocket,"

Lomack snapped. "I'll have to get in touch with my bank. But you'll get it."

Dallas eyed him. "You mentioned a trail herd. How far away is this herd?"

"Less than thirty miles, and driving nearer."

Dallas did some calculating in her mind. "I might accept cattle, rather than money," she said. "I believe you said it was a stock herd. That means cows and young stock. I would consider taking, say, four hundred head, provided your cattle are in good condition."

"Four hundred head," Lomack scoffed. "I could have got twenty thousand at Dodge for . . ."

"I'll cut my offer to three hundred and fifty—provided I have the pick of your herd."

Lomack began to swell up angrily, but Sid Ferris said bitingly, "We'll take it, Wyatt. It's the best offer she'll make. She's hard formation."

"All right," Lomack growled grudgingly. "Now, where do we find Jess Steele?"

"I'll meet my end of the bargain when the cattle are in my possession," Dallas said. "I'll get my horse and go with you."

Sid Ferris said, "You must hate Jess Steele. What did he do to you?"

"I understand he is a murderer," Dallas shrugged. "I feel that I am only doing my duty in helping bring him to justice."

She got her harness horse and rigged it with a sidesaddle. They did not offer to assist her nor to help her mount. She held that against them, aware of their scorn for her and the bargain she was driving for a man's life.

She said to Emil, "I may be gone a day or two. I have business to transact in town.

It was mid-afternoon when Jay rode into the flat on Latigo Creek. Emil was planing a window frame.

"Mis' Carver ain't here," Emil informed him. "She pulled out a couple hours ago fer town."

"I just came up the trail from Spearhead," Jay said. "I didn't meet her."

Emil shrugged. "All I know is what she told me when she rode away with two men."

"Two men? Who were they?"

Emil said shortly, "How would I know? Strangers, they were."

Jay hesitated, suddenly shrinking from his next question, fearing its answer. "What did they look like, Emil?" he finally asked slowly.

Emil sniffed and went back to his planing. "Couldn't say. My eyes ain't so sharp any more. All I could make out was thet the smallest one wore a white collar an' a string tie."

Jay stood gazing unseeingly at the old man. He had come here, wanting to see Dallas to reassure himself of something. For he knew that Lily's attitude toward Dallas had its basis in Frank Spain's death. He was remembering the warning Dallas had voiced against Lily. He thought again of the burning of the hay shack.

He finally mounted and headed back to the road to Yellow House. He had not been far ahead of Lily and the crew, and at the fork he saw by the fresh hoof tracks that they had passed by during his side trip, and were now ahead of him on their way to the ranch.

Then he pulled up as Otis Haskell's buggy came in view from the direction of town. Otis halted his rig. Amelia sat beside him in the buggy. This was a changed Amelia. Her dark eyes held a peace and a full maturity and met Jay's without apology or evasion. Her face seemed even thinner than before, but the anxious, pushing need for attention was gone from her, and in its place was a serenity that gave her a beauty that was much finer, and subdued.

Amelia looked now what she was—a married woman who belonged where she was, at her husband's side. Jay saw also a sober pride in Otis, and he guessed that Amelia had made her confession to him, and that now there was between them a complete and lasting understanding.

"Is Miss Carver at Frank's place?" Otis asked.

"No. Only Emil Voss. He says she left for Spearhead a few hours ago."

"We must have missed her on the trail," Otis said. "We will go on to Yellow House for the night, and try to see her tomorrow."

There was a grimness and an unyielding purpose in Otis that Jay did not understand.

He rode ahead of them, sensing they wanted no company, and outdistanced them on the remainder of the journey to Yellow House.

It was sundown when he dismounted at the corral and stripped his horse. The crew and the pool owners had arrived ahead of him, and were scattered around the bunkhouse, and there was little talk or lightness.

Lily was in the cookhouse helping Sabrina Moon get the meal started. Otis and Amelia Haskell pulled in as Jay was caring for his horse, and Lily came to welcome them. Then she ushered them to the main house to quarter them for the night.

Jay now saw Will Overmire sitting on the gallery with Homer Ring, smoking a stogie.

Ben Tracy had come to the corral to join Jay. Ben said, "Lily stopped by the Doc's office as we rode through Spearhead today, and asked him to join the party."

She always turns to Overmire when she needs help, Jay reflected.

Ward was up and around, now, but uncertain on his legs and amazingly pale. He was ragingly resentful of his inability to ride with them. "Just a damned leppie," he told Jay. "Useless as an unweaned calf."

24

All of the men ate in the cookhouse, with Lily and Sabrina serving the table. Then they slept until an hour before dawn. By daybreak they were at the corral, catching up horses.

Jay discovered that Will Overmire was rigging a horse also. The doctor wore a holster gun, and had a rifle in the saddle boot.

"This is hardly the place for a sawbones," Jay said.

"On the contrary I'm afraid a sawbone will be much in demand before this day's work is over," Overmire shrugged. "Do you aim to do your operating with a six-gun?"

Overmire smiled. "If necessary."

Then, as Jay started to turn away, Overmire halted him. "By the way, Steele, if . . ."

Jay pulled up. "Steele?" he challenged softly.

Overmire was unruffled. "If anything should happen to me there is an envelope in my desk in my office in Spearhead which has your name on it. Top left drawer. You can break the lock."

Jay's gaze was flat, hard in the faint light of the corral lantern. "A letter written by Lily Benton, maybe?" he said.

"Not the one you are thinking of," Overmire said, keeping his voice low so that none of the others could hear. "That one was never written."

"Never written?"

"No. That was a bluff. She was afraid of you at that time, and invented that story about the letter. But this other matter is very real. It is not a letter. It is a copy of a formal, sworn deposition that Lily made in regard to an event that occurred in Concho, Texas, some six years ago. It is an eye witness account of what she saw and heard. It is powerful evidence that, because of the time element, there is great doubt that Jess Steele could have fired those two shots through the rear window of the saloon that killed Mason and Vince Lomack that night."

Jay stood waiting.

"The original of that deposition is in the hands of the governor of Texas," Overmire said. "Lily made the sworn statement some time ago. She sent it to Amos Dean, our own senator, and he turned it over to one of the Texas senators, who is insisting on a full investigation of the Lomack murders."

There was a silence. "Don't judge her too harshly, Steele," Overmire said, his voice gentle. "Up to that time she had not been sure. Even now her deposition is far from certain exoneration of you. It is only her word against many. But it would help at a trial."

Jay mounted, rode to where Lily sat on her horse, waiting for the men. He looked at her in the faint light of dawn. "So there never was any letter," he said slowly.

She straightened, and finally murmured, "No."

"And the reason you didn't write it was because you never believed I murdered Mason and Vince Lomack that night in Concho."

She considered that for a time. "There was always a doubt in my mind. I saw you ride off the street around the corner of the saloon, and the shots came in the next instant. It did not seem to me that you could have got to the rear of the place in that second or two."

"You're a little late with your story," Jay said.

"I told Dad what I had seen, and we went to the sheriff that same night," she said steadily. "But I was scoffed at. I was six years younger, then, you must remember. A girl of eighteen. And, after all, I wasn't sure. They convinced me I had miscalculated the time. After all, Jess Steele had a reputation as a gunman.

Dad and I knew nothing about the real situation, for we were strangers in Texas. We were told you were a killer. You had been painted with a black brush, as had all the remaining Fence Cutters."

"But that doubt in your mind didn't prevent you from using the threat of a hangrope to drag me to heel for your own purposes, now that you're older and more experienced," Jay said.

"I used you," she answered unflinchingly. "You were a weapon that was forced into my hand by necessity. But you must remember that, if there was a doubt in my mind, there was also every indication that you were guilty. It wasn't until Steve's death that I was sure."

"Why did Steve's death convince you?"

"It wasn't exactly his death. It was knowing you better. And knowing Ben and the others. They are listed as outlaws also. They're charged with holdups they never committed. Ben told me they had rustled cattle, but never did many of the things they are blamed for, and I believe him."

She paused for a time, then went on. "And . . . and if you were really the kind of a man who would kill like that you would have thrown in with McColl against me in the first place. It wasn't fear of exposure that impelled you to accept the job as my range boss. The real reason was that you knew my cause was just. Fundamentally, it's your nature to oppose men like Hodge McColl and Wyatt Lomack and Sid Ferris."

"You paint me as too high-minded, Lily," Jay said. "I had intended to ride as soon as Ward was able to travel, and never come back."

"You would never have gone through with it," she said positively. "You fought for Pitchfork, risked your life. And Steve lost his life in the fight. You would never have quit. There's a stubborn antagonism in you toward anything dishonest or unjust. And a loyalty to those you believe in."

Her voice suddenly became shaky. "Sometimes that loyalty is misplaced."

"You leave me no ground to stand on, Lily," Jay said. "The fight was mine from the start, as well as yours. You know that. When you forced me into it you did only what I had about made up my mind to do. But I suspected your motives. I misjudged you from the start. I misjudged you the day the hay shack burned."

"I know," she said.

Will Overmire joined them. "And now you both understand each other."

"But we still strike sparks when we meet," Lily said wanly.

Jay pulled a long breath into his throat. The threat of the gallows had eased a little . . . but only a little.

"The name," he said wearily, "is still Webb. Jay Webb. I'm afraid the law in Texas won't see it the way you do, Lily."

He lifted an arm to the others. "All right, men."

They rode away with him into the strengthening daylight. Jay saw that Lily was with them, riding at Overmire's side. He found himself suddenly, fiercely resentful of the tall doctor's presence. And after that there was only an emptiness in his mind.

260

25

At noon they sighted a far, saffron haze of dust.
Presently, from a ridge, they saw the Lomack herd.

It was some three miles away, spread loosely in a
clearing on the timbered bench. The cattle seemed to
be still on graze for the day, and riders were working
the herd on cutting horses.

Jay rode ahead with Ben and Pooley Moon for a
closer look. Reaching cover half a mile from the scene
they watched the operation.

Lomack's men were cutting cows from the main
herd, running them to where branding fires were
burning. There, bulldoggers were throwing the animals, hog-tying them, and heated irons were hissing
on hides. The rebranded cows were being thrown into
a separate holdout beyond the big herd.

Pooley had brought field glasses. Jay took them
now, and brought a freshly worked cow into sharp
focus. A numbing shock drove through him. The vent
across the Double Arrow insignia was plain. Also a
new rib brand. The fresh mark was a Rafter S—Frank
Spain's iron.

Jay swung the glasses to a young woman, riding
sidesaddle. Dallas Carver. A crawling horror grew in
him. Her horse was jaded, and she was dust-pow-
dered, but she wore a posture of forceful triumph that
was above weariness.

With her were Sid Ferris and Wyatt Lomack. His

face bloodless under his tan, Jay watched for a long time.

He at last passed the glasses to Ben. "How many head do you count in that rebrand?" he asked in a monotone.

"Close to three hundred, an' more being cut to it," Ben said reluctantly.

Jay said, his voice thin and faraway, "Ten thousand dollars in gold or cattle! She preferred cattle. Frank Spain must have talked after all—to her."

Wonderingly he realized that his only emotion was revulsion toward Dallas. That and nothing more. There was no sense of loss in his heart. He knew now that this monstrous thing fitted in with Frank Spain's death, and with the minor matter of the burning of the hay shack.

Finally he took the glasses again. He had hoped he could drive the Double Arrow herd from this range without meeting Ferris and Lomack face to face. But this hope was gone, for they knew he was here, and were paying the price of the reward for that information.

He studied the situation. The Lomack herd was thirsty after a day in dry camp, and the cattle were nervous.

Next water would be at Wagon Creek, some six miles north. There the country was rough, broken by washes and cedar brakes.

The branding ended. The bulldoggers were through, and the fires were being kicked into extinction. The herd was shoved into motion, the cattle stringing out in trail formation.

The rebranded cut was being hazed along toward Wagon Creek also, held apart from the main drive by two Arrow riders. Dallas Carver traveled along with these cattle.

Wyatt Lomack and Sid Ferris sat apart on their horses, talking earnestly. Ferris once pointed in the direction in which Yellow House lay, but Lomack kept shaking his head. Ferris seemed to give in reluctantly to Lomack's point of view, and they finally rode to help with the herd.

It was as though Sid Ferris had agreed to put off for a time a matter that he had wanted to settle immediately. Jay, as surely as though he had heard their words, knew that he had been the subject of their discussion.

"They'll reach Wagon about dark," Jay said. "And we'll hit them there. That's a good place to scatter a drive."

As they returned to their horses Jay discovered Lily waiting back in the timber. She had followed them. She carried field glasses also, and that meant she had witnessed this delivery of cattle to Dallas Carver.

She avoided Jay's eyes. She mounted, joined them without a word, and rode silently back to where the others were waiting. She remained in the background, saying nothing, while Jay made his report to the men.

"Don't let yourselves be caught between running cattle and a coulee," Jay concluded. "And if anybody shoots at you, shoot back and shoot straight."

They kept in touch with the Double Arrow drive as

it moved northward toward Wagon Creek. Dallas Carver's cattle were still being trailed apart from the main herd.

"Miss Carver has bought that bunch from Lomack and Ferris for a certain price," Jay told the Pitchfork riders. "Her cattle will have to take their chances along with the Double Arrows when we start 'em running."

The afternoon was turning sultry hot again. White thunderheads formed over the Wardrums and began towering massively in the sky as the day advanced. Sullen black bellies were showing in those clouds.

The gathering storm moved out from the mountains before sundown, bringing a gray and threatening twilight. Heat lightning flickered over the plains to the east where darkness was already setting in.

They pulled up in the gloom of brush half a mile from Wagon Creek and waited. Presently the point of the Lomack drive came in sight. The thirsty cattle, with the scent of the creek in their nostrils, were moving at a half-trot, their white eyeballs showing. The animals were tuned to the electric threat of the coming storm.

The point rolled past, and the swing riders came in sight. Jay made out Sid Ferris. Farther back on this same flank Wyatt Lomack rode into view.

Lightning darted across the black sky, marking in sharp relief the frightening boil of clouds overhead. Jay said, "Here it comes. Ride into them along with the thunderclap."

They drove spurs to their horses, bursting from

cover in a skirmish line, yelling and waving slickers.

The thunder exploded at the same instant, its deep concussion reaching to a man's marrow.

The echo of the thunder was picked up by a nearer, sustained roar of hooves as the Double Arrow herd wheeled away from the attack on its flank, and broke into full stampede.

Lightning blazed now, flash upon flash, and the thunder rolled in waves of violence. The rain came, along with a blast of icy wind and a rush of hail that was in chill contrast to the former oppressive heat.

Brush and cutbanks and coulees lay athwart the path of the stampede. Jay glimpsed Dallas, quirting her horse and riding to safety out of the way of the oncoming cattle.

Her rebranded cut was running also. Jay saw a wing of the massed cattle shearing off over the lip of a coulee to his left, taking the biggest part of Dallas' cattle with them to destruction.

To his right more cattle were piling up beneath the cut banks of a brush-masked tributary stream. The lightning revealed a solid mass of cattle wedged in this deadfall, with others using their bodies as a bridge.

The remainder of the herd was scattering into the brush and timber and still running. The rain, mixed with bursts of hail, reached a blinding peak, then tapered off as swiftly as it had started. The sky began to lighten as the storm rolled eastward.

A few shots had been fired by Double Arrow riders in the first minute or two, but that had ended quickly, for it had become impossible to distinguish friend from foe in the confusion.

There was no point in pressing the attack, for the stampede was complete and devastating. Jay turned to pull clear. Well to his left he saw Ben and Trent Craig and Mario also wheeling to withdraw from the brush. And beyond them he sighted Lily.

Then, to his right, he glimpsed another rider bigger, bulkier. Wyatt Lomack!

Jay swung his horse instantly, turning toward this man. He heard Lily call desperately, helplessly, "No!"

He did not answer. He roweled his horse ahead through the brush. "Wyatt!"

The big man twisted in the saddle. They were a rope's length apart in the gray twilight, but Lomack knew! He knew instantly!

"I believe you wanted to see me, Wyatt!" Jay said.

Lomack drove from the saddle, hitting the ground on the offside of his horse, with the animal shielding him.

Jay left his horse at the same instant, landing in a half-crouch. They held that position for a taut moment as each measured his chances and his disadvantages.

Lomack then fired beneath the neck of his horse. He missed, and the animal broke away from him, leaving him exposed.

Jay could have killed him then. He held his fire. "You don't seem surprised to find me in this range, Wyatt," he said.

Lomack shot twice, but Jay had dropped flat, and the bullets again went wide.

Lomack retreated a dozen feet to the only tree within reach. It was a small cedar, clear of limbs for a dozen feet, and was too slender to entirely hide his bulk. He stood edged to it.

"You paid your ten thousand in cattle to learn I was in this country, Wyatt," Jay said. "It wasn't worth the price."

Lomack lifted a wild, nerve-shrilled shout. "Sid! Sid! This way. It's Jess Steele!"

Jay heard Sid Ferris yell a response. And behind him in the brush Lily was screaming, and Ben Tracy was shouting something and riding toward the scene.

Then Sid Ferris loomed out of the twilight. He had on a slicker, but his white collar identified him. He had Jay flanked.

Jay rose to one knee. Lomack was shooting at him now, and screaming. "Get him, Sid! Get him!"

Sid Ferris fired at Jay and missed. He did not have a chance to shoot again, for Jay tripped the hammer of his gun. Jay's slug tore through Ferris at the waist, doubling him in the saddle.

At the same instant a bullet from Lomack's gun caught the brim of Jay's hat and tore it from his head with astounding violence.

Ben Tracy's voice boomed behind Jay, "Hold it, Wyatt!"

But Wyatt Lomack had jammed fresh shells into his gun, and was bearing down for another shot at Jay.

Ben fired, then fired again. Lomack went reeling back, and finally fell on his back a dozen feet from the tree he had used as a shield.

Sid Ferris was now slipping from his horse, which had gone to pitching and finally fell headlong. He was dragged by a stirrup for a few yards until his boot pulled off, and he lay there, a crumpled, mud-caked shape, while his horse went buck-jumping off into the brush.

Ben Tracy said in a high, taut voice, "I always figured Sid would spook if a good man looked him in the eye. He wasted his shot."

Jay lowered his gun. Lily came spurring through the thickets and leaped from her horse. Mike Cavanaugh and Trent Craig arrived.

Jay walked to where Wyatt Lomack lay. Lomack was still alive, but pumping blood from a hole in his right lung. Jay bent over him.

"Ferris is done for too, Wyatt," he said. "He can't help you now. You killed your father and brother that night in Concho, didn't you, so that you would have all of the Double Arrow for yourself?"

"Sid!" Lomack tried to shout, but it was only a gasp.

"He's lying over there with a bullet in him," Jay said. "You haven't got much time, Wyatt. Make it clean. You killed them, didn't you? And you wanted me dead, knowing that as long as I was alive the truth might come out."

Lomack's head dropped back. He looked at Jay with the resignation of a man dying in defeat. "It was Ferris," he gasped. "He did it. He . . ."

Then Lomack was gone. Jay walked to where Sid Ferris lay. Ferris was still breathing, but, like Lomack, he was going.

"You heard that, Sid," Jay said. "Wyatt confessed that you killed Mason and Vince Lomack. Do you want to add anything to that statement?"

Sid Ferris gazed up at Jay and his smile was gray and scornful and unyielding. "Wyatt always was a rat," he murmured. Then he was dead.

Jay straightened. After a time he and Ben looked at each other. "We'll never know now which one of them did the actual shooting," Ben said. "It was probably Sid. But Wyatt was in on it. Sid forced him to turn over a half share in the Double Arrow afterwards as part of the deal."

The Pitchfork men were all gathering now. Tom Faye and Yancey Tolliver brought with them a Double Arrow rider whom they had rounded up.

Jay pointed to the bodies of Lomack and Ferris. "They're through," he said. "Who was the segundo in your crew?"

"I guess that'd be me," the man said.

"You're free to gather up what cattle you can and head out of this range by the way you came in," Jay said. "If you come back you'll never get through with a single head alive."

The man looked at the bodies and shrugged. "There don't seem to be much point in goin' ahead," he admitted.

Dallas Carver was also rounded up. Pooley Moon had found her, screaming hysterically, and trying to gather some of the scattered cattle that had been rebranded by the Rafter S iron. She was wild-eyed, her hair stringing down her narrow face.

"You—you murderer!" she screeched at Jay.

"Dallas," he said. "You'll have a lifetime remembering that you lost more than ten thousand dollars' worth of cattle today. That, I'm afraid, will be your only regret."

He walked away, found his horse. He mounted, and the others caught up their horses too and followed him, leaving the Double Arrow men to take care of their dead.

Lily Benton rode with Will Overmire in the background, staying away from Jay.

Somewhere along the way Dallas Carver left them, riding away alone. She was heading for her tent on Latigo Creek.

Lily made no attempt to stop her. There would be no point in telling her that Frank's place was lost to her also. Otis Haskell had talked to Lily the previous night at Yellow House. He had told how Dallas had blackmailed Amelia. Otis was canceling the transfer of the mortgage, which had been held up, pending settlement of Frank's estate. Dallas had lost her last hold in the Wardrum country.

It was past midnight when they pulled into Yellow House and unsaddled.

Lily walked at once to the house, and went in alone. Will Overmire stood gazing after her. He turned and looked at Jay, who had also stood watching her.

Jay said, "Always be faithful to her, Overmire. If you give her so much as a moment's worry you'll have me to answer to."

Overmire sighed, and said, "You are not worth it,

Webb, or Steele or whatever name you intend to go by. I would have made her a better husband, but it seems I have to tell you that I'm not the man Lily Benton is weeping for in that house right now."

Jay said, "That can't be true, after the things I've said to her."

Then he walked to the house. The living room door was open, the room dark, deserted. But faint lamplight drifted from the hall to the right, which led to the bedrooms.

Jay heard subdued sounds now . . . the misery of a girl in tears. He walked down the hall, the ring of his spurs loud on the cedar floor. The sounds choked off, and utter silence came.

He stood before the door beneath which light showed. "Lily," he said. "Lily!"

Presently she opened the door. She had pulled off her saddle garb and had donned a nightgown, and now had thrown her quilted robe around her shoulders, and was holding it clutched about her.

She had the bright stain of tears on her cheeks. She stood gazing at him, offering nothing, expecting nothing.

"It is Overmire you should have," Jay said. "But I've also known how it was with me, even before you kissed me that day. But I would not let myself forgive you for forcing your will on me. And also for once believing that I might kill you to silence you."

"Yes," she said. "I did fear you at first."

"But you were sure of me weeks ago. You wanted me to leave this range only because you feared for me, instead of for yourself. You didn't want me killed by Sid Ferris or Lomack."

Color was high and rich in her throat, and her eyes were soft. "Yes," she said shakily.

Sabrina Moon's nasal voice spoke from the open door of an adjoining room. "Lily Benton! Close that door. You're not dressed decent."

Jay drew Lily against him, and her lips were wild with the waiting and the longing and the sweetness that was to repay for all their differences.

"This is scandalous," Sabrina said, but there was no disapproval now in the way she said it.

Then Sabrina closed the door of her own room, leaving them there alone.

Center Point Publishing
600 Brooks Road ● PO Box 1
Thorndike ME 04986-0001 USA

(207) 568-3717

US & Canada:
1 800 929-9108